Shielded Mates Volume 1

A Guardians of Chaos Duet

C.D. Gorri

Shielded Mates Volume 1
A Guardians of Chaos Duet

Featuring:
Wolf Shield
Dragon Shield

Guardians of Chaos Books 1 & 2
by C.D. Gorri
Edited by BookNookNuts
Copyright 2021, 2022 C.D. Gorri, NJ

To the loyal readers of LLS,
You are the best! <3
Xoxo,
C.D.

STOP! Before you go, sign up for my newsletter and get the latest on
my releases, giveaways, freebies and more:
https://www.cdgorri.com/newsletter

This is a work of fiction. All of the characters, names, places, organizations, and events portrayed in this novel are either part of the author's imagination and/or used fictitiously and are not to be construed as real. Any resemblance to any person, living or dead, actual events, locales or organizations is entirely coincidental. This eBook is licensed for your personal enjoyment only. All rights are reserved. No part of this book is to be reproduced, scanned, downloaded, printed, or distributed in any manner whatsoever without written permission from the author. Please do not participate in or encourage piracy of any materials in violation of the author's rights. Thank you for respecting the hard work of this author.

WOLF SHIELD

GUARDIANS OF CHAOS 1

BLURB

She's a normal caught in a supernatural war, and he's the only man who can save her.

Hudson Stormwolfe is a Guardian of Chaos. His order is tasked with keeping magic free to ensure the flourishment of supernaturals through innovative thought and creativity without fear of persecution.

But there are those who wish to put a cap on freedom. A group called the Loyalists have sworn themselves enemies of the Guardians and all they stand for. They want the power to control all magic.

Fergie McAndrews is a typical normal with an atypical obsession for shoes. Her no nonsense attitude has gotten her in trouble with previous employers, but she is determined to make this new job work. She even goes so far as to put in overtime.

But what was with the creepy green goons who wanted to take a bite out of the pleasantly plump female? Tossed into a fight between supernaturals, the human woman is about to get got until he steps in.

Storm can't help but be drawn to the curvy female. Her voice, her scent, her smile all call to his inner Wolf. Ready or not, this Guardian has found his fated mate, but can he save the fiery redhead from harm and convince her she belongs to him?

Storm will do anything to claim his mate, even promise to keep her in the ridiculously expensive shoes she favors.

Guardians of Chaos Pledge

I am the watcher in the storm.
I am the iron shield.
I protect against those who seek to control the wild nature
of magic.
I am the guardian of chaos.
To thrive, we must be free.
From chaos comes creation.

PROLOGUE

"Why are we traipsing through the fucking swamp to meet your so-called contact, Fur?" Hudson Stormwolfe, or Storm as he was known, growled at his friend and fellow Guardian, "a goddamn coffee shop wouldn't do?"

The Horse Shifter snorted as Storm stepped in a hole cursing quietly as a trickle of slimy sludge slipped inside his once clean steel-toed boots.

"Oh, you are going to scrape these clean," he shot at Furio.

"Dude, just watch your step," Furio retorted making a show of how easily his long legs ate up the muddy landscape.

Fuck him, snarled Storm's Wolf. Trudging through

the muck was not his animal's idea of a good time. Give him a dense, clean forest any day. Storm only agreed to accompany Furio because Kingston told him to go.

Their leader could be a hard ass at times, but no one fucked with the Dragon Shifter just lately. Not because they were afraid, but for other reasons. Losing one's mate could really fuck a guy up inside. Besides, Storm had liked Neela, may she rest in peace for eternity.

Damn the Loyalists. Those bastards were nothing more than terrorists and fanatics attacking supernatural creatures and hoarding magic for their own nefarious purposes. They wanted to control and siphon out the one thing every supernatural needed to live with their leaders as the gatekeepers. That thing was of course magic itself.

Loyalists believed that common folk had no business accessing magic. They wanted to keep it for the elite, the wealthy, and basically anyone who did what they said. They were nothing more than pirates and madmen as far as Storm was concerned.

They had been around for nearly as long as the Guardians of Chaos. Storm was proud to call himself a Guardian. He was more than able and willing to do his part to ensure freedom for all supernatural-kind.

Even after all this time, those bastards still failed to gain the momentum necessary to achieve their goals. Their terroristic acts were the stuff of nightmares. Especially this latest attack on the Guardians' leader. The heinous crime was without precedent.

It still left a bad taste in Storm's mouth. He gritted his teeth as his mind still tried to take in the fact she was gone. Neela Baldric, the beloved mate of their once fearless leader, was brutally attacked while on her way to the supermarket.

The gentlewoman was a rare and precious creature and was mated to his superior, Kingston Baldric, for many years. She'd only just succumbed to her wounds a few months ago, leaving all of them bereft of her company, but none so much as Kingston.

"We all miss her, bro," Furio said, and Storm realized he'd been projecting.

Fuck. He hated it when he did that. Though truthfully, it wouldn't have mattered. Furio felt her loss as well. Everyone in Kingston's group of Guardians felt the loss keenly.

These kinds of terroristic acts were the new tool the Loyalists used to persuade mainstream paranormal society to their way of thinking. Blackmail, bribery, murder, mayhem, all elements of destruction that this so-called law-abiding organization stooped to in order to fulfill their aims.

Not on his watch, Storm vowed to himself. It was his job and that of all the Guardians to stop those bastards and ensure freedom for their kind.

"Sorry," Storm muttered, "still, we had to meet in a fucking swamp, Furio?"

"What swamp, bro? We're in Secaucus," Furio opened his arms wide and gestured to the thick, musty smelling wetland they were currently stalking through.

It was just a little past ten o'clock at night, but summer in the Garden State meant hot and sticky. Especially in that small portion of undeveloped marshlands. Storm growled when his foot sank yet again, ankle-deep, into another muddy hole.

Goddamn it, he grimaced, and slapped his friend in the back of the head. Then he counted to three like he'd been told to do by another of their own, Egros, a male Witch who thought the Wolf Shifter would have better control if he could simply manage his anger.

Yeah. Right. The hell with counting. He was going to kick Furio's ass when they were done here.

"Half the fucking state is a swamp," Storm growled, shaking the muck off his foot, "I thought you were born here?"

"I was. Born and bred in Hoboken, *cumpy*."

"What?"

"Nothin' man, just some local slang from when I was a kid. Anyway, you're shittin' me right, New Jersey isn't a swamp," snorted the Stallion Shifter.

Storm rolled his eyes and blew out a breath. What was he going to do with this guy? Thirty years as a Guardian, and Furio was still a rookie to Storm, who'd spoke his vows over a hundred years ago this past April.

As a Wolf Shifter, he had a longer than average life expectancy, which had only increased when he'd pledged his allegiance to serve all the supernatural creatures living on this planet as a Guardian. He'd fought too many battles to count, but the work was meaningful. Protecting freedom always was.

It had been the same for his grandfather, who'd raised him just outside the boundaries of the Pack where his father still ruled as Alpha. His older brother was the heir which usually meant younger brothers were ousted or had to challenge for positions in the Pack. Rather than stay and fight for his dominance in the place of his birth, he'd left.

Storm respected tradition, but he had had a higher calling to serve. The Guardians of Chaos were an elite order of supernaturals. The higher ups did not want it said they were showing favoritism to any specific Pack, Clan, Coven or what have you, so they composed each unit of a mix of *supes*. It took years to build the kind of team Storm was a part of.

Furio might be considered new, but he was still one of them. So fine, maybe Storm wouldn't kick his ass outright, but he could best him in training. That would satisfy both his Wolf and human sides.

"Did you hear Kingston has a meeting with the Assembly next week to discuss Neela's passing?" Furio spoke in a low voice, but with his supernaturally enhanced senses, Storm heard him just fine.

"I did. The Assembly, are all former Guardians, they will understand Kingston's loss and will likely support his call to mount a hunt for the Loyalist who'd ordered the hit," Storm responded.

"We're not Enforcers, Storm. Their job is to police the paranormal peoples of the earth, not ours. Guardians of Chaos don't promote actual chaos, right?" asked Furio, and he was right to a point.

"Look, we are called Guardians of Chaos, because from chaos, aka freedom, comes creativity. If we lose that, we perish. A Guardian is the ultimate protector of free thought, and therefore, the champion of creation itself. Neela was a cherished female and Kingston's to protect and to avenge. We might not understand what it is like to be mated, Furio, but he has rights and this did happen because of our war," Storm responded.

"All for magic? Neela was killed so the Loyalists could control magic? How would that even happen?"

"No, she was killed to break us. Without our leader, the Loyalists hope to win whatever scheme they are hatching and believe me, they are always plotting something. Whoever controls magic, controls us all," he grunted.

The way Storm understood it, magic was a finite thing, like ore, it was distributed organically, used, and recycled by each supernatural group as needed. The ancient ones, gods, goddesses, or what have you created magic out of chaos for each paranormal species to grow and take shape.

"What would they do, if they had it all?" Furio asked.

"What's with all the fucking questions?" growled Storm.

It was not for any one of them to control the others' usage of this gift. It went against their very nature as magical creatures.

Storm understood this. It was why he'd never looked back after leaving the Black Moon Pack to follow in his grandfather's footsteps. With his father still ruling and his brother as heir, his life there would have been difficult to say the least.

He was too dominant. More so than his old man, yet the tradition dictated that the second son could not be Alpha.

Leaving was his only option, and his grandfather had ensured that he had all the knowledge he needed before his time came. Storm had joined the crusade against those who sought to rule over the entire supernatural world before he was old enough to vote. He knew his duty was no longer to Pack, but to his band of Guardians.

Which was why he was wading through the last thick patch of swampland left undeveloped in Secaucus, New Jersey, home of the best outlet shopping this side of the Hudson River for which he was named, at the behest of one of his own.

Fucking Furio.

"Sorry, *cump*, talking helps pass the time. Anyway, my CI prefers to be away from prying eyes, you know he's part Goblin, and more than a little skittish."

"Yeah, well, what news does he have, anyway?"

"He thinks he found the Loyalists' new headquarters. It was too good a tip to pass up. He's supposed to have the GPS coordinates for me tonight."

"Shit. That is important. But he couldn't have texted them?"

"Nah," Furio shook his head, causing his long hair, which was bound in a leather thong to sway side to side, mimicking that of his shifted form.

He stopped to touch one of the long overgrown cattails they'd passed, and Storm stilled in his tracks, wondering if he heard something. Like a woman breathing or humming or something. But how could that be? They were in the middle of nowhere. Furio dropped the cattail and turned toward the soft, and admittedly pleasant, vocals.

"Hey, you hear that?" Furio asked.

Storm raised his hand to quiet the other man. His Wolf was at full attention. A warm breeze blew in their direction, and he breathed it in deep siphoning through the various layers, hoping to identify whatever made that sound.

Along with the heavy scent of the dense and decaying vegetation, came another, lighter, much more pleasant fragrance. It sifted through Storm's highly acute olfactory system, teasing and tempting his senses. Whatever it was, Storm wanted more.

His Wolf's ears worked to zero in on the source of both the sounds and the tantalizing fragrance that seemed too soft, too fine for the misty marshlands of Secaucus, New Jersey.

"It's like brown sugar and marzipan," he murmured as the sweet fragrance danced across his senses, like something out of a dream.

"What?" laughed Furio, but he ignored the Stallion.

He knew better than to go traipsing off after a phantom scent, but there was something about it. Something all too tempting and familiar. Storm's Wolf perked up. He growled low and deep as he took in another breath.

That scent, that crazy good scent, was like a shock to the system, but not necessarily unpleasant. More like an awakening. Storm noticed the Stallion Shifter walking through the thicket towards that divine fragrance, and the Wolf inside of him snarled.

"What the fuck, *cump*?" Furio asked.

Storm shook his head. What the fuck was wrong with him? Furio was his friend and fellow Guardian.

It didn't matter. It upset the Wolf. Storm shook his head and tried to silence the beast, but his animal was insistent. He needed to beat his friend to the source of that heavenly scent.

"Shit," he growled.

He hurried past the Stallion, using his superior

height to gain the advantage, despite Furio's better speed. The Stallion couldn't beat him there. Storm would not allow it. He leapt over fallen trees and shrubs, avoiding the holes that had gotten him twice already in the deceptively soft, wet earth, until he reached the edge of what seemed to be a parking lot.

The heavy breathing coming from behind him told the Wolf that Furio had managed to keep pace, but the Stallion needed to hit the gym more if he was out of breath. It was shameful for a Guardian to be so easily exhausted. Then again, when had he ever beaten the Horse Shifter in a race?

"Damn, Storm, I never saw you run so fast," he huffed and Storm blinked in surprise, "shit, if I'd have known this lot was so close, I wouldn't have made us park behind the stadium and walk," the Stallion sucked in air greedily.

"Shhh," Storm held up his hand for silence.

His Wolf's enhanced vision allowed him to make out the details of the scene before him. They were just outside the fenced in parking lot of some kind of building. There was a municipal sign hanging up not too far away.

It was late at night, so it wasn't the courthouse, and there were no cop cars parked outside, so it wasn't a police station either. He looked around for any other indication of what the older cement building was. Ah, another dented sign.

"It's a library," Furio whispered.

"I see that," Storm growled.

He was angry and on edge, and he had no fucking idea why. His entire body vibrated with energy. He was not nervous, just impatient, he realized. That was odd, too.

What could he possibly be waiting for here? His Wolf dripped saliva from his fangs as he waited in that metaphysical plane where he rested until Storm called to him. He tried to consider what led him there, but all coherent thought fled his brain the second *she* came into view.

The strange woman was all the way on the other end of the tiny parking lot. A tall security fence and a good fifty feet of black asphalt stood between the female and the place where the two Guardians lurked, but Storm could still make out every detail of the stunning creature.

"She's a little round, but I always did like a girl with some cushion for the pushin'," Furio elbowed him jokingly, but his words enraged Storm.

The Wolf inside of him snarled and growled and before he could stop himself, he had Furio by the collar of his shirt. He'd lifted the Stallion a good foot off the ground before shock had him dropping his friend.

"The fuck?" Furio choked and rubbed his bruised neck.

Storm ignored him, eyes glued to the woman in the ankle-length skirt and short-sleeved blouse. She wore shiny red shoes with high spindle-like heels. *Stilettos*, he thought, and for the first time he understood why they were called that.

They might not be good for running, but the long, skinny heels could pierce a man's heart just like the stealthy blade someone named them after. As it was, he more than appreciated the way the shiny red heels lengthened her legs and caused her hips to sway seductively in the yellowish glow of the streetlights.

Her hair was pulled back in a loose bun. She'd obviously tried to tame her fiery red locks, but curls still fell around her lovely face. Storm observed the subtle highlights and lowlights in her hair color even in the diminished light, noting with pleasure her eyelashes held the same coppery tinge.

So, she was a natural redhead. Good. He did not like artificial things. Unlike most redheads who leaned towards fair-skinned, this beautiful woman had a healthy bronze glow to her. Her whiskey brown eyes were large and bright in the darkness.

He appreciated her plump pink lips, straight nose, and stubborn little chin. She was a knockout. The most gorgeous creature he'd ever laid eyes on.

Storm was thunderstruck. He watched her innocently sashay across the otherwise deserted parking lot to a beat up looking pick-up truck.

Hmm. Odd car choice, he thought.

That was all he had time to think as three men crept out of the shadows and circled the tiny female. Blood rushed through his being and he couldn't make out what was being said.

Whatever it was, didn't matter. One of them dared grab her arm and tossed her purse aside. Storm's fangs lengthened and claws popped free of his nails. The sound of her scream woke something furious inside of him. His entire body trembled with the strength of his fury. He needed to get to her. Now. There was no time to lose.

"Uh, what is that?" Furio tapped his shoulder and Storm turned and snarled.

His friend pointed down. Storm looked and took a step back in surprise. His palms were glowing. Small blue lights were circling both hands. His feet and legs were covered in what looked like shadowy black smoke billowing skywards. It was magic. He knew that much. It didn't hurt, but he'd never felt it before.

"Holy shit, Storm! Do you know what this means?"

Then it hit him. The reason for all the sudden changes. He turned to Furio and growled one word.

"Mine."

His female shrieked and hit the ground, and the Wolf inside him howled in fury.

Protect, the Wolf demanded.

He barely blinked his eyes, then he was directly in front of the female. It was like he'd moved through time and space. Storm appeared in front of her, shielding her from the soon-to-be-dead men who dared touch what was his.

He lifted his lip and snarled at the three assholes. It was nothing more than legend, he'd always thought. A fairy tale to keep younger *supes* from leaving the order. But he might have to change his mind.

He lifted his fists, still glowing with blue magic, and slammed it into the face of the first one of the three to launch an attack against him. Sparks flew, as did the assailant's teeth.

"What are you waiting for," Storm said to the other two.

He smiled wickedly. Looked like even Shifter fairy tales were true sometimes. It was rumored that the Guardians were blessed by the Fates that upon finding their true mates they would receive certain magical benefits to promote honoring their vows till death.

Stronger together, those were the words etched inside the doorway of the Keep. Now Storm finally understood their meaning.

"Mine," he looked down into startled butterscotch eyes.

He knew without doubt; the woman was his mate, and he would shield her from harm.

Always.

ONE

What a day! Fergie McAndrews headed towards the pick-up truck she'd borrowed from her roommate for work that morning.

Of course, the thirty-thousand dollar certified used luxury car she'd splurged on earlier in the year was in the shop. Again.

Just another in a long line of bad decisions. After leaving a perfectly good job for a startup company, she was laid off three weeks ago and had to borrow money from her parents to pay rent. Wasn't that humiliating?

"This is the last time, Ferg," her step-monster had said after she'd Venmo'd the money to her.

God forbid the mechanic call and tell her the car was ready. She wouldn't be able to pick it up for another week. That was when she got her first paycheck from her newest gig at L-Corp. Not a startup, but an older company with new offices in Bayonne, which was only a half-hour commute.

But to commute, you needed a car. Fergie had no choice but to borrow the old pick-up from her best friend and roommate, Jessenia Banks. It wasn't like she needed the truck. She worked from home these days. Besides, Fergie promised to fill it up and have it washed.

She huffed out a breath. It'd been a really long day. A crappy one too. Fergie wanted to love her new job. Really, she did. But so far, it was the pits. If Fergie wanted to be a librarian, she would've been one.

Research was her jam. Well, when it was interesting. She had a knack for sniffing out information and compiling easy-to-read spreadsheets and timelines. It wasn't the hard work that annoyed her. Her complaint was the content. The actual stuff her new boss had her looking up. It was beyond boring.

Why an enormous conglomerate like L-Corp needed old land surveys, cross-referenced with newspaper reports on accidents, crimes, etcetera. She had no idea. She'd been at it for weeks now. So far, she'd researched six locations given via GPS coordinates across Hudson County. Her new boss wanted everything, every little insignificant piece of information she could dig up.

That was the easy part. It was the hassle of the actual job that really made her want to give up. Every day she had to drive to Bayonne to pick up her work laptop she'd dropped off the night before with all of that day's findings. Every single night they wiped her computer clean.

Like she was going to run away with the secrets of what happened on 2nd and Washington sixty-years ago. Can you say paranoid? Ugh.

Fergie had always looked forward to working for a huge global company. It was supposed to be her ticket out of the Garden State. Travelling the globe, seeing new thi. Butngs, visiting far-off places was always a secret dream of hers. Well, that, and having her own walk-in closet full of gorgeous designer shoes.

Best secret dream evah! In her opinion, anyway. What woman didn't love shoes? Fergie hummed as she daydreamed about rows and rows of Blahnik's, Jimmy Choo's, Garavani's, Ferragamo's, and her personal favorites, Louboutin's on every shelf!

Don't judge. Fergie wasn't shallow, she just liked pretty things. Haters gonna hate. But every time she ran across a thrift or second-chance store, she'd search high and low to see what they had. That was how she'd scored the pumps on her feet.

They made her feel good about herself. Being five-foot two-inches short with more curves than a race-track, Fergie had had more than her fair share of self-esteem issues growing up. Alright, so she was chubby. She could admit that proudly now.

If everyone looked the same, the world would be one boring as hell place. Fergie liked herself perfectly fine these days, in spite of all the times her step-monster tried to make her diet growing up. So she liked food and shoes. Big deal.

She worked hard to feed and clothe herself, so as far as she was concerned, no one had a right to comment. So what if she wanted some excitement in her life? Fergie was aware she was better off than most, but what was wrong with having goals?

She'd spent a lot of time thinking about how a woman like her could have an adventure. Travelling was the only thing she could think of. Of course, she'd been hoping this job would be the answer to that. Even travelling for work was better than being stuck.

Sigh.

So far, her plans had fallen flat, but hey, at least she was earning a paycheck. Her new boss, Mr. Offner, might be a strange man, but he signed her checks, and that was enough for now. Fergie had never seen more than a glimpse of him. All of her instructions usually came via email.

Most of the time she was able to compile her research quickly, then she'd head back to the office to organize it into neat little spreadsheets, and finally, she'd hand it all in with her laptop. But not today.

Mr. Offner sent her an email detailing everything she could dig up on one of the oldest places on record in the county. Of course, land surveys that old, along with police reports, newspaper articles, deeds, and sales records were nowhere she could easily access them.

After wasting hours at both the court house and municipal building, Fergie had been directed to the *second* public library. Apparently anything over a hundred years old was filed away in the godforsaken place. She'd been shocked to find an entire room filled with musty old archives. And wouldn't you know it, there was no cell service and no internet access. Plus, their phone lines were down. She'd had to photograph each page using her cell. When she got home later, she would send those photos like a fax to her boss along with her spreadsheet. If she could manage that before collapsing into bed.

Boy, was she tired! She should've gone home ages ago, but Fergie was no quitter. Only once did she skip out of the library to grab a venti mocha latte with skim. She so loved curbside delivery!

Then she'd headed back over to the Second Free Public Library down on Paterson Plank Road. Properly caffeinated, she'd hunkered down and got to doing more of the work she was being paid to do.

Why the old building was called the second library was a mystery to her. One she didn't really care about, so, whatever.

Her job was to gather all the info she could on some old, currently vacant, piece of land formerly owned by Abel Smith. Mr. Offner, and therefore L-Corp, wanted every scrap of info she could muster up on the land which included a burial plot that had its own creepy folklore surrounding it.

Not her concern, she told herself, though some stories made the hair on the back of her neck stand on end. The land was bisected by Secaucus road and was actually not too far from the very library where she now found herself.

Fergie stopped walking and scolded herself for behaving like a schoolgirl. She was a professional adult woman, for Pete's sake! Her dedication to finding out miniscule details had earned her a GPA of 3.96 in college, and she'd taken that work ethic and experience with her wherever she went after graduating.

Fairy tales and campfire stories aside, she would give all the information to Mr. Offner tomorrow. She might not have the job of her dreams, but at least she could pay her bills. For now, she'd settle for that.

"Two hours to find the musty old ledger," she mumbled aloud while digging for the keys.

It was dark out and she was alone. That always made her nervous. Talking out loud helped calm her irrational fears. Adult or not, nobody liked being alone in a dark, creepy parking lot in the middle of the night. At least, Fergie didn't.

She'd prefer being back inside that horrible little room, reading the small handwritten columns in those old ledgers. And that had been no picnic either. After begging the nerdy little clerk to let her stay late, promising to lock up, she'd spent a total of six hours in the awful place. It was a wonder her eyes still worked.

She blew out a breath. Where the heck were the truck keys? She grabbed her cell phone. Of course, she still had zero bars, so no service, but oh well, at least she could use it as a flashlight. Just what she wanted from a nine-hundred dollar smart phone. Thank God they had monthly payment plans.

"Stupid piece of junk," Fergie blew out a breath and rummaged through her purse.

It was already after ten. She could probably wait

till morning to bring her computer back to the office. She didn't use it anyway. All her info was on her phone. Besides, right then, all she wanted was sleep.

Fergie dropped the phone back in her bag. She'd located the keys and hummed to herself as she headed towards her borrowed truck. Her new scanning app was really something. She would use it as soon as she woke up and email her boss.

Mr. Offner was sure to be impressed with it. The software allowed her to convert images, like the ones she took of the ledgers and hand-drawn maps, into readable and printable PDFs. She wanted to make a good impression, and who knows, maybe she could land a promotion that would get her out of all this scut work.

One thing she knew for certain, Fergie could live the whole rest of her life and never step foot in that creepy ass parking lot or the old second library again. Who thought it was a good idea to put this place all the way on the edge of town?

There wasn't a drive thru or gas station anywhere in the vicinity. Just an old patch of marshland, which now that she thought of it, meant tons of creepy crawlies. Fergie loved animals, but not the kind that lived there. Rats, snakes, spiders, and bird-sized mosquitos.

Ew. She shivered and picked up the pace. It had been hot all day, and the local vegetation stunk something awful. She swatted away one huge bloodsucking fiend of an insect and crinkled her nose.

How Fergie could still smell the stink of the swamp with her allergies was beyond her? Speaking of which, it was way past the time she normally took her meds. She stopped walking again and started to dig through her pocketbook for her regularly prescribed allergy meds. If she didn't take them at the same time every night, they didn't work. A noise brought her head up, and she turned around fast.

"Hello, anyone there?" she questioned the dimly lit parking lot, feeling a tad foolish for doing so.

Too many scary movies, she scolded herself. She bent her head to check for the pills once more when the sound returned. Except this time it was directly behind her, making her jump.

Fergie whirled around and came face to face with three monstrously tall men. Her would-be assailants were all huge compared to her, even with heels on. She couldn't really make out their faces in the dim streetlights, but what she could see made her shudder.

Was it possible for three men to all have the same scale-like scars on their skin? Wait, was their skin green?

"Hello yourself," one of the men said, "*what'sssss* in the bag?"

"Holy shit," Fergie gasped in horror.

The speaker opened his mouth, and she swore she saw a row of needlelike teeth and a long, forked tongue poking out.

What the fucking fuck? Fergie swallowed. Hard.

Two

efore she could think to run or move at all, the strange-looking man ripped her purse right out of her hands and tossed it on the ground behind him.

Shit. Her keys were still inside the bag. Sure she knew there was always a chance of violence happening to a woman alone at night, she'd even read about an increase in muggings in town, but she'd never imagined it could happen to her.

She straightened her back, Fergie wasn't about to play the victim. Not for anyone. Cupping her hand around the lipstick tube she'd managed to grab, she addressed the would-be muggers as she'd been taught in her self-defense class back when she was still in school.

"Look, just take the bag, and leave me alone," she said in a firm voice.

"Well, now boys, we got *oursssselves* a *feissssty* one," the largest attacker hissed his words.

Fergie's eyes darted from one to the next. This was so not going to end in her favor. She squeezed the tube of lipstick, holding it as if it were a lifeline. Fergie was in trouble and she knew it.

Oh well, she *might as well go down swinging*. Fergie lifted her hand around the tube of lipstick in a defensive position.

"Stand back! I've got pepper spray!" she lied, and the three of them laughed.

Rude! She narrowed her eyes at the three hulking men. This was not going to end well.

"Good, I like 'em *ssssspicy*," one of them said.

"First of all, you guys need to see a speech therapist. And maybe a dermatologist, too. I can help you find one. I am good at finding things. Just let me grab my phone," she took a step towards her purse, but one of the three blocked her path.

Whoa. She didn't even see him move. Something was not right here. Fergie backed up a step, watching in horror as vertical lids flicked over that assailant's eyes.

Like Jessenia's pet lizard's eyes, she whimpered. Panic set in. These dudes were so not normal. Fergie dropped her lipstick, ignoring the snickers of another of the trio.

"What the h-hell?" she stuttered.

Okay, Fergie maybe spent a lot of her time daydreaming with her head buried in books or scouring websites for info when she was between jobs. It was one of her vices, or so people said. Personally, she didn't see the problem with being a closet-nerd.

She just loved to read. Still, never in all the time she'd spent looking up facts and studying lore, had she ever thought to come face to face with any of the wacky creatures in her books and websites.

She clenched her jaw, this was real. Her own eyes weren't playing tricks on her. These men were not human.

"Oh, *ssssweeetie*, you'll hurt our feelings," the third one inched closer, "we *jusssst* want a *tasssste*."

"You can just back the hell up!" she held up her hand in a feeble attempt to ward off the brute, "What the hell are you guys?" she asked again.

"You're about to find out," the biggest of the three reached out and grabbed her arm.

He pulled and Fergie, being herself, slid on the slick asphalt. To keep from toppling forward, she had no choice but to grab onto her attacker with her free hand. When she looked down, she saw with growing horror that his skin was covered with green mottled scales and he was oozing some kind of slime. But that wasn't what made her scream, it was the long, gnarly claws that tipped his freakishly, strong hands.

"Ouch," Fergie pulled back from him, shifting her weight too fast in her high heels.

She fell backwards, landing on her ass, which of course, made her scream again. The asphalt was uneven and damn it, it was hard too. It stung even her plump bottom, but that still didn't hurt as much as the three long scratches on her forearm.

"I'm bleeding!" she shrieked once she realized he broke skin.

Red droplets welled up from the laceration and she suddenly felt woozy. She looked up and was confused. The giant reptile-man who'd just attacked her was flying.

Wait, not flying exactly. He was being lifted into the air, and, *ooh*, tossed away like the piece of trash he was! But what if whoever just attacked him was coming after her next? Fergie swallowed down her next scream and found the source of her assailant's sudden airborne abilities.

Holy hotness. She stole a quick glance at the man, all six and a half feet of him, that stood in a defensive position in front of her. The hiss of her remaining attackers had her eyes darting to them, but the resounding snarl coming from her rescuer brought it back to him.

Up and up she looked to search out the source of that ferocious sound. She wanted to see his face, to look into his eyes to determine if he was friend or foe. Fergie had to work to ignore the warm feeling that grew deep in the pit of her stomach as she first took in the pair of large, muddy boots.

Those were followed by big, strong calves, and thick, muscular thighs encased in tight denim. She bit her tongue, glancing over the impossibly large bulge beneath the stranger's fly, and allowed her gaze to travel even further up. She noted with giddy pleasure the rock hard abs, defined pecs, and bulging arms that were outlined to perfection in the thin white cotton t-shirt he wore.

Finally, she got a look at her hero's face. Fergie almost swallowed her tongue as her eyes met the glittering sapphire stare of the hottest guy she'd ever seen. Dark, short-cropped curls crowned his head, complete with a smattering of facial hair that seemed to thicken before her eyes. A trick of the light no doubt, but it was his rough-hewn features that made him all the more mouthwatering.

The stranger seemed to growl at her, but she was

positive he wasn't hostile. Somehow, she knew he was there to help. Just like she knew out of all the men there, he was the deadliest.

"Are you okay?" he growled, and she nodded in turn.

Knowing he was on her side made her tingle all over. No, Fergie wasn't scared of him. He was definitely stronger, rougher, and tougher than those other guys, and that knowledge warmed her further still. The stranger nodded once at her, his eyes glowing in the darkness. Nope, frightened was not the word she would use to describe her reaction to the man.

Turned on. Lustful. Okay, plain old *horny* were all better words for what she was feeling. His nostrils flared slightly, and his gaze dropped to her blouse where her hardened nipples were surely visible through the light cream-colored fabric.

Damn girl. This was so not the right time for her headlights to be on and her panties to grow damp. The heated look lasted for only a flash, but in that brief moment he'd managed to take her in from top to bottom in a way that made her want to climb up his mountain of a body and take him for a ride.

Yowza. She had never had such a knee-jerk reaction to a man before. Never felt this kind of sudden and fierce attraction to one. It was like her body recognized him as its master and was demanding some attention.

What the hell was going on? Fergie shook her head and his gaze returned once more to where her wound was now full-on bleeding.

Oh, great. More blood. She felt dizzy as she watched the red liquid pool and drip down to her lap. Her skirt sucked up the droplets, turning the smart khaki into a muddy color in the darkness. Fergie felt nauseous, but before she could give in to that unpleasant sensation, her attention snapped back to him.

Her hero's eyes seemed to glow even brighter than before. A trick of the light, maybe? Then a louder, more menacing snarl ripped from his throat and she gasped in surprise. That sound was not altogether human. She cried out a warning just as the stranger turned lightning quick to meet the oncoming lunge of the remaining two goons.

"Watch out!"

Fergie remained frozen in place on the ground. She was in shock, she realized. Or at least she was until one of the men landed right next to her and reached for her heel clad foot.

"Oh, no you don't, these are *Christian Louboutin's*," she grumbled and kicked at the man's green tinted hand, "do you have any idea how many days I went without lunch to buy these!"

She kicked at him again but missed as he seemed to float out of reach. Like his buddy before him, green-boy here floated up and tossed away from her before she could connect. Too bad. She really wanted to kick his ass for ruining her outfit.

She didn't have time to reflect on that as two firm hands suddenly wrapped around her arms. Fergie squealed at the sudden appearance of a pony-tail wearing man. He pulled her to the side and squatted down.

"Miss," he nodded his head, "I think we better get you out of here," he picked her up off the ground.

Fergie hardly had time to catch a breath before the large man stood her on her feet and shoved her behind him. He'd moved so fast, she hardly noticed it. Taller than her rescuer, but not as muscular, and not as devastatingly gorgeous in her opinion.

Still, he seemed to be protecting her. He backed up a step, and she did the same, reaching out to hold his arm as her heels slid again on something she'd rather not think about.

Her rescuer had beaten the stuffing out of those three punks. Like literally.

There were copious amounts of blood, not hers,

ooze, a few actual teeth, and other crap on the pavement. She backed up another step and squeaked as she slid again. Fergie squeezed pony-tail man's arm tighter.

The other man whom she thought of as her *rescuer* turned around at the sound. Having pummeled the last of the three assailants into dust, he was now free to come over and introduce himself. Or so she hoped.

Fergie wanted to whoop with joy! She was so happy to have gotten out of the whole thing relatively unscathed, and all thanks to him.

Can you say swoon? Fergie waited for him to meet her stare so she could thank him, but his focus seemed to be on where her hand gripped the other man's arm. Letting go as if she'd been burned, she swallowed down the odd sensation of guilt that suddenly filled her.

"Storm, now listen up, *cump*, I just got her out of the way. I didn't do a thing to her," the man who'd picked her up off the ground had both his hands in the air as if in surrender, and she could certainly see why.

Her rescuer had steam coming out of his ears. Okay, not steam, but he seemed to be smoking. Again, literally, and she meant that in its correct sense, not the modern way of misusing and abusing the word.

Actual tendrils of black and gray smoke seemed to surround his body, and that wasn't all. Electric blue lights glowed and circled his hands.

"Um, what's going on?" she swallowed nervously.

"Storm, man, I swear," pony-tail tried again.

All that begging didn't help much. Her rescuer seemed to blink from the place he'd been standing to the space directly in front of her. He growled fiercely and drew back his bloodied fist, socking pony-tail man right in the face, while snarling a word that suspiciously sounded like *mine*.

Dizzy from her ordeal and from having the person she was leaning on so abruptly removed from her grasp, Fergie blinked rapidly as he turned to catch her. He wasn't a lizard, but he was surely something else. Something *other*, she thought definitively.

His eyes glowed like little blue lasers and long fangs appeared when he opened his mouth. He was a bit furrier than before. His beard appeared thicker, and his once short, curly hair, longer now than it had been when she'd first spied the sexy warrior.

That wasn't right. No, it was more than not right. It was impossible. A wave of dizziness swept over her, more than she should've felt from the minor blood loss. Her rescuer tightened his hold on her arms.

The last few minutes had been the craziest in her entire life. Maybe she needed a moment for her brain to catch up. Fergie held her spinning head with one hand and tried to catch her breath.

"Easy," the stranger's deep whisper sent chills through her body.

He released her slowly and held his hand out, *his claw-tipped hand*, in case she stumbled. Eyes wide, Fergie stared at the sharp looking appendage. The man frowned and closed his fist to hide his nails, but it was too late. She wobbled unsteadily, and he raised his hand once more. This time, she squeaked.

"Sorry about that, it's just my Wolf. He is still agitated," he grumbled the explanation, but all she heard was the word *wolf*.

"I'm sorry, what?" she stopped and looked at him dead on.

"My Wolf," he repeated.

"Ooh-kayy," she knew her eyebrows were some-where up in her hairline, but what else could she say.

Dizziness hit her again, and she blinked her eyes. Shit. This had never happened to her. Oh hell.

"Um, Mr. Wolf?" she cleared her throat.

"Yes," he said one eyebrow quirked.

"I think, I'm gonna," but that was all she got out before blackness swallowed her.

Well, damn.

THREE

"Damn it, Storm," Kingston Baldric, Dragon Shifter and leader of Storm's unit frowned at him.

The Guardians of Chaos had few rules, but the ones they did have were important. Like the one about no unannounced visitors, especially of the human kind. But what was he to do? Storm held his ground while the Dragon growled from his position in the hallway of the Keep.

He wasn't fool enough to answer the angry Dragon. He simply slipped past his leader with the woman from the lot cradled protectively in his arms. He stalked the hallways to his room. The door opened on its own, and he took that for the Keep's blessing on his decision to aid the female.

He placed her down gently on his bed, already having refused to put her in any guest room. Not even their own medical examination room was good enough for her. She was his to help.

There were currently six Guardians in their unit and of the six, two were crowding his space. Storm was the sole Wolf Shifter. Furio, the Horse Shifter, had his head stuck inside the doorway. Kingston, the Diamond Dragon and their leader was growling and frowning from his stance.

Missing were Byram, the sole Vampire of the unit, Elena, a Panther and the only female, and Egros, a male Witch formerly of the Coven Realta. With Kingston's mate there had been seven, but now that Neela had been stolen from them, their numbers had diminished by one.

The Keep, the name they called their castle, was located deep in the pine barrens of South Jersey. Their only neighbor was a Jersey Devil Shifter and his family, but other than that, they were a good hour from any city or town. The location was good for keeping their work a secret from the humans.

He normally didn't mind the isolation of the Keep, or the way they all intruded on one another's privacy, entering private rooms without knocking and so forth. But now he felt anxious to the point of agitation.

It was the first time he could recall feeling so protective of his privacy. It was obvious why, mating fever was upon him. He just hadn't been prepared for the onslaught to be so great.

Amassed of enchanted stone and steel, the very walls that surrounded him were made of magic. The kind he'd vowed to protect. Almost intuitive, the Keep was the safest place he knew, while providing the utmost comfort for its inhabitants.

It wasn't the *where* that bothered his Wolf at the moment, it was more the *who*. Four males and one female lived there with him. All of them were currently unmated.

Yes, his beast recognized the pain that seemed to emanate from their leader after the loss of his mate and as such he knew Kingston was no threat to his female. But still. There were others. Including that idiot Horse who'd touched her at the lot.

Storm's Wolf would simply not allow anyone near her. He could not let his mate out of his sight. The beast was riding him hard. The animal in him knew who and what she was to him. He demanded she be marked and claimed.

"No. You will not mark her unless we know for certain she is what you say she is, and not unless she agrees to it. That is an order," Kingston practically roared, but Storm's Wolf didn't give a fuck.

Yes, he was projecting again. That kind of telepathic sympathy was useful when their unit was in battle, but that was the second time in as many hours he'd slipped and allowed his thoughts to be known. Mating fever was fucking with his sense of balance.

"She is mine, King," he began.

"You can't start thinking with your dick, Storm, we need you here with us," Kingston returned, "Besides, you don't know if she's *truly* yours."

"Yes, I do. When she was in danger, I was able to use powers I never had. It's the sign of a true mate."

"I saw it too, Kingston," Furio added.

The Stallion Shifter was sporting a black eye and stood as far away from Storm's bedroom door as the hall would allow. Smart man. While Storm wasn't proud of himself for punching him in the face, his animal did find some pleasure in knowing he'd hit the man for touching his woman. Never mind what he did to those asshole reptile Shifters.

"How did clean up go?" he asked his leader.

"Fine. Byram said there wasn't much left of the two men, but he recognized one as a Loyalist sympathizer," Kingston narrowed his gold eyes at him.

"Two, there were three of them," Storm interrupted.

"Yeah, well, you must've missed at least one of their carotid arteries then. And why were you there to begin with?"

"To talk to his fucking informant," Storm growled.

He didn't like the questions. He didn't want them in his room. He just wanted her to wake up.

"Uh, anyway, Byram found my informant in the back seat of a car not too far from the lot," Furio interrupted, "he was missing his head though."

"Shit. So, it was an ambush," Storm concluded.

As a Vampire, Byram would've been able to pick up the blood trail of the Reptilian Shifters and the Goblin informant. The Loyalists had no shame apparently. They would hire anyone. Even a bunch of half-wits who didn't seem to know they should never bring a human into the war between supernatural factions. The Dragon Shifter's voice shook him from his reverie, and Storm focused on the golden-eyed man.

"It would seem that way. The woman was working you guessed?"

"Well, I snagged her computer, but she doesn't seem to be a librarian," Furio interjected.

"You stole her things back at the library?" Storm asked.

"Not stole, *borrowed*, so we could learn why those goons wanted her," he insisted.

"It doesn't matter. You have to bring her back," Kingston said.

"No," he snarled, "that fucking Gila Shifter scratched her. She could be infected."

"Well, we won't know that if you don't let Byram near her."

"I could claim her. My bite will remove any toxins," he started.

"I already told you, no," the Dragon snapped at him.

Storm snarled, though he averted his eyes out of respect for their leader. He'd vowed to follow Kingston in all things, but this was not part of his duty to the man or the Guardians.

No one had the right to interfere between mates. Not even him. His Wolf bristled. The beast was not happy with Kingston's declaration. The thought of anyone, especially that bloodsucker Byram going anywhere near his mate, was liable to drive Storm crazy. She was an innocent, and she was his alone to protect.

"Kingston, my Wolf just can't do that, you know what this is like. She is my mate, I can't let anyone else near her. I can't let her go. She is too soft for this cruel world."

"Storm-"

"No. If the Loyalists know about her, if that bastard who got away told them about my reaction to being near her, then her life is in danger."

He could not let her go without knowing she was safe. Maybe not even then. His soft mate had been in the wrong place at the wrong time. Through no fault of her own she'd become the target of his worst enemy.

"The Loyalists have already killed one mate. They can't have another," he gritted his teeth as he spoke.

Kingston might be angry with him, but there was no way in hell he was letting her go. She was far too precious. He wanted this conversation over and the two men gone. He was the only one who could protect her. It was his duty. His privilege even.

Mine, his Wolf pressed him and Storm closed his eyes. He counted to three. He knew that Shifters could be possessive assholes, and something inside of him admitted that he wasn't above that.

"Storm, you need to bring her back. You cannot mate her until you explain things, and then only if she agrees. That's an order."

FOUR

Fergie's head was pounding. What the heck happened? She'd been on her way out of that old library after having a super-not-fun time researching old land surveys. It had been late at night. No biggie there. It wasn't like she'd had anywhere else to go.

Just home to Jessenia, her snarky as fuck roommate, and to Jeeves her fluffy, but moody rescue cat. Damn feline was going to be the death of her. Shit. She was late feeding him. He hated that. Usually paid her back with a nice surprise on her pillow.

Sigh. What time was it anyway?

"Owie," she tried to sit up, but it felt like there were a million drums being pounded enthusiastically by a bunch of no talented musicians right inside her head.

Dang. Had she been drinking? She hadn't felt this bad since that time Jessenia had insisted Margarita Mondays were a thing now. Fergie had jumped all over that.

Besides Margaritas were awesome and had minimal calories, unlike her favorite drink. Who knew Pina Coladas were like the whale of all alcoholic beverages in terms of caloric weight gaining potential?

Alas, she'd vowed Margarita Mondays were never to be heard from again after she'd technically lost her job at Shethler Real Estate because of one such Monday evening. That was like four or five jobs ago, but it still stung.

Crawling into work three hours late hadn't gone over well with the slimeball Mr. Shethler or his stupid name. Yep, you guessed it. The gross middle aged man had offered her a way to make up for it, but she resigned with a hard pass.

Water under the bridge, as the saying goes. It was all good. Time had healed those wounds, and she had a new job at L-Corp.

Okay, so back to the *where-exactly-was-she-now* part of the program. Wherever she was, this bed was super comfortable.

Mmm, she ran her hands over the silky sheets and thick, warm comforter. Definitely not hers. The ratty old blanket she'd had since college now sported several tears from too many washes. Her fingers and toes always got stuck in the darn thing.

She should replace it, but priorities. A girl had to have those. For Fergie, when it came to shoes or blankets, the former won every single time. Hands down. Speaking of her shoes.

"Owie," she moaned again as another wave of pain hit her right between the eyes when she'd tried to sit up too fast.

"Here," a deep voice said from very near, "easy now."

A powerful hand supported her lower back, helping her to sit up as she tried to take in her surroundings. It was dark inside the room. Really dark. But still, there was the odd sensation that she was safe.

Hmm. Maybe her scare-o-meter was broken or something. She was quite certain it should frighten her, waking up in a strange place with a massive headache, and feeling altogether rundown. But nope.

In fact, the big, warm hand on her back was rather soothing through the fabric of her blouse. Fergie blinked slowly and turned to look at her host. Her mouth went dry as she drank him in with her eyes.

Big, dark, glossy curls sat atop his head, cerulean blue eyes watched her from a tanned face framed by thick, inky lashes. She had the feeling she knew him. A spring of recognition bubbled up inside of her, and she found herself smiling like an idiot.

Where had she seen him before? It was there in her foggy brain, but it wasn't clear yet. He didn't smile back, but she got the impression he was pleased by her reaction. His breathing was slow and steady, with deep, careful inhales, follow by slow, deliberate exhales. She'd never found breathing sexy. Until now.

OMG. She was really losing her grip on reality if the way he breathed turned her on. Where had she picked him up anyway?

Then it hit her. Images of the almost too-handsome man with glowing blue eyes fighting a band of lizard men came rushing through her brain as she started to recall what had happened earlier that night.

"I was attacked," her scratchy voice reached her own ears, and she winced at the pain it caused her to speak.

"Don't worry about that now. Here, drink this. It's water," the owner of the pleasantly rugged voice handed her a cool glass filled with what she assumed was water.

Fergie was too thirsty to question it. Besides, she trusted him for whatever reason. Tipping back the glass, she drank greedily allowing the icy cold water to soothe her rough throat.

She'd finished the entire thing before she realized it. Her cheeks grew warm with embarrassment as she handed him back the now empty container. Fergie always did have a large appetite whether it be for food, drink, books, or what have you.

"Thank you," she said, and cleared her throat, "I don't mean to sound ungrateful, but can I ask you a question?"

"Of course," he nodded.

"Who are you? Where am I? Can I call an Uber from here?"

"That's more than a question."

"Sorry, but I need answers."

"Okay, I understand, but you went a little fast back there. Are you okay?" he seemed hypnotized by her mouth.

Fergie bit her lip nervously before she replied, ignoring his question when she did. The real answer was no. She was not okay. Her eyes darted around the room.

It was big. Like bigger than her first apartment.

Neat, but lived in. That was nice. She wasn't much of a neat freak herself. There was a huge entertainment center. A comfy looking couch that she could just imagine being curled up on with a bucket of popcorn and a certain blue-eyed stud.

The curtains were an ugly plaid, but they could be changed. And as for the sports memorabilia that decorated one wall, well, she supposed they could be tidied, but she would leave it. She liked sports herself.

What the fuck, Fergie? You movin' in? She shook her head to stop her dangerously delusional daydreaming. She'd just met the guy. And not under anything even resembling normal circumstances.

"What happened back there?"

The handsome stranger did not smile as he considered his words. She usually appreciated a man who thought before he spoke, but at the moment she just wanted to know if any of what she'd been through was real or if it was some kind of hallucination brought on by toxic fumes from the swamp.

Wishful thinking she supposed. She was far too practical a person for her own good. There was just no way in hell she was going to come to grips with what had happened. Not yet any way.

"Look, let's start with something easy. My name is Hudson Stormwolfe."

"I'm Fergie. Where are we?"

"Hello, Fergie. We are in a house that I share with five others, but this is my room. You're safe here."

"Am I?" she snorted.

"Of course, you are always safe with me," he frowned as if it bothered him that she questioned his sincerity.

Oh well, she didn't have the time or patience to deal with his fragile male ego. Fergie had to get back to her apartment, her roommate, and her cat. It might not be much, but it was her life. She took a fortifying breath and looked down at the bandage on her arm.

Beneath the carefully applied wrappings the scratch she'd received from one of those green-skinned weirdos burned like hell. She bit back a groan and flexed her fingers to test out the tightness of her skin.

Well, that sucked, but a little antibiotic treatment should fix her right up. She tossed the blanket away from her legs more determined than ever to get home via the local urgent care facility as soon as possible.

She might need stitches, she thought with a shudder. Fergie did not do needles, which was why even though she was a fan of body art, she did not have a single tattoo or piercing anywhere on her frame. She compensated for it the best way she knew how, with expensive designer shoes of course.

Why would a woman, especially one her size, want to walk on ridiculously tall, skinny heels? To that annoying question Fergie had one standard answer:

Life's short, bitches, make sure your heels aren't.

Speaking of heels. This was only the second time she'd worn the *Pigalle Follies* from an older, but still classic Christian Louboutin line. She'd discovered the red patent leather babies by chance at a new second-hand shop in Morris County. And they were just her size.

One look down her body had Fergie letting loose a shriek that would have made a banshee proud. Something only she could achieve, according to her late paternal grandmother, Nana McAndrews.

Her Irish side tended to run a bit to the fantastical, whereas her Italian blood had her moods running hotter than all the levels of hell in Dante's Inferno. That last bit was according to her father and step-monster. She didn't hate her dad's wife. She just didn't like her either.

"What is it? Are you injured?" Mr. Tall and Growly dropped to his knees beside the bed and ran his large hands over *and under* her blouse and torn skirt.

His hands brushed down her legs, removing the cause of her upset, mainly the scuffed beyond repair red heels, and managed to turn her mind to other small bits that needed some attention. She assumed he was checking for breaks and bruises, but Fergie could not stop the direction of her wayward, and entirely lustful, thoughts.

A strange, tingly sensation started in the pit of her stomach as his long, callused fingers continued searching her limbs for injury. Of course, their hurried movement slowed once his eyes met her heavy-lidded gaze. His hands slowed as they reached mid-thigh. That maddening, sizzling touch changed from perfunctory to passionate.

Exciting her as he drew little circles over her suddenly too warm flesh. Fergie bit her lip to stop herself from groaning out loud. When was the last time someone, anyone, had touched her like that?

He dropped his hands as if he'd been burned and turned around. She watched the muscles in his back ripple as he sucked in great, big gulps of air. Like he'd just run a marathon or something. Fergie was having a hard time herself. She nearly swayed right off the bed. Would have to, had he not turned around, steadying her before she could topple like the mass of boneless woman she currently was.

Holy shit, was that hot. Hudson Stormwolfe, was that his real name, was more man than anyone she'd ever met. She seemed to lose all train of thought at his sudden nearness. Dang. What had she been doing? Oh, right. Her heels.

"Those shoes cost me two weeks salary," she was so busy concentrating on just remembering how to breathe, that she didn't care at all about how shallow she sounded.

"I see, I'm sorry about that," he said and his gravelly voice sent little shocks of awareness right through to her core, "well, besides the shoes, does anything else hurt?"

"My arm is still throbbing."

"It does? I cleaned the wound before I bandaged it. I also applied some healing salve, but you should know, it could still be infected."

"Ugh, I was afraid of that," she frowned down at the bandage.

Crap like that always happened to her. She had the worst immune system. Anytime she caught the slightest little cold it was a month in bed or else she never got better. She couldn't even imagine what this would do to her. She looked up and found herself captivated by his intense stare.

The man had the craziest blue eyes she ever saw, not crazy like mental, just really, really blue. Like little pools of the purest water and boy did she really want to dive right in. She blinked and tried to shake herself from the spell he seemed to weave so effortlessly around her.

"Thank you so much for all your help, but I have to go, I need to stop at urgent care."

"Urgent care?"

"Yeah, you know, one of those budget clinics that've been popping up all over the state."

"Look, if you aren't feeling well, I'd rather you stayed-"

"No, really, I couldn't," she blushed, "it's just a scratch.

A knock at the door brought both their heads up and Fergie was grateful for the respite. Any more meaningful staring and she'd be volunteering to strip her clothes off for the man.

"Come in," bit off Hudson, but she could tell he was not happy about it. Even odder was the way he covered her back up with the blanket.

Fergie looked up and her mouth dropped open. Was everyone here gorgeous? Hudson snarled and looked from her to the visitor and back again with one eyebrow raised.

"Hello, my name is Byram. I'm a friend of Storm's here," he said to her as he entered the light.

He was tall and lithe with light brown hair combed

away from his almost too handsome face. The man was positively pretty she thought a little enviously. He seemed to know that and he smiled a bit sheepishly.

"Byram," Hudson nodded at him expectantly.

"I've come to inspect the wound. If I may?"

FIVE

His female was wounded and in a strange place, but she wasn't afraid. That was a good sign, he noted with some pride.

Her brown sugar and almond scent filled his room, and he knew it would leave its mark on his sheets. Might as well get used to this semi state of arousal he grimaced as he tried to sit next to her and found his pants a bit snug.

It was hard enough wanting to lay claim to her with increasing urgency every second they spent together, but now that the Vampire was in his room, he damn near lost control.

Byram was a good man. He was a Guardian before Storm and they'd worked beside one another for nearly a century. But he couldn't help it. He did not want the suave aristocratic bloodsucker near his mate.

Shit. Guilt filled him at the unkind thought. When he took his pledge, Byram vowed he would never drink from an unwilling donor. He got his blood from a bank, actually. Storm knew this, but his Wolf wasn't as politically correct as the man.

"Easy, brother," Byram said in a low voice as he carefully opened his medical bag.

"Will it leave a scar?" Fergie asked interrupting their little convo.

"No," Storm answered her before Byram could.

It was more promise than threat, but Byram still snorted at the implication. Good. Fucker should be aware if he hurt her, Storm would be hurting him.

"My dear, I will be gentle I promise. Let me see your arm, please and thank you," he said.

Storm always wondered at the traces of his British heritage that sometimes lingered in his accent and cadence of speech. He knew it had been hundreds of years since the Vampire had set foot in the place of his birth, but still, he often wondered at it.

"Ouch," Fergie gasped then giggled.

"I haven't removed the bandage yet," Byram said and smirked.

"I know I was just getting ready. Hudson? Will you

hold my hand?" she bit her lip, and he moved closer to her.

It was good that she wanted him for comfort. A sign that maybe she was feeling some of the same formidable attraction he was. Mating fever affected humans, he knew, but he'd never seen it or experienced it before.

"Here now, he won't hurt you," Storm took her small hand in his and held it as she'd asked.

Such a platonic touch, and yet he felt it all the way down to his marrow. The healthy bronze glow he'd noted in the dark parking lot was a bit paler now after the incident and her consequential wound. Byram unwrapped the bandage carefully, he had to give him credit.

The scent of antiseptic, blood, and Gila Shifter venom reached his nostrils making his Wolf pace in agitation. Something was wrong. The wound was not healing.

"Is it bad? Do I need stitches?"

"No stitches, but I am afraid it's infected," Byram's steel gaze met Storm's, and he knew immediately there was something wrong.

"You know, maybe you can help me? You see, Hudson here hasn't answered my questions yet, but maybe you can," she narrowed her eyes at the deep gauges on her arm.

"If I can," Byram nodded, ignoring Storm's warning look.

"What were those guys who attacked me? Some kind of role-playing groupies or something. Were they in costume? I mean I know some people have strange fetishes. I once saw a picture of some guy who had these little plates implanted underneath his skin so he could resemble a freaking dragon, you believe that?" she was rambling nervously, but Storm couldn't help but think she was adorable.

"Uh, actually, maybe Storm can better answer your questions when he gets back, I need him to help me get some things from my room to treat this," Byram nodded at him.

"Sure," Storm answered.

He needed to do something to keep his mind off the fact that she was lying in his bed. His eyes glanced down as he pictured the way his hands had roamed over her lush curves just minutes ago.

"Storm?"

"Yes, I will be right there," he said to Byram as the Vampire stood to leave, "You will wait? I can have food brought?" he asked her.

"No, I'm fine," she said a little too brightly.

Storm narrowed his eyes, but he had little choice.

She might not know she was his mate, but he did and he had a duty to her. One he relished.

He followed the trail the Vampire left down the hall to his room and Storm entered without knocking.

"Well?"

"Oh, you're welcome, Storm, it is my privilege to help your mate," he snorted as he rummaged through vials in the medicine locker in his room.

"I apologize, Byram, of course I am grateful, but what is wrong?"

"What's wrong is her blood is infected. Something is not right with the Gila Shifter's venom. I don't know how, but it seems to have increased in potency tenfold."

"That's impossible. The mucus those Shifters make should have only a mild effect on even normals," Storm growled.

"Yes, well, this poison is much stronger than anything we have ever seen. I've never come across the likes of it. She will need help fighting otherwise she could lose her arm, and worse than that."

"No, I won't let that happen."

"I understand, Storm, but can I ask why you haven't just told her what she is to you? Your bite would be of more help than anything I have here."

Storm growled and paced the room. He knew his

bite would heal the lovely creature that was his mate, but fucking Kingston and his damn rules. But the Dragon had lived longer than any of them. He had suffered losses none of them had ever known. He was the glue that kept their unit together. Storm owed him obedience.

"I am forbidden to claim her until she knows everything."

"I see," said Byram, "well, Kingston knows best. I have some elixir made from evening primrose and devil's weed which should help slow the venom until you get that all sorted."

"Are you sure it will help?" Storm's worry increased, and he zeroed in on the man.

"You needn't search me for deception, Storm, I would never hurt what is yours," Byram spoke calmly, but Storm could feel his hurt.

Shit. He didn't mean that. Storm knew his words were truth, but he was out of sorts when it came to Fergie. Did having a mate make all men mad? Probably. But it was worth it or so he'd been told.

"She is special, Byram. I can't explain it exactly, but she brings new meaning to me and my Wolf."

"I understand, brother," Byram said, "let's get this to her.

The sounds of feet running and a squealed scream met Storm's ears, and he hurried to open the door.

"What the hell is going on here?" came a roar he knew to be Kingston's followed by a thud.

By the time Storm rounded the bend he saw two things, Furio splayed on the floor with his head in his hands and his little mate wielding the baseball bat he'd had hanging on his wall signed by Don Mattingly in 1985 when he'd received the American League award for MVP. That was a fun year for baseball if he recalled correctly.

Of course, that had nothing to do with why his mate was currently barefooted and swinging said bat against his fellow Guardian's head. Storm grimaced. That was going to leave a mark.

"Oh my God! Why'd you sneak up on me like that?" raged Fergie at the Horse Shifter who seemed dazed.

And no wonder, thought Storm as he took in the lump forming on his forehead. His gaze shifted to his mate's, and he frowned. Her color did not look good.

She swayed a little as she stood one her feet and closed her eyes. Storm ran to her side. He took the bat from her fingers, supporting her frame while she clung to him.

"What happened?"

"Oh, thank God!" she gripped his arm tightly and he could see she was looking a little peaked.

"Byram, can you help Furio?"

"On it," the Vampire said, and sounded as if he was fighting his own laughter as well.

"Come on, sweet," he bent and scooped her in his arms, taking the bat from her hands as he did so.

"Really, I'm too heavy for you to keep picking me up like this," she swallowed after she finished speaking.

Storm frowned. He knew she was feeling dizzy again. The effects of the venom were getting worse. He needed to do something, but first he had to set the record straight.

"You are not too heavy," he stated. In fact, he rather liked the feel of her slight weight in his arms. She was perfect for him. The Fates had designed her so, and he was more than grateful.

"I, uh, think I need to lie down," her mouth was close to his as she spoke.

So close he couldn't resist brushing against her lips with his.

Mine, his Wolf growled.

Six

ergie damn near swooned as he brushed a perfectly gentlemanly kiss on her mouth and set her back down on the bed in his room. How did that happen?

His hot blue gaze travelled down her body and she followed, noting with horror her skirt was basically gone. She squeaked and let go of his neck, both hands worked hard to hold the torn sides of the long khaki confection together.

Well, dang. She was down a pair of heels and a skirt. Was someone trying to tell her something about her fashion choices or what? The big man snorted, and she looked up which had him clearing his throat to cover the sound.

Great. The smart maxi-skirt had once had a small slit that ended with a rather cute red-threaded heart sewn just under her knee, but it was now torn all the way up to her underwear line. Embarrassment rushed through her, heating her cheeks again. She could only imagine what was going through Hudson's brain.

First, she attacked his buddy with a baseball bat, then she was half-naked in his bed. Again. He definitely thought she was nuts, and that wasn't the worst thing he could imagine in her opinion.

OMG. What if he thought she was trying to seduce him? Panicked eyes found his, and she sucked in a breath.

Fat chance of that, Fergie. Look at the man. Hudson Stormwolfe was ridiculously hot, and from the many luxurious items decorating his extra-large bedroom, he was loaded.

Doubly blessed, gorgeous and rich, not to mention one hell of an MMA fighter. The man was unlike anyone she'd ever met. Way out of her league. In fact, Fergie knew he wasn't lacking in the female companionship department. And didn't that just make her sick?

Ugh. She squirmed on the bed. There was just too much of Fergie on display for her own comfort. She was out of sorts and in pain from her ordeal. Bloody, bruised, and not to mention, horny. It was nuts. She felt an insane amount of attraction for the man and he was little more than a stranger.

Not true, a voice inside her seemed to say. It was the same voice that encouraged her to eat that second helping of dessert on a regular basis or to switch jobs on a whim. She really needed to start ignoring that asshole voice.

"Are you alright?" his deeply masculine voice broke through her rambling thoughts and she exhaled.

"Yep, peachy," she snorted.

Shit. Every time she moved the fabric seemed to get further apart revealing more of her ultra-chubby thighs. She cringed, pushing that negative thought from her mind.

How long had she worked on developing a positive self-image? Too long for her to start that crap now. That was it. She was giving up.

"Excuse me," Fergie let go of the skirt and looked at him hoping he would get the hint and back up so she could stand. No such luck, as it turned out.

"There's no rush for you to leave," Hudson began.

Was it her imagination or did he move closer? She couldn't stop looking at his face. Strong jawline, straight nose, plump, kissable lips.

Ahem, knock it off, she scolded herself. If she didn't

stop it soon, she was going to jump him. But Fergie wasn't sure her fragile mind could take rejection. She was better off playing it safe and leaving before she made an ass of herself.

"I'd like to make sure you're a hundred percent alright first," he continued.

"Your doctor friend said I just needed to heal, and you said it yourself, I'm not bruised anywhere else as far as either of us can see," her response was low and breathy. It didn't sound like her at all.

"Except for your shoes," he replied, and there was that sinfully seductive grin again.

The one that made Fergie want to just sit there and stare at him for the next thousand years or so. When the hell had she ever been so corny about a man? She wondered. Probably never. But Hudson Stormwolfe was unlike any other man she'd ever met. He called to something inside her, not just her body, she realized, but to her heart and soul. Uh oh. She must be delirious.

"I'd like to replace them," he said, "your shoes, that is, since they mean that much to you."

"What? Oh no, I couldn't let you do that," she cleared her throat and shook her head, "I apologize if I came off as shallow, I just, uh, like shoes," her cheeks were flaming now.

"It's not shallow to like nice things and I could never think badly about you, sweet. Besides, it would be my pleasure."

Somehow, he was even closer to her than before. So much so, she breathed in the faint peppermint fragrance that seemed to cling to him along with another deeper, masculine scent that made her stomach clench.

Whoa. He really was massive. With shoulders easily twice the width of her own, Hudson was powerfully built. Strong, as he'd already demonstrated, and tall. He loomed over her position on his bed and she realized she'd never felt quite so small.

"What are you six-foot three?" she asked.

Her pulse was racing and heart pounded inside her chest. It was crazy. Inappropriate. Definitely the wrong time. And yet Fergie was completely and overwhelmingly attracted to the man.

"Six-foot five," he grunted.

"Whoa. That's big."

Were all her responses going to be so blasé? She shuddered at the thought. She couldn't do this here with him. Flirting was not her strong suit.

She needed a different atmosphere. A change of clothes. A pair of clean, unbroken gorgeousness on her feet to help boost her confidence.

She couldn't even imagine what she looked like. Then again her rescuer, *Hudson Stormwolfe*, she savored his name in her mind, did not seem to care about her current state of dishevelment.

"I got over a foot on you, tidbit," he grinned.

"That's not hard to do," she laughed.

"I like the sound of your laughter. You should do it more."

"Oh, yeah?"

"Yes," was his only reply.

Awareness seemed to kindle between them, fanning the flame to her already heightened state of arousal. His size, his scent, the heat radiating from his impossibly large frame, were attractive to her. Everything about him was.

She breathed in the airy light scent of mint and man, and a soft moan slipped past her lips. What was it about this man that made her want to reach up and run her fingers along the bit of scruff that only made him even more handsome? She was not a particularly forward person when it came to sex. She liked sex. She'd had it before, though for the most part it had been rather unsuccessful. Still, she'd never actually initiated the act before, but for him she seemed to lose all inhibitions.

"This isn't normal for me," she blurted, eyes going wide at her own brashness.

"I know what you mean," he murmured and inched closer.

Fergie's eyes dropped to half-mast. Her nipples pebbled inside the bra making the normally soft fabric feel abrasive to her tender flesh. She couldn't seem to control her body's reactions to his presence.

All her girly bits seemed to be paying very close attention to the man. She knew all the reasons she should get up and leave, but for some reason, she didn't want to.

Fergie trusted him. To take care of her, to treat her well, and keep her safe. It was unexplainable, but she just did. Warning bells sounded in her head, but her heart ignored them. It wasn't every day a man who looked like that came along and made her feel like she was the sexiest thing on the planet.

Not even close, she thought. Really, when was the last time Fergie felt this way? There was only one honest answer, and that was never.

She decided to throw caution to the wind. Chances like this didn't grow on trees. Not in New Jersey at any rate. His big body seemed to give off heat, warming her, tempting her. Yes, she wanted him closer.

Wanted his mouth on hers. His skin touching, arming hers. His hands on her body.

Yes, she wanted him. Right then and there.

"Who are you?" she whispered as he leaned down, eyes opened, and brushed his hard lips across her mouth.

"You know who I am, *nushe*," he breathed the strange word into her mouth as he fully claimed her lips this time around.

Fergie didn't have a single defense against him. She craved his kiss more than anything else in the world. The sense of rightness was nearly overwhelming as his tongue entered her mouth and dueled with hers.

Yes, she thought as he pulled moan after moan from her throat. He was one hell of a kisser. Fergie reveled in it. She clung to his shoulders, needing his hard body to steady hers.

A deep, throbbing ache flared to life inside of her, starting between her legs. Fergie whimpered as if he was touching her there. She could almost feel him stroking her swollen flesh with those magnificently long fingers of his.

Thankfully, her skirt was already ripped making it easier to maneuver. She opened her legs wide enough to cradle his hard form as he pushed her down into the mattress and settled over her.

She loved the feeling of his weight pressing down on her. So dominant, so possessively male. A whimper escaped her throat as he held her face and tilted it to the side. Right where he wanted her, he held her still with one hand, and plundered her mouth with his.

He felt so damn good. Fergie moaned and wiggled beneath him. Holy shit. She could've come without him ever doing more than just that. Her brain was screaming at her to slow down, but she didn't want to.

"This is too fast," she managed.

Hell no, she wanted to scream at herself. She didn't want him to stop. On the contrary, she wanted him to keep going. Hudson Stormwolfe might've been a stranger a few hours ago, but she felt closer to him than anyone else in the world.

"But it feels so good, sweet," he growled and nipped her earlobe sending tendrils of desire unfurling through her body, "doesn't it feel good?"

"Yes," she moaned, unable or unwilling to lie, take your pick.

He was so much more handsome than any other man she'd ever seen. Glowing blue eyes, strong features, perfect body. And yet that wasn't all. She seemed to know instinctively that he was good and kind.

And how she wanted him. Hell, Fergie was

desperate to have him. She was on fire, burning with need, and he seemed to know it.

Intuitively, he gave her what she wanted. Like he knew how she felt before she did. Anticipating her desires before she even knew what they were, he growled and deepened the kiss. Tracing every dip and mound, every curve with his hands and mouth, Hudson unraveled all her secrets, wrecking her for any other man. She moaned around that clever tongue of his, welcoming his invasion as his hard, muscled body moved against hers in a pantomime of what was to come.

Hopefully, the both of them, she thought wickedly. Hell, she basked in the naughty little image of him entering her with that wonderfully large erection she felt pressing against her. Moisture flooded her panties, and Fergie groaned again.

"Mine," Hudson grunted her new favorite word.

It was so hot and raw. The possessive word was not something she'd ever heard during sex, but she liked it. A lot. He kissed her neck and chin, before reclaiming her mouth as his hands dipped between her legs for a teasing little rub.

He didn't let up, not for a second. He just kept kissing her. Pinning her to the bed with his hard body, stroking her mouth with his insanely adept tongue. Fuck, Fergie meant it when she'd said he was hard.

Every inch of his superb physique was corded with thick ropes of muscle. She ran her hands down his back, tracing the ripples as he moved on top of her. His denim covered cock pressed against her core, teasing her with promises of pleasure to come.

Too many clothes stood between them, too many restraints. No sooner had she had that thought then he'd reared up as if he'd read her mind. He worked her blouse open and removed his t-shirt at the same time so she could look and touch to her heart's content.

"So beautiful, *nushe*," he grunted, freeing one berry-tipped mound from the confines of her ugly, but comfortable support bra, "so sweet."

"Yes," she echoed the sentiment.

Her eyes ate up every tanned inch of his gloriously hot body. Fingers traced his pecs, arms, and abs, so immersed was she that she hardly knew what he was doing until she felt his mouth close over her breast.

Fergie moaned aloud as he suckled the hardened nub. Spikes of pleasure shot through her. They were both panting with desire by the time his head came up. She was truly desperate now. She wanted him to shuck away the rest of their clothing, to bury himself deep within her heat.

"Want you, *nushe*," he growled.

"Yes," she groaned her assent as he released her nipple only to lick the valley between her breasts, upwards to her neck, her chin, and back to her open mouth.

"You taste like marzipan," he whispered kissing her and molding her flesh to his hands.

She'd never had anything like this happen to her. What was this godlike man doing with a chubby ginger like her? He pulled away from her, blue eyes scowling at her.

"You're fucking gorgeous. Every strand of that fiery mane of yours, every curve of this spectacular body is perfect. You were made for me, *nushe*, and this," he cupped her sex, "this is mine. I'm going to take you here with my mouth, my fingers, and my cock. You want that?"

She swallowed hard and nodded her head. Yes, she wanted that. Wanted him. So damn much.

"Gonna make you come so hard you won't remember your name."

"It's Fergie," she whimpered.

She was uncertain whether she'd told him her name before, but if they were going to do this, she wanted to make sure he'd damn well remember it.

"My name is Fergie McAndrews."

"You are mine, sweet Fergie McAndrews," he growled and brought her mouth to his, the hand on her throat tightening ever-so-slightly, "if you want me to stop, tell me now, because once I start, there isn't a thing in heaven or earth that will stop me from claiming you."

SEVEN

There. He explained it, Storm thought as he gazed into his mate's gleaming butterscotch eyes.

She was so fucking beautiful. His mind was a buzzing whirl of activity with ways to please her. Like all the cogs in his clock decided to activate at once, and every single one of them was focused on one thing. *Her.*

Fuck, he was trembling like a green pup. His dick hard as steel, he whined with need as he brushed his cloth-covered hardness against her. The Wolf inside him growled, pressing against his skin. The beast wanted out, to take part in the claiming.

True, Kingston had warned him against doing just that, but Storm knew what he was doing. Fuck it all, he thought, that damned interfering Dragon could not stop him now.

Not when his sweet mate was moaning enticingly against his invading tongue. She was so sinfully sexy, he damn near spilled his seed in his pants. He wasn't going against orders. Not exactly. Kingston said Storm had to explain the situation to his mate before he could claim her.

Well, he just did. Didn't he? All he needed was her answer.

"Well, *nushe*? Will you let me have you?" he asked, a slight tendril of fear that she'd reject him held him still.

"Yes please," she whispered and covered his chin, his neck, and finally, his mouth with whisper light kisses.

That was it. He had her assent. Storm growled and took control of her kiss. He was now a Wolf on a mission. Pressing her down into the bed, he hovered above her luscious form. Then he moved.

Tearing the jeans from his overheated body, he was gratified to see the widening and apparent appreciation in her big brown eyes as she took in his naked form.

He was fascinated by that look. Storm had never seen eyes that particular shade of brown. They were more like molten caramel than chocolate, maybe honey or butterscotch were better descriptions.

Whatever. He was a Wolf not a poet. All he knew was her eyes were incredible. Beautiful and bright, and in the center of each was a ring of amber flame. His *nushe* was fiery inside and out. A spicy little morsel, and his alone.

Storm licked the seam of his lips as he took in her own spectacular form from head to toe. She was a curvy goddess of a woman. The perfect mate and exactly what he'd always wanted. He tugged her bra off, using his razor-sharp claws to cut through the wide straps of the functional underwear.

It was a plain, simple garment, but he found it sexy as hell. Besides, it was the treasures it kept hidden from him that held his true interest. Storm growled softly. He looked his fill before reaching out a hand to touch.

She was pale there and on her soft belly, unlike the lightly tanned skin across her chest and arms. Another slice and away fell her torn skirt leaving her in nothing except a pair of pretty little pink panties. Too bad those had to go too.

His female, his *Fergie*, he thought, testing the sound of her name in his mind, whimpered as he skimmed the sensitive flesh of her stomach with his lips and fingertips. He'd already stroked along her sweet sex, but now he would claim her with his mouth.

Face to face with the tiny swatch of damp cloth that attempted to hide his prize from him, he took a deep breath. The scent of her arousal mixed with the subtle almond sweetness that was all her reached his sensitive nostrils.

His inner Wolf howled and snapped his jaws, demanding the man do something already. He leaned closer and placed his open mouth on her heat, sucking her plump lips through the thin cotton covering.

Mine. The sentiment echoed through him like a trumpet blast. He sucked again. Hard. Fergie bucked her hips and gasped. Her wide eyes met his, and a louder growl reverberated through him. Storm snagged her panties in his fingers and tugged until they snapped.

"Mine," he growled aloud.

His sweet *nushe* nodded her head and Storm's Wolf howled in triumph. Keeping her eyes locked with his, he dipped down to taste her honey sweet nectar straight from the source. Fergie nearly bucked him off of her, that was how strong his little mate truly was, as he lapped at her heat. But Storm held true, swallowing down every drop of her moisture until it ran down his chin.

His sweet Fergie's hands found his hair, but she wasn't tugging him away. Oh no, not his *nushe*. He growled in delight as she shoved him closer, grinding her sex on his face, chasing the satisfaction only he could deliver.

He felt the first ripple of her release and went for broke, knowing he had to strike while she was high on pure pleasure. Storm reared up, gripping his cock at the base, he placed himself at her entrance.

He met her eyes looking for any sign of discomfort or change of heart and thankfully found none. Fuck, she felt good as he pressed inside her slickness. Perfect, he thought and sunk into her velvet heat deeper.

So deep. He stretched her tightness until she fit him like a glove. Out he inched, mourning the temporary loss of her sublime sex, and growling his pleasure when he drove in once again. In and out, he repeated the move. Withdraw, enter with hard, precise flexes of his hips that had them both grunting.

Her orgasm grew and grew, coursing through her until she screamed with it. The spasms caused her channel to squeeze him tightly. It wouldn't be long till he followed her lead into sweet oblivion, but he had to claim her first.

Storm thrust once, twice, three times, until her moans reached a crescendo. Then he struck with his

Wolf's fangs. He bit down on that tender place between her neck and shoulder, slicing through her soft skin like butter.

The Wolf inside him howled, demanding blood and he swallowed down her life's fluid greedily, sealing the bond the Fates had begun between them. He sealed the wound with his saliva tossing his head back. Storm's triumphant howl was met with her own scream of completion as another wave of bliss washed over them both.

Exhausted and overwhelmed no doubt, his mate's eyes drifted closed. Finally, the beast within him seemed to cease his snarling and Storm tugged her closer, wrapping her soft form in his arms.

Power pulsed through his body and he felt those same changes that had taken place during the battle earlier that night take shape inside of him. Their *mate-bond* thrummed in his ears.

He could already feel his Shifter strength working to heal her from her attack. His Wolf's saliva would clean her blood of the venom from that Lizard fuck who dared hurt her. His claiming bite might have other side effects, but it was too early to tell. At the very least she should get some of the benefits of his kind.

She was his now, and that was enough of a benefit for him. He had never felt more whole. A Guardian's true mate was a rare thing, he knew and understood that. Storm thanked the Fates for the gift of her and for the added strength that would help him protect her. What had she called it? Blinking. He smiled at the memory.

His newfound powers would allow him to call upon deeper magic than he ever had before. It was like blinking, he thought, the way he moved during the fight. The black smoke that had whirled around him was as if made from the shadows themselves, and now, he had the ability to move through them or between them as it were.

The other surprise benefit were the whirls of blue energy that he'd always called upon to aid him in shifting between shapes. Only now, that energy was tangible, making his punches and kicks that much more powerful in battle.

Yes, he liked the increase in strength. He would use it to keep his *nushe* safe. Odd how that word flowed so easily when he spoke to her. His grandfather was only a quarter Lenape, but he still had Native American blood and the term of endearment was perfect for his mate. His beloved *nushe*. The woman who now owned his heart. Storm exhaled.

"Rest now, *nushe*," he said and draped a sheet over them both.

He listened to her steady breathing until he felt himself drifting off beside her. It didn't matter what his leader had said. Fergie was his now.

His to love and his to shield.

Eight

alk about Déjà vu, she blinked slowly and took in her strange surroundings. Okay, not as strange as the first time around, she snorted then covered her mouth and looked at the huge sleeping male next to her.

OMG. Fergie could not believe what she'd done. Holy shit. She'd had dirty, muff-diving, mind-blowing sex with a complete fucking stranger.

She kept her hands over her mouth and nose to stop from snorting again at her ridiculous thoughts. But yeah, he was literally a *fucking* stranger, cause, *hello*, she so tapped that fine ass of his. Score one for fluffy chicks everywhere! And she'd barely even spoken to the gorgeous hunk of man.

Dang. She shook her head. Bad jokes aside, she had to get out of there. There was such a thing as wearing out one's welcome.

Besides, Fergie needed to think. Now that the body was finally satisfied, because again let's face it, the second she'd seen the guy her ovaries basically exploded. She was like one huge hormone. And that was putting it mildly.

Yeah, she needed to put together the pieces of what had happened over the last twenty-four hours. Regretfully, she slid out from under her lover's arm careful not to wake him. Good thing he was a heavy sleeper.

He exhaled a deep breath and turned onto his side giving her a splendid view of his nibble-worthy glutes. And, she noted with pleasure, he did not snore.

God he was cute. His thick glossy curls were deliciously mussed, and the hard slash of his mouth was more relaxed in sleep. He looked good enough to eat. Definitely good enough for round two.

No, bad girl! She scolded herself and inched across the floor. Crap. She was buck ass naked and her clothes were torn. She couldn't even look at her heels. What was she going to do?

Good thing the man whose bones she'd oh-so-willingly jumped was a certifiable giant otherwise it might be difficult for her chubby ass to sneak out and commence with her well-deserved walk of shame.

Fergie opened the bottom drawer of a sleek black dresser and peeked inside. Score two for her! She grabbed a pair of clean sweatpants and a matching black hoodie and shrugged into them. Carefully, she snagged her scuffed and broken heels, because maybe there was a shoe repair service that could work miracles somewhere out there. Positive attitude and delightfully sore body intact, she inched out the door.

"Shit," she whispered and leaned against the wall in the hallway.

Where the fuck was she? The hallway looked a little like that dungeon room at that medieval tournament dining place she'd gone to for her twelfth birthday. Stone walls were decorated with rich tapestries and gleaming weapons. The occasional piece of sports memorabilia among them.

Okay, so maybe Hudson was some kind of rich eccentric. Fergie didn't know, and truthfully, she didn't care. She wanted to be gone before tall, dark, and sexy woke up.

Having to witness the moment he realized he'd been high off the adrenaline from the fight, and that was the only reason he'd fallen into bed with a plump little ginger from the other side of the tracks was not on her to-do list.

Fergie tiptoed down the impossibly long hallway. At least there was a long plush runner along the undoubtedly cold stone floors, she nodded as she continued barefoot on her way towards what she could only hope was a kitchen and a telephone. Ooh, and a bathroom.

She should've checked for one of those first, she supposed. Of course, now that she'd thought about it, the need to tinkle was all she could focus on.

Ugh. Pressing her legs tightly together, she hurried down the hall until she came to a right turn which she quickly followed. Finally, she saw a door similar to her, *uh*, to Hudson's room, and she tried the handle.

Unlocked. Thank heavens, she thought as she listened to the satisfying click of the knob before pushing it in.

"Please be a bathroom," she whispered as she looked into the room.

Soft light filled the space from a tall lamp in the far corner. Crap. It was another bedroom. It took a moment for her to adjust to the dimness, and even when she did, Fergie was still unprepared for the shock of what waited inside.

Her eyes widened and she bit back a scream as she

took in the huge black panther in the center of the room. Glossy fur, glowing pink eyes, and humongous teeth. The animal's claws clicked on the wood floor as it stepped closer to where she was standing. Her pulse sped up and the big cat turned and hissed at Fergie.

"Oh fuck," she whimpered, and took a step back, but the big kitty didn't like that. Not one bit.

It advanced on Fergie, slinking across the room one step at a time. She kept moving until her back hit the wall and the snarling, growling beast continued to close in on her. It pressed forward until its dripping fangs were the only thing she could see.

"Elena, back off," growled a familiar voice, and Fergie turned to see Hudson standing in the hallway.

She had never been so happy to see anyone in her life. Relief poured through her, but it was short lived as he continued to frown in her direction. The black cat hissed again, and Fergie closed her eyes tight and whimpered.

"Elena, back the fuck off," he said again.

The cat must be his pet or something, she figured, because after hissing once more at Fergie, the creature suddenly bounded off. It went back inside the room from whence it came and slammed the door shut.

Hmm, that was odd. Did panthers close doors?

"You left," he growled, and stalked towards her.

"What the hell was that?" she asked ignoring his statement.

"That was a Panther. You. Left."

"What are you like the Tiger King of New Jersey or something?"

"The *what*?" he cocked his head to the side.

"Ugh, never mind," she walked past him, determined to ignore the pull of his fabulous body clad only in a pair of unbuttoned jeans.

Seriously, if she thought he looked good enough to eat before that was only because she had yet to see him like this. All of her girly bits stood up and screamed for attention the second her eyes landed on him. A fact that scared the shit out of her. She'd never been so out of control of her own body before.

Hell, she hadn't even realized she'd stopped walking until he stood directly behind her. The steel bands that were his arms wrapped around her body and large, warm hands squeezed her tight. She felt his hot breath on the back of her neck to the place where he'd kissed her so roughly the night before. Damn, but she loved every second of it.

When his lips found the spot where she'd undoubtedly sported a hickey, lightning bolts of desire and need spiked through her. She craved him. Wanted his touch like she wanted air to breathe. He was in her blood, channeling a path straight to her sex which throbbed with a longing only he could fulfill.

"Mine," he whispered and kissed that spot again.

Fergie wanted desperately to give in to his caveman-like claim, but this was the twenty-first century. Men didn't simply beat their chests and proclaim a person as their property. Even if the thought of him doing just that made her a sopping wet bundle of needy nerves.

"I need a bathroom, and a phone," she said, ignoring her flights of fancy.

This was just a strangely hot one-night stand. No matter what this man thought right now, it would be over sooner than later anyway.

She was just avoiding the muddy confusion that would inevitably end with her gaining fifteen pounds from all the chocolate ice cream therapy she would no doubt need once he dumped her fluffy ass.

"Of course," he said, and took her hand, tugging her back down the hallway to his bedroom door, which for some reason seemed a much shorter trip on the return.

"Everything you need is waiting for you. I will get us some food, and then we can talk," he walked her inside the bedroom to a gleaming blue door off to the left of the bed.

That was funny. She hadn't noticed it earlier. She nodded her head and smiled her thanks. A shower did sound marvelous.

Inside the enormous bathroom, Fergie gasped at the size of the bathtub. It was like a miniature swimming pool. She opened the drawers of the vanity and found a brand new toothbrush still in the package, her favorite brand of toothpaste and mouthwash next to it.

That was odd, she thought but decided to go with it. Turning the crystal knob of the faucet towards the red tab, she watched a moment as the tub began to fill with warm water. Perfect, she thought and went to use the toilet before washing her hands and brushing her teeth. Afterwards, she climbed into the mini-pool.

"Oh," she sighed and allowed the water, which was at the exact temperature she'd always strived to get somewhere between hot and lobster boil and leaned her head back.

The bandage on her arm had come loose in the water and she unwrapped it hesitating at first. She wasn't good with blood and gore, but this was her body, damn it, and she swallowed down any repulsion she felt.

"Whoa," she murmured and twisted her arm this way and that.

The huge, gaping wound from the night before

had receded to two pencil thin marks that looked weeks old. Astonishing. A knock on the door brought her head up, and she panicked for a moment.

"When you're ready, I'll take you to the dining room. Breakfast is being prepared now," he said through the door.

"Okay. I'll be a few minutes," she bit her lip and picked up the soap.

After washing her body and shampooing her hair, Fergie drained the water from the tub and stood up. She twisted a second crystal knob and watched in amazement as some of the stones in the wall pushed forward creating a sort of natural spout from the ceiling.

A second later, clear, warm water poured down on top of her, rinsing the remaining suds clean from her body. She gasped in happy surprise as the stream rained down on her from that stone spout much like a waterfall.

She couldn't call it a shower really, it was much more beautiful and decadent than any showerhead she'd ever seen. Large enough for two, to be sure. She allowed one, *or three*, images of Hudson to enter her mind and bit back a moan as she pictured him in the water with her.

Flashes of last night flittered through her brain and

Fergie whimpered. No. She could not go there right now. She shut off the water abruptly, determined to get back on track.

Fergie needed to go home. She had to check in with Jessenia and go to her job. That in mind, she grabbed a fluffy blue towel off of the shelf and patted her body dry, loving the plush feel of the luxuriously thick terrycloth.

After taming her tangled mass of hair into something much more manageable, she grabbed a piece of ribbon and tied it back. Then, she applied some lotion to her skin, which tended to dry out easily, and used the unopened stick of lavender deodorant she found under the sink.

It was really strange that he seemed to have everything she needed. Like the bathroom came equipped with all of her favorite things. All she did was think of them, and when she opened a drawer, they were there. Like magic.

Nah. She shook her head. Her taste was pretty generic when it came to toiletries. Chances were *Mr. Studly* probably ordered the stuff in bulk for his nightly conquests.

Kudos to the big guy, she supposed. He was hot. Hot guys get laid. Period.

There was nothing she could do about the stab of

jealousy that went through her at the thought of him with other women.

Forget about that, she told herself firmly. On to the next issue. Clothes, or her lack thereof. She looked around for the sweats she'd borrowed, but they were nowhere to be seen. Exasperated, she exited the bathroom with the towel wrapped firmly around her.

"Hey," Fergie stopped in her tracks as she took in the naked backside of Hudson Stormwolfe bent over while he tugged on a pair of jeans.

He turned around before zipping up, and she got a scandalous view of his short-cropped pubes. Since when did that turn her on? Well, how about, since the owner of said pubes had the most amazingly defined *V* that led straight to them.

Gulp. He grinned at her knowingly, but Fergie did her best to ignore the sinfully sexy expression. His glossy curls were glistening with damp and she realized he must've also taken a shower. Somewhere else, obviously. He froze her with his glittering sapphire eyes and she held herself still even though he seemed to devour her from head to toe with his gaze. She wished she had something else on besides a towel, or even better, nothing at all.

"Uh, I don't have any clothes," she stated the obvious.

She backed up a step as he stalked across the room towards her, his long legs ate up the space far too quickly for her to have time to do more than simply blink and breathe. Her own stare had been so riveted to his, Fergie hadn't noticed the Neiman Marcus bag in his hand.

"For you," he said and one side of his mouth tilted up in what she suspected was as close to a smile as he was going to give her.

"Thanks," she said and took the bag, "when did you get this?" she gestured to the bag.

Fergie motioned for him to turn around before she rummaged through it. Hudson snorted and grinned but did as she'd indicated. Allowing her some semblance of privacy.

"I ordered them online, and had a friend go by to pick them up," he said.

Fergie gasped as she withdrew a beautiful sheer, navy blue panty and camisole set in her exact size. She removed the tags and slipped them on loving the feel of the incredibly soft fabric. Next was a wraparound dress in a matching color with tiny little red flowers dancing across the material. It was simply gorgeous.

Even better was a certain box she recognized beneath it. Fergie's heart pounded as she lifted it out of the bag and opened it. Inside were a pair of

Louboutin's identical to the ones she'd ruined the night before.

Her mouth went dry. She couldn't take them. Could she? When she looked up it was to find those sapphire eyes glittering in appreciation as they took her in from head to toe.

"Allow me," he said and knelt at her feet placing one hand on his shoulder as he lifted one foot, then the other and slid them into the shoes.

"Perfect," he said.

"They're beautiful," Fergie agreed with pleasure as she slid into the perfectly designed footwear. Only, the man wasn't looking at her feet. He was staring at her.

"Breakfast?" she asked, breaking that stare with the one thing she was sure anyone would believe when they looked at her, that she was hungry of course.

What they wouldn't believe was that Fergie wasn't noshing for food. *Uh uh*. She wanted him.

Something inside of her seemed to light up just being near him, something growly, with a mind and possibly a voice of its own. She knew one thing for sure, when the whispered word entered her head, it hadn't originated with her.

Yes, it came from inside of her, but it was separated too. No matter how much she wanted to agree with the simple monosyllabic declaration and the sentiment that went along with it, whispers of apprehension filled her.

Fergie shook her head and exhaled. But that didn't matter, the voice spoke to her again. Louder.

Mine.

NINE

Storm led his mate to the kitchen after hearing her simple request for breakfast. What a thoughtless oaf he'd been to forget to feed his precious female! He noted her wary expression and realized he was growling again. Shit. He always seemed to be doing that around her.

"Sorry," he said, "this way."

The corridors of the Keep could go on forever if you didn't have a clear destination in mind. It was designed that way to stop intruders and burglars by keeping them busy for hours, days, or sometimes longer. Enchantments and wards such as those were set up all around the large and ancient castle.

Built on sacred Lenape tribal lands, the added

magic of the Shifters, Vampires, Witches, and Fae who'd lived there over the years only served to build up its stores.

"When walking about this place make sure you know exactly where you want to end up or you could be lost," he mumbled to caution her.

"Really? You should maybe think about an intercom system cause, well, it is a really big house, with um, wild animals lurking about."

He grunted. Shit. He'd forgotten about her meeting with Elena in her Panther form. The woman was the only female Guardian in the Keep. She was a good fighter. Tough as nails and loyal too. Of course, he didn't like that she'd scared his mate, but that was his fault not hers.

"So, Hudson," his *nushe* interrupted his train of thought, "are you going to explain what that was back there?" she asked the question he'd been dreading to answer.

He held out a chair for her in the informal dining room. The walls were painted a soft gray with little adornment. It felt wrong to him for the first time ever. Like there should be paintings on the wall and flowers on the enormous granite rectangle that served as the table and was always cold to the touch.

He pushed her chair in gently and started removing the silver covers to the steaming chafing dishes that held just under a dozen varieties of food. He'd always appreciated the Keep's mystical ability to have food ready and waiting for each of its dwellers. The Guardians had become accustomed to having hot meals whenever they wanted. A special gift, one he was even more grateful to have now that he had someone to share it with.

"This looks fantastic," she eyed the dishes of perfectly cooked bacon, scrambled eggs, miniature quiches, toasted slices of Italian bread dripping butter, bite sized fruit Danishes, thinly sliced tomatoes with olive oil drizzled on top, and golden hash browns, "um, before we eat don't you think we should talk?"

"I will tell you everything you want to know, *nushe*, but first let me feed you," he began filling her plate with little bits of delicacies he thought she'd like while she poured them both coffee from the steaming silver service.

Something inside of him was aware of her in a way he'd never noticed any other being before. The way her fiery mane seemed to curl at the ends just around her shoulders had his hands itching to stroke the soft strands. The tiny hum of pleasure when she took her first sip of coffee made his jeans a little bit tighter and his own breathing a bit heavier.

Damn. He had it bad. He shook his head and placed the dish in front of her, noting her surprise. Okay, maybe he went a little overboard, but she was such a tiny little thing. He wanted her safe, healthy, and happy above all else.

Storm sat next to her and accepted the cup she offered, losing himself for a moment in her almost too pretty eyes. He knew he had more explaining to do, but he didn't want to ruin the moment.

"This is a feast. How did you have time to prepare all this and shower?" she asked, but before he could answer they were interrupted.

"Oh ho, this is some fancy spread," Furio trotted into the dining room and Storm cursed under his breath.

"Oh, uh, I apologize about the bat," she whispered embarrassed.

"No worries, I'm good."

"Wow, I thought I gave you a lump?" she stared at the Stallion's head in wonder and Storm cleared his throat.

"Uh, I'm a fast healer," shrugged his friend.

Shit. He might have a bit more explaining to do

than he realized. Furio snorted amusedly which only served to annoy Storm's Wolf further. He growled at the Stallion who ignored him and zeroed in on his mate with a wide shit-eating grin.

Oh hell fucking no, Storm growled louder ignoring Fergie's openmouthed stare for the moment.

"So, tell me all about yourself, gorgeous," the Stallion winked at his mate.

He waited for the rage to come, but Storm's Wolf merely chuffed in disgust. The animal within him seemed more at ease now that his luscious mate wore his bite-mark on her neck where all could see.

The permanent symbol that would always remain a part of her smooth skin was not the only sign that she was mated. It was in the scent she bore as well. Something his beast recognized and cherished. A sweet seductive mixture of her natural sugary almond fragrance and his own minty masculine musk.

The result was fucking perfect, in his not-so-humble opinion. Just watching her smile and joke with Furio without wanting to kill the man was a pleasant change. She seemed to be taking everything in stride so far. So much so, it humbled him. She was really a treasure. *His treasure*. Storm was one lucky Wolf.

"Okay, so I remember you from last night," she

quirked her head to the side and Storm's heart damn near tripped in his chest.

"That's right, I was with Storm."

"Why do you all call him that? His name is Hudson-"

"Because he'd bite my head off if I called him that."

"I prefer, Storm, from my friends," he answered.

"Did you want me to call you that?' she asked.

"You can call me anything you like," he said, and it was true.

"Alright then, Hudson," she smiled shyly.

Storm's heart pounded inside his chest. So damn hard it nearly burst through his ribs. No, he didn't mind if she called him by his given name.

"Anyway, how are you feeling?" Furio asked.

"Good, thank you. Actually, the scratch is pretty much all gone," she marveled and held up her wrist.

"I see. It's to be expected after the mate bite," the Stallion picked up a slice of tomato and popped it in his mouth.

"I'm sorry, what?" Fergie asked.

"Uh, Furio," Storm didn't like the stunned look on her face.

He knew it was because he'd failed to really tell her what it all meant. Shit. He'd thought to do that now, over breakfast, without an audience. Motioning with his hand for pony boy to shut the fuck up wasn't working though, and the idiot kept right on.

"Well, the old Wolf got you to mate him right? So, once he bit you, he transferred some of his magic to you. Congrats by the way."

"I'm sorry, say that again," she placed her napkin down and sat back in the chair.

"Furio!"

"No, I want to hear what he has to say," she said sweetly and smiled at the other man, "what's a mate bite?"

"Uh," finally the idiot caught on and closed his mouth.

"We can talk about this," Storm started when her whiskey eyes flashed at him nervously.

"Oh, shit, you didn't tell her she was your mate? You didn't explain about the mate bite and what it meant? What the fuck were you thinking, *cump*?"

"It was a little hard to think at the time," he growled, but Furio just glared back at him.

"Kingston said not to mate her until you explained."

"And I did, I told her she was mine," Storm growled back at the other Guardian.

"Okay, I am just gonna go on my way now. So, this was fun," she smiled tightly, "but, uh, no worries, boys.

You're fine. I'm, uh, just gonna call an Uber," Fergie stood up.

"*Nushe*, please, you have to listen," he tried.

"My name is Fergie, not *nushe*, whatever that means, and you two are crazy, so I'm just going to leave now," she backed away from his touch and that hurt more than he cared to admit, "I will send you money to pay for the new clothes and shoes," she gestured to the new outfit he'd gotten for her.

Fuck.

This was not going how he'd planned. His Wolf started snarling all over again. One thing was certain, he could not let her leave him.

"Dude, you need to stop growling at your mate, you are scaring her," Furio chastised him.

Shit.

He hadn't even realized what he was doing. Looking at her wan face and tense expression and the Horse was right. He was scaring her.

"I wasn't-"

"W-Why do you sound like an animal when you do that?" she kept walking backwards until her back hit the wall.

"That's cause we're Shifters, babe, we have dual natures, sort of like animal spirit guides, but we can wear their fur when called upon," Furio winked.

"What? Shifters? Look, I don't know what you are both into, but I need to go to work."

"*Nushe*, last night was special. You can't just go-"

"Like hell I can't, buddy!" she yelled.

A look he much preferred to the scared uncertain expression she wore moments ago. He could handle her being mad at him, but not scared. Never that.

"What is going on in here?" Kingston stalked inside the dining room and took in the two Shifters and the human woman in one glance.

His golden eyes slammed into Storm and the Wolf felt his Alpha's anger down to his furry tail.

Well, shit. This whole thing truly sucked. Storm had no idea how it had all gone sideways and so fast too.

"Miss? Are you okay?" the leader of their unit raised his hands and addressed Fergie like she was a frightened animal.

"I, I think so, but he's growling like some mad dog, and this one here keeps talking about Shifters, mating, biting, and I just really need to leave."

"Okay, try to calm yourself. If you take a right down this corridor and a left at the end you will arrive at the front door. Wait for me there, and I will take you where you need to go," Kingston stated.

"Alright, but I want my phone," she demanded.

"I will see to that myself," Kingston replied.

"Fergie, please wait," Storm nearly lost control of his Wolf then, the animal pressed against his skin, scratching and snapping his jaws angrily at the thought of the Dragon or anyone taking his mate.

"Stand down, Storm," the Dragon commanded, but the Wolf wouldn't hear of it.

"Oh my God," Fergie covered her mouth with her hand and took off down the hall.

Four hands held him back as he tried to go after her. He couldn't stop the snarls and growls from spilling out of his throat, but he would never hurt her. She had to know that.

"Come on, man," Furio grunted and held on tightly, "you're losing your shit, Storm."

"I told you not to mate her unless you explained it all, Guardian! You disobeyed and now you will reap what you've sewn," the Dragon growled.

"She's mine," Storm insisted, and felt himself lose control of his Shift.

The whine of his Wolf followed by a long, mournful howl fell from his lupine lips. Furio and Kingston held firm until the latter rose up, allowing some of his Dragon to fill his face.

"You will obey me, Guardian, I am the Alpha here," Kingston stated, "I will take the human home and she will be safe. After I come back, we will discuss your transgressions and find a solution for this mess you've created. Now, you will remain here while I tend to the female," his final words were infused with his Alpha powers, a command Storm could not simply shake off.

He sat on his hind legs and snarled at his leader. Fuck him for vowing to obey the pompous son of a bitch to begin with. He wanted to tear into him, to meet his beast claw to claw, fang to fang, to fight for the honor of escorting his mate home.

"Come on, bro, these are not your real feelings. It's just mating fever," Furio attempted to soothe him, but Storm merely growled at the Horse.

He was burning with the need to chase down his mate, but his Alpha's command was final. He had no choice, but to wait.

"Come on, *cumpy*. You know Kingston will make sure she's safe. You can sit here growling at me or we can come up with a plan for you to woo her later on," Furio tried to reason with him.

Finally, Storm saw the logic in his statements. He took a deep, calming breath and exchanged fur for skin once more. Walking over to the large buffet against the opposite wall, he opened a drawer for some extra clothing they kept there for random Shifts such as his.

Tugging on the sweats, Storm listened for the sounds of Kingston's tires speeding away. He closed his eyes when he found the bittersweet noise and felt his heart squeeze inside his chest more and more with each foot of space that lapsed between him and his mate.

Nushe, his Wolf cried.

TEN

"So, you're Hudson's boss?" Fergie tried anything to break the ice between her and the rather formidable looking man who was currently driving her back to her apartment.

"Yes, in a matter of speaking. Did you just call him Hudson?" his lips quirked.

"Yeah, that's his name, right?"

"I suppose it is," the stranger nodded.

The stranger was handsome, she supposed, but not like *him*. Hudson Stormwolfe was in a class all by himself as far as she was concerned. Too bad he was batshit fucking crazy.

She closed her eyes to catch her breath for a moment. There was something really weird about what they'd all been talking about in that dining room.

Shifters and mate bites, it was like something out of a fantasy novel.

"So, uh," she began, "I need to pick up my roommate's truck at the library," she said and rattled off the address.

"Sure," he nodded, "I think we have other things to discuss as well."

"Like what?" she pretended she didn't know what he was talking about. Somehow it seemed easier.

"Like Shifters and the fact that you mated one of my Guardians."

"Okay, just hold on, what the hell are Shifters? And what is that word *mated* supposed to mean? Like sex? Cause I am not discussing that with you," her inner sass demon had just woken up it would seem, but Fergie was on a roll now and she was not going to stop until she had some answers, "and when you say *guardian*, do you mean like your *ward*? Like something out of a Bronte novel?"

The man had the audacity to chuckle. He pulled up at the scene of the crime, where she'd been attacked the night before and Fergie shuddered.

"Is this where it happened?"

"Yes," she said and swallowed down a lump of fear.

It tasted bitter, but for some reason she knew she was safe now. Perhaps it was because of the giant black wolf that was watching her from behind the fence. She didn't think to mention it, merely met the beautiful beast's piercing blue eyes before turning back to the man who'd driven her back to the parking lot where she'd left Jessenia's truck.

It didn't matter. He seemed to already spot the wolf in the marshes, and he was not happy about it. His eyes flashed gold and her inner warning bells went off, but still, she felt the need to speak up for the beautiful animal.

"It's not hurting anyone," she said ready to defend the creature with fur so dark it reminded her of a midnight sky.

"No, he's not hurting anyone, but he's also disobeying a direct order," he grunted.

"Look, what's your name?"

"I am Kingston Baldric. I am one of those Shifters, Furio was talking about. Like Hudson Stormwolfe, or Storm as we call him. He is one of my Guardians, and no, I don't mean in some gothic novel kind of way. In fact, he should have explained all of this to you last night before he bit and mated you," he was talking to her, or so she thought, but for some reason his eyes were glued on the black wolf.

"You all keep talking in riddles. Shifters, bites, mates, marks? What does it all mean?"

"This is going to sound strange, Ms. McAndrews, but since you are already halfway there, I will simply say it. Storm, Furio, Elena, and myself are what the supernatural world calls Shifters. You met Byram too, and he's a Vampire."

"Uh-"

"Shifters are dual-natured beings who share our souls with that of an animal or creature thought to be mythological. Storm is a Wolf Shifter."

"So, he's a Werewolf?"

"Yes," he chuckled, "but not in the way you mean. He shares his soul with a Wolf and he can, therefore, communicate with that part of himself, draw on the power of the beast, and shift into his animal with the help of magic."

"Okay, so Werewolves are real and now magic is real too?" she hedged.

"Yes. Magic is real. So real, in fact that we, those of us who live in the Keep where you spent the night, have all vowed to protect it. We are the Guardians of Chaos, and I am the leader of our unit."

"Of course you are," she muttered and went for the door.

She really needed to get off the crazy-town train. Like now. Good sex was no excuse for losing her mind.

"Okay, let me try this another way. The men who

attacked you," he said stopping her in her tracks, "what did they look like."

"I don't know. They were weirdos. Probably a cult or something."

"Why do you say that?"

"Because they had plastic surgery or makeup to make them look not human. Green skin, weird eyes, fangs, and claws," she shrugged trying to minimize how afraid she'd been.

"They were Shifters, Fergie. Gila Shifters to be exact. Like people, not all Shifters are good," he said apologetically.

"Great. Now, I am supposed to worry about man-animal-monsters getting me?"

"There are female Shifters as well. I believe you walked into Elena's room back at the Keep while she was in her animal form. She is a Black Panther Shifter."

"You mean the big black panther with the pink eyes? Holy shit," she gasped.

"Yes," he nodded.

"Uh, I don't have the keys for the truck. They were in my bag, it got snatched from me last night. My roommate is going to kill me," she grabbed the door handle anxious to put some distance between herself and the strange man.

"I have them here he said and held out her ruined purse."

"There was more stuff in here. Dammit."

"We can search the ground for it," he suggested and his gold eyes looked kind as he began to help her.

"What about the Wolf?" she asked though she wasn't really afraid of the animal.

In fact, the Wolf seemed the lesser of two evils when faced with Kingston. For some reason, the man gave off a seriously weird vibe. Like he was more than just the six and a half-foot tall massively muscled male in front of her. As if that was not intimidating enough.

"He will not cross the fence. At least, not right now," Kingston said.

Fergie frowned and exited the luxury vehicle with less speed than she'd intended. She walked on her new Louboutin's to where she'd been attacked the night before. For some reason, everything he'd told her seemed to resonate with the truth. But how could she believe such nonsense?

"There's my change purse," she muttered.

Kingston bent to retrieve the small bag from the ground. It had been tossed aside like so much garbage. A few other items that had spilled from her bag were scattered about, and he retrieved those as well.

Yikes. Having the man handle one of her tampons

was just a tad embarrassing, but oh well. The Wolf growled from the opposite side of the fence when Kingston handed her one item after the other, and something warmed inside of her.

"Knock it off," Kingston grunted, but she couldn't imagine why.

She stared at the beautiful animal who seemed exceedingly familiar to her. The dark, glossy fur and bright electric blue eyes reminded her of someone. Her pulse raced as the sound of his growl grew louder, calling to her. Fergie turned slowly to face him.

Oh shit.

"Ms. McAndrews," Kingston addressed her, but she couldn't answer him yet.

It was as if she were frozen to the spot. Her heart pounded and blood thundered in her ears. She tried to swallow, but her throat was dry and she couldn't manage it. The magnificent animal moved closer to the gate, his long tongue licked his muzzle as he watched her like the predator he was.

Fergie closed her eyes and placed her hand over her chest, rubbing the spot where her heart was suddenly beating so rapidly. The Wolf whined and her eyes shot back to his.

She really needed to have her head examined. First, she'd been attacked, then rescued, then she'd jumped into bed with one of the guys who did the rescuing, and now she was talking about the possibility that that guy could turn into a Wolf. This was so not okay.

"There is no need for guilt. The need to connect is extraordinarily strong, oftentimes impossible to ignore between mates. That is why we Shifters call it *mating fever*," Kingston appeared directly in front of her and held out the keys, "here are your keys."

"Thanks, uh, you know I don't normally jump in the sack with someone I just met."

"I see," he smirked, "would you feel better if I told you it was fate?"

"Ha! No, not really."

"I am being serious, Ms. McAndrews," he frowned at her and for some reason Fergie felt like a kid being scolded by her school principal, "Hudson Stormwolfe is your fated mate. It is why you feel so strongly about him, why you *jumped in the sack* with him almost immediately. You could not stop it any more than you could stop the tide changing."

"I don't believe in Fate. Everything I do is by choice."

"Yes, that too. Fate does not take away choices per se."

"Doesn't it? Look, if you're trying to explain why

someone like Hudson would fall into bed with someone like me-"

"Not at all. I understand I may have misspoke. Please, suffice it to say that last night you met and were marked by your fated mate. He is a Wolf Shifter and a Guardian of Chaos, which means you can expect some sort of magical boon if you will-"

"I didn't ask for any magical anything-"

"Don't be so quick to refuse what you don't yet understand," he said and his eyes took on a faraway look that made her feel an overwhelming sense of sympathy for the man.

"I have to go to work," she whispered, but it was just an excuse and they both knew it.

"Fate can be a right bastard, Ms. McAndrews, but it is still a force to be reckoned with. You see that Wolf there is not just a wild creature any more than I am just a man standing in front of you. It is Storm, or, *Hudson*, as you call him," he gestured to the animal behind the fence.

Fergie's eyes widened. This whole thing was getting weird. It was simply too much for her under-caffeinated brain to comprehend.

"I need to get to work," she repeated shaking her head back and forth, "I'm sorry, if I could have your address so I could re-pay Hudson for the clothes, I would appreciate it," she managed to say without spilling the tears that swam in her eyes.

"Alright. If that is all you can take for now, I do understand. What's your cell phone number? I'll text you with all the information you asked for."

She told it to him and walked to Jessenia's pick-up. Thank goodness her friend ran her cooking vlog from their apartment. She rarely needed the truck for more than grocery shopping and even that she accomplished with delivery these days.

Fergie ignored the Wolf's mournful whine and opened the driver's door. At least the truck wasn't damaged. Thank God for small favors. She stepped inside and started the engine, waving a half-hearted goodbye as she drove past Kingston.

He stood by his car with his hand on the back of the enormous black Wolf who watched her go with sad blue eyes. Both seemed to be waiting for her to leave.

She blinked against the onslaught of tears that had started to run down her face. Fergie was not a crier by nature, but this was really too much. Shifters, mates, magic. Who wouldn't be in tears by now?

Ugh. Fergie had no time for this. She needed to get her head on straight. Her new job at L-Corp was on the line, and she needed the money more than ever.

Repaying the man she'd slept with for the delicious

underthings, the dress, and the new shoes was tantamount. She did not want to have any debt looming between them. Not when she was so unsure about what had happened.

Accepting extravagant gifts from virtual strangers was not something she'd ever done before. Okay, so the man was not exactly a stranger. He had seen, kissed, licked, and fucked every inch of her silly. Her body hummed with remembering, but her heart squeezed tight.

It all seemed part of some dream. Like it wasn't real. Only the pleasant ache of her well-satisfied body reminded her it had actually happened. That and the sudden abiding sadness that seemed to well up when she thought of never seeing him again.

She found her cell phone at the bottom of her broken bag and dug it out while she waited for the traffic light to change. Her roommate would certainly be awake by now.

"Fergie! OMG! Where the heck are you? You didn't come home, I was worried sick-"

"Jess, I'm sorry. Look, I had the craziest night."

"Is my truck okay? Are you?"

"Yes, to both, and thanks for giving the truck top billing," she snarked.

"Hey, the last time you borrowed her, she came home with two new dents, fuck you very much."

"Ha, funny. Like you can even tell with this pile of junk," she smiled broadly, tears forgotten as she bantered with her BFF.

"Seriously though, Ferg, you okay?"

"Yeah, uh, can you meet me for lunch?"

"Of course, I'll just meet you. Tell me what time and where."

Fergie closed her eyes and thanked God for her roommate. She really needed a friend right now, and despite her unhealthy attachment to the piece of junk Fergie was currently driving, Jessenia was the absolute best friend she'd ever had.

"I'm going in late, so I'll take lunch at one," she said and gave her the address to her new office building.

Exhausted, confused, and unreasonably heart-achy, Fergie entered the L-Corp offices with a drawn-out sigh a few minutes after she hung up on Jessenia. She went to drop her keys in her purse and moaned in annoyance. Dang it! She'd left the damaged bag along with her cell phone in the truck.

"Just perfect," she sighed.

Oh well. She would have to grab her phone when she went for lunch with Jessenia. No big deal. First, she needed to find out if she still had a job. She smoothed the front of her dress and closed her eyes for a brief second.

Hudson had outdone himself with this number. The man had guessed her exact size in everything, and she had to admit the clothes and shoes felt divine. They bolstered her esteem, but at the same time they reminded her of him.

She definitely needed time to think, but afterwards she really wanted to talk to him. Her stomach clenched, and she frowned. Fergie's biological clock ran on a strict calendar. She was not due to have her period for another couple of weeks. The strange mild cramping passed, but it did leave her a little breathless.

"You got this," she gave herself a little pep talk as she punched in the security code on the pad by the double glass doors she'd been given in order to access the inner offices.

Her new Louboutin's made a light clicking sound as she crossed the tiled floor to where her desk sat. Not that she spent much time there, but she needed to talk to Mr. Offner to tell him what had happened the night before. The company had a strict policy and not only had she missed the drop off with the laptop, but she no longer had the laptop. Shit. She'd forgotten it at Hudson's. She closed her eyes, this was not going to be easy. And she thought explaining her tardiness was rough.

She opened her eyes and looked around the room. That was odd. The lights were off and no one seemed to be inside. She'd been so absorbed in her own thoughts she hadn't realized it at first.

"Hello?" she called out and pressed a hand to her chest.

Her heart was pounding and that strange cramp in her stomach was back. What the fuck? As if she hadn't just been through enough. An attempted mugging and God knows what else, a night of unprecedented explosive sex with a man who made her heart and body simply sing, then finding out said man was actually some kind of fairy tale creature.

She wasn't keeping score or anything, but Fergie definitely thought she was due for a little break. Like maybe a smooth day at work where her boss understood her plight without her having to beg for forgiveness?

"A little late are we, Ms. McAndrews," Mr. Offner startled her as he stepped out of the shadows in the corner of the room where her desk sat.

Fergie yelped in surprise. Yikes. When the hell had she ever made that noise? She inhaled and crinkled her nose immediately against the offensive stench in the room. Was it her boss?

The older man's age spotted skin was a little slimy looking even in the unlit room. From sweat perhaps, she wondered. She recoiled after sniffing again.

Ugh. He did stink. Like unwashed armpit and something else. Something rancid and sweet like this one time when she had been defrosting a steak in the fridge. The piece of meat had slipped between the shelves and she'd forgotten about it until it started to rot and stunk up the whole damn refrigerator.

So gross. She'd had to use baking soda and white vinegar, the one for cleaning not for salads, to get the stink out. Why would her boss smell like that?

"Oh, you scared me," she plastered a fake smile to her face, "I'm sorry, Mr. Offner, I had car trouble," she lied.

For some reason, she wanted, *nope*, that was too mild a word. It was way more than *want*. Fergie *needed*, to leave. Like now.

Alarm bells went off inside her brain, and she felt herself starting to panic. What was going on here? Another man slid out of the shadows and stopped next to Mr. Offner. Fergie swallowed and moved back a step wincing at the click of her heels in the suddenly too quiet room.

This was so not good. She looked from her boss to the man next to him. It couldn't be, could it? But there was no denying the truth, Fergie recognized the green-tinted skin and angry yellow eyes. Of course, now the man, *er*, Shifter, was sporting a few bruises. Probably got those from Hudson, she thought with mild satisfaction. Funny, she'd never been bloodthirsty, but now she was practically trembling with the need for revenge.

"You," she spat the word.

She forced herself to swallow down a scream, putting her hand over her mouth to stem the sound as the man's skin became a mottled, darker green color before her very eyes.

"Hello again, *sssslut*," his vertical eyelids blinked rapidly over yellow eyes distracting her from his words.

"It seems you have been busy, Ms. McAndrews. A mating mark is quite the prize, is it not? Tell me, where is this Wolf of yours?"

"I don't know what you are talking about," she replied.

"That's a shame really. Good secretaries are so hard to find," Mr. Offner said.

"Hey, I am a research assistant, buddy! And that guy is not normal, in fact, he attacked me last night," she pointed at the lizard-man and took another step back only to bump into something. The wall, perhaps?

Said wall hissed in her ear and this time she did scream. Fergie whirled around. Another green-skinned assailant with scales and a forked tongue closed in on her. He grabbed her face with his claw-tipped hands and she struggled to get away. It was no use. He was too strong.

"*Thissss* one is *ssssweet*," he leaned forward, licking her face.

Fergie grabbed his arm in an effort to move him, growling in disgust. He simply squeezed her face harder. She was not going down like this. Not without a fight. She let her hand fly and smacked the beast across his scaly face.

"You bitch," he drew his fist back, and she closed her eyes waiting for impact. Thankfully, it never came.

"No more of that," Mr. Offner snapped.

When she opened her eyes, it was to see the Shifter struggling to drop his arm which seemed frozen in place. The good news was he let go of her and she scrambled away from him. Her cheeks hurt, and she rubbed her jaw.

"She is far too valuable a hostage for you to kill with your poisoned tongue or bruise with your fists."

"She hit me," said the man.

"Yes, she did, but it does not matter. We will use her to break the Guardians. We will make them pay," he cackled evilly, but Fergie was having a difficult time following since she was currently seeing spots.

The place on her cheek where the guy had licked her was burning and tingling like when she'd gotten a bite from a jellyfish down the shore last year. Her stomach cramped and chest squeezed.

Shit. Fergie did not want to pass out in front of these three, but she didn't think she had a choice. The spots swimming in front of her eyes grew darker. She tried to walk, but she couldn't move, her arms and legs felt so very heavy.

She fell to the floor, unable to move any part of her body as Mr. Offner leaned over her with that same evil smile and that horrible stench clinging to him.

"There now Ms. McAndrews, you will be easier to handle like this. Pick her up," he ordered his men.

Fergie tried to scream, but she couldn't make a sound. Panic had her pulse racing, as she struggled to stay awake. She did not want the darkness to take her, didn't want to be at Mr. Offner's mercy. He was dangerous, evil.

Where were they taking her? Would she survive? Questions flooded her brain as she was lifted and thrown over a huge shoulder like a sack of potatoes.

Terror and regret warred with each other and she couldn't wipe the tears that leaked out of her eyes.

Hudson, she screamed inside her mind's eye for him. She wanted Hudson. Why did she leave him like that? Was she so jaded a woman she couldn't admit what she'd felt from the minute she'd seen him in that parking lot.

Who cares if it was crazy or too soon? Fergie was in love with the big sexy man. It was too late now anyway. She was going to die, and he would never know how she felt about him.

Everyone always said stupid shit like how they were going to live each day like it was their last, but how many really did it. No one. Not one person she knew would ever admit so easily how they felt about another.

She couldn't think why. Why was it so important for people to deny their emotions? She didn't want it to end like this. To have it be over before it began. One night wasn't enough. Fergie wanted more. She was greedy, she supposed, but so what?

Hudson, I'm so sorry I didn't give us a chance. I love you, my beautiful Wolf, she thought as the blackness closed in on her.

And then, nothing.

ELEVEN

"What the fuck, Storm," Kingston growled at him the second his mate drove away.

Storm whined from his lupine throat and moved to follow her, but that damned Dragon grabbed him by the scruff. He was probably the only man in the world who could get away with such a move, but that was only because the Wolf knew his Alpha.

There was that one little fact. But he also knew that even his Wolf's sharp teeth would barely scratch the Dragon Shifter's tough as nails hide. The fucker.

"That is because I am a Diamond Dragon, fuck-wad. Your teeth would break. Now, get in the back," the Dragon commanded and Storm obeyed, albeit reluctantly.

He wouldn't risk changing to his human form in public when anyone could be watching. Especially in this age of smart phone recordings and vloggers posting every dang thing as a supernatural phenomenon.

The world kind of sucked for paranormals these days. But whatever. He didn't care about any of that right then. No, he only wanted his mate.

The need to follow her, to ensure her safety burned within him. But first things first. Storm supposed he'd earned the tongue lashing he was currently receiving from his boss. Kingston stopped in the large circular driveway once they'd made it back to the Keep. He was too damned far away from her, he snarled. He ignored the Dragon's slamming of the car door and shifted back to his skin before exiting. Storm stalked into the house naked, and like most of his kind, he did not give a fuck.

Nudity was commonplace among Shifters since you couldn't keep your clothes on when swapping skins. Of course, it was bad etiquette to stare when someone was naked. No one did. At least, no one who didn't want to get their asses beat.

"Well, what do you have to say for yourself?" Furio

met him at the door and *tsked* the Wolf Shifter as if he were an errant pup.

"Don't fuck with me right now, Furio," he growled and marched to his room to snag some clothes.

"Have all of you forgotten your vows? Everyone to the conference room now," Kingston bellowed from down the hall.

As their leader his word was law. Even the Keep knew that. Any wards or magical sound blockers were immediately disabled whenever Kingston used his Alpha voice.

"What is going on?" yawned Elena as she entered the conference room.

Furio mouthed something to her, but Storm didn't pay attention. Every fiber of his being was on alert. With his mate so far away, their tentative bond was stretched.

Something ached deep within him, like a nervous energy or sense of foreboding. Dammit, why didn't he take her cell number? He kept rubbing his chest with the palm of his hand as if that could stop the pain. But there was only one thing on the planet that could do that.

Fergie, both his Wolf and his heart seemed to cry out for her. One night of having her in his arms had completely changed Storm. He was wrecked, broken, lost without her. Storm was used to being a rough and tough kind of a man. A dominant Wolf Shifter, he was normally fierce and in control. His work as a Guardian had mainly consisted of kicking ass and taking names.

Storm liked his job. He was good at it. But now that he'd met his mate, she was the only thing he wanted. The new power she'd unleashed inside of him pulsed and pressed against his skin. Different from his Wolf, and yet born of the same source, it sought its other half, hungry for her soothing presence.

"Enough!" yelled Kingston.

The entire room stilled. Present were Furio, Elena, Kingston, of course, Storm, and Byram. Egros, their resident Witch, was out on a recon mission. He was a secretive male, but Storm respected the man.

"Ah, so now that Storm is officially mated, might I offer congratulations," Byram crossed his legs and leaned back in his chair in that elegant manner only someone born five-hundred years ago could get away with.

Tall, pale, with a deceptively lithe body type, the Vampire was possibly the strongest being in the room. There was some question on whether or not he could beat the Diamond Dragon in sheer strength, but Storm had his doubts.

He did not answer the Vampire with words, merely nodded his head. There was nothing to be said. Joy was something he should be feeling, but Fergie had left him. He had failed in his duty to explain to her what it meant to be his mate and he'd lost the only woman he would ever care about.

Shame filled him, anger too. At himself of course, for his own rash behavior. He ignored the unladylike snort that came from Elena.

"You should have heeded me," Kingston growled, "now you have marked a human. I had to explain our kind to her where you failed to do so. Do you know how much fun that was? Trying to tell a *normal* what we are and what we do? She is a human woman, Storm. I don't even think she registered a single word of it. She will need time, Storm, and now, because you went off half-cocked, you are compromised and will be useless out in the field."

"Uh, I think it was pretty full-cocked, sir," Furio interrupted, and earned himself a smack to the back of the head from Elena, "What? My room is right next to his," he shrugged.

"Oh, shut up," Elena hissed.

"I can't say I regret it, Kingston. I am sorry I disobeyed, but this is stronger than your position as my Alpha. The woman is my most cherished fated mate.

Even you can't fight the Fates," he stated with more calm than he felt.

"Is it true, about you getting a bonus power? I didn't get to ask you that earlier," Byram inquired.

Storm nodded. The whole room seemed to still. Yes, of course, now he had everyone's attention. Hell, he felt their keen interest down to his bones. Kissing and telling wasn't really his style, but this went beyond that.

They revered fated mates in his world and all too rare an occurrence. He was the only one of them to have found his fated mate while being occupied as a Guardian of Chaos. His position was one of duty and honor. He'd always thought it must be difficult to have a mate while serving the paranormal world in such a capacity, but now that he'd found her he knew she would only make him stronger and better.

Kingston was already mated when he'd joined them, which was why Storm figured the Dragon had never received an additional power boost. Perhaps those were only for Guardians at the time of their service?

"Well? Are you going to tell them?" Furio smirked.

"What? Oh, yes. It was strange because I merely recognized something special about her when suddenly she was in trouble," Storm recalled, "I barely considered that she was my mate, when I felt this strange electrical hum all over my body. When I looked down, I saw swirls of black smoke circling my frame and flashes of blue light around my fists. Then, it was like I was speeding through time and space, blinking, she called it, from one place to the next."

"Walking through shadows," Byram said with awe evident in his slightly accented voice.

"Yes," Storm nodded, "I walked through shadows to get to her."

As he said it, he rubbed his chest harder. Something was wrong. Something beyond his missing his new mate. He frowned.

"Okay, we need to discuss this further. As you know, mated Guardians live here in the Keep, but I did not get the impression Ms. McAndrews would be moving in anytime soon," Kingston began.

"The fuck do you know about it," Storm growled at his leader.

"I was not trying to offend you, Storm," he began but the Wolf in him was seeing red.

Was the Dragon trying to keep his mate from him? Had his leader done something or said something to make her not want him anymore. Irrational, yes, but he couldn't help it. His inner beast was about a half a second away from ripping out of his skin and into his Alpha.

"Storm, look at me."

Storm did as he was asked and looked at the tall Dragon. He was bristling inside. The Wolf didn't care if he was stronger and bigger or the Alpha. If he thought to keep him from his mate, Storm would challenge him.

"All I meant was that she is a human, and this situation will need delicacy," Kingston glowered at the sudden ringing of his cell phone.

Storm was almost grateful for the interruption. A second longer and he'd have been one big, furry, pissed off Wolf. Good thing too. The Keep had a way of getting even with people who did not follow its rules. The old place didn't take too kindly to Shifters suddenly changing in its halls.

Too many ruined furniture pieces and scratched floors to repair, he supposed. Last time he'd shifted during a fight with Furio, the Keep had served him cold tuna salad sandwiches for breakfast, lunch, and dinner every day for a month.

Storm hated tuna salad. Especially with raisins and apples. But, no matter what he'd put on his plate, even if ordered out, that was what he'd wound up eating.

So, yeah, there would be no Wolfing out, he

scolded himself. All of the Guardians present in the conference room waited while Kingston answered his cell phone. His surprised expression quickly turned to anger, then something else as he barked off short answers.

"Hello? What? Yes, I know her. Listen to me, you have to get out of there. Leave the garage right now. You could be in danger. No, don't panic. Get to a public place, then text me where you are. My name is Kingston Baldric. Fergie McAndrews is a friend of my associate. We are on our way, and we will explain everything when we get there," he growled.

"What's wrong?" Furio asked.

"It's Fergie," Storm knew instinctively, and panic rose inside of him.

"All of you get in the car. Egros isn't here or we'd use the portal," Kingston growled.

Once outside the Dragon Shifter removed his shoes and clothing, he tossed them at Storm who jumped in the front seat and gripped the dashboard. His Wolf pressed him hard, but the man was positively shocked when he realized just what Kingston had planned.

In a blur of motion, he'd shifted into a two-ton Diamond Dragon with bright, clear scales and glowing gold eyes. He would be able to cloak himself from the humans with his Dragon magic and get them to where they were going in record time.

Whatever was going on, Storm knew instinctively that it involved his mate. His Wolf snarled and snapped his teeth in his mind's eye. The phone inside Kingston's belongings buzzed, and Storm grabbed it.

"Hello," he growled.

"Who is this?" a strange female answered, "Where's the other guy?"

"He's indisposed. You called about Fergie. What's wrong? Where is she?"

"Well, that's just it. I was supposed to meet her for lunch at her new job, but there's no one here. Just her car, well, actually it's my truck. She's been borrowing it. Anyway her cell was inside and this was the last number that texted her, so I took a chance."

"My name is Hudson Stormwolfe, Miss?"

"Jessenia Banks or Jess. I'm Fergie's roommate and I don't know who you are, but I am very worried. Your friend said not to call the cops. I'll give you the benefit of the doubt, but unless I'm not convinced by what you have to say, I will be making that call."

"No! I mean, *please* just wait until we meet in person. The police won't be able to help you."

"Fine, but you have a lot to explain-"

"I know. Can you tell me what she said when you last spoke?"

"She just said something happened last night. She didn't make it home, and that is not typical of her. Fergie didn't sound bad when I spoke to her this morning. Just like she'd been crying a bit-"

"What? She was crying?" his chest tightened.

"Look, I don't know you, but your friend said he could help. I'm waiting at *Corner Coffee* on 4th Street. If you're not here in fifteen minutes, I'm calling the police and going back to the garage."

"We will be there," he growled and clicked end.

What the fuck? He'd made his mate cry. What kind of insensitive asshole did that? Anger and despair waged a war inside of him, and by the time Kingston landed their car in an empty parking lot as close to the coffee shop as he dared, Storm was in one hell of a bad mood. He was a growling, snarling beast.

"Move over," Kingston opened the door and grunted as he shoved on his pants and shirt.

He took the wheel out of Storm's hands and started the car having already heard the address to where Jessenia, Fergie's roommate, was waiting.

When they entered the shop, Storm's eyes zeroed in on the only woman sitting alone at one of the small booths. She had dark hair in a messy bun with an untouched cup of coffee sitting in front of her. Her eyes narrowed at him first, then on every member of his unit, landing a tad bit longer on Furio than any of the others. The Stallion snorted, nostrils flaring as he stared back at her.

Storm shoved ahead of him. He did not have time to deal with whatever show of dominance his buddy was currently engaging in with a human in a crowded coffee shop. Kingston, Byram, and Elena followed him, leaving Furio to bring up the rear.

The five enormous Shifters had to squeeze between chairs to reach the isolated booth. Good thinking on her part. They really did not need to be overheard

"Jessenia Banks? I'm Hudson Stormwolfe, we spoke on the phone," he said, careful to contain his growl, "now, what happened?"

"First off, who the fuck are you people? How do you know Fergie?" she leaned forward and inhaled briefly.

Her dark eyes darted to his face then to the rest of the Guardians with him, lingering only for a moment on Furio. She shook her head and closed her eyes.

"Shit, you guys are all supernaturals. Shifters, right and one Vampire?" she asked.

Two of the men squeezed into the bench with

Elena opting to sit next to Jessenia. The Black Panther sniffed and smirked when she turned to meet Kingston's and Storm's stares. They were the only two left standing.

"She's a Witch," Elena said.

"Shh," Jessenia's eyes darted around the small coffee shop, "yes, but I'm more of a kitchen Witch really, and you are all Guardians of Chaos. I can see it in your auras. Now, answer me this, how does a unit in one of the most elite forces in the supernatural world get mixed up with my very human roommate?"

The group of Guardians all looked at one another then back at the tiny, but fierce kitchen Witch. Her magic might be on the smaller side, but there was no doubt she was a devoted friend. Fergie clearly had a special place inside her heart, and that made her important to Storm.

"She is my mate," Storm answered honestly.

It was the least he could do. In that one word, he imbued all the feelings he had for the redheaded mortal who was now forever bound to him by the sacred bite he had given her.

Rumors of Shifters and supes going mad when faced with losing their mates had always troubled the Wolf, but it was one of those things he'd never thought could happen to him. It had been too far removed from his realm of possibilities.

Arrogant. That was the word he'd use to describe his actions or lack thereof when it came to his mate. He'd been a foolish, arrogant ass. Storm had experience with this sort of thing. All of them had. They'd each worried about Kingston after he lost his own mate, but he'd personally had no idea what the Diamond Dragon faced until now.

Just being separated from her was driving him crazy. There was only one possible recourse. He needed to find her, he needed to make sure his fated mate was safe and sound. And he needed to do that now.

"Oh gods! Well, you fucked that up, didn't you?" she slapped the table and rolled her eyes at him.

"I plan on making it up to her," he growled back at the sassy Witch.

"How do I even know she wants you, Fido?"

"Because she let me mark her," he snarled, the woman was too darn snarky for his liking, but he'd put up with that and more to get to his mate, "You tell me, is Fergie the type of woman to fall into bed with just anybody?"

"No way, you jerk! Fergie is not like that."

"Of course she's not! My mate is an honorable

woman. She is fucking perfect! Now, please, help me find her."

"Hmm," she seemed to be making up her mind.

It took a moment, but she nodded once, decision made. Storm exhaled heavily. She was going to trust them. Thank fuck.

"Please, what do you know?" he begged.

"Look, she was supposed to meet me for lunch and when I Uber'd to her new job, the office building was empty. Like completely empty. And uh, I sort of smelled Shifters there too."

"What kind?" Storm growled.

"Lizard. Gila to be exact."

TWELVE

ergie knew something was immediately wrong from the moment she opened her eyes.

What the hell? This was the second time in as many days that she'd woken up in a strange place. Her vision was a little hazy and her stomach hurt like a sonovabitch.

Last time was infinitely better, she reasoned as she tried to sit up and found she could not. Instead of being surrounded by the mouthwatering minty scent that was Hudson Stormwolfe, and his piercing blue eyes gazing hungrily at her, Fergie had been kidnapped.

Bound with handcuffs to a metal cot in some kind of old store room or closet that stunk worse than

Offner. Like mildew and mold, cockroaches and rats. *Ew.*

"Hello!" she screamed and struggled against the metal cuffs that were slicing into her wrists and ankles.

Shit. She looked down and saw her bare feet poking up at the foot of the old metal bedframe. Her new shoes were gone.

"What the fuck?" she grunted.

Was the universe conspiring to take every pair of Louboutin's she owned right off of her body? She huffed out a breath, blowing back a mass of curls that had fallen into her face. She realized quickly that she wasn't able to do much more than a crunch position, and as a certified and proud fluffy woman of the twenty-first century, Fergie so was not the type to do any sort of exercise. Not even by accident. She lay back down immediately.

"Well, damn. This really sucks," she spoke aloud to no one at all.

She relaxed her body once more. Testing her handcuffs again, she grunted as she pulled and pushed only to discover that absolutely nothing had changed.

Fergie was trapped. Snatched up by her putrid smelling *ex*-boss! She didn't really know Mr. Offner well, but he was involved with some bad Lizard hitmen or some shit.

The man was at least eighty-years old. Stooped back, full of wrinkles, he walked with a cane, and slicked the small white tuft of hair that grew on the back of his head down with some kind of old people pomade that made it appear a sickly yellow color.

His hands were covered in age spots and his nails were kinda long for a man. She never noticed his odor before today, but it could've knocked her out on its own, without any help from his minion.

When she'd landed the job, she thought he was simply a figurehead for L-Corp. She had no idea he actually ran things until she was assigned to be his assistant.

It had only been a few weeks, but she'd quickly learned what her boss wanted from her. The man was all about information, and getting his facts in detailed sheets, and the company laptop back in the building before the end of the business day each and every day.

They would wipe her computer and she would pick it up along with whatever she was assigned to research the next day. It wasn't fun or exciting, but that was what Fergie was hired to do. Research and a ton of it.

Land surveys, maps, old newspaper articles and police reports. She'd compiled massive amounts of information, most of it exceedingly obscure. If a report took several days to build, she still had no access to her PC after hours. All the new information would have to be added the next day in its own separate sheet.

Tedious and annoying, but that was how it was done. She'd never missed a single day. Except for last night of course, she thought grimly. Her research at the library had taken a long time, and she'd left her laptop in the lock box in the boot of Jess's pick-up truck.

Hell, if that man wanted her research he only had to ask. Not tie her up for fuck's sake. The sounds of heavy footsteps followed by a slower, more deliberate gait brought her head up. Good, she had a bone to pick with her so-called kidnappers.

The door flew open and the two goons with green-tinted skin entered the musty room where Fergie was currently tied to a stinking dirty, she didn't even want to think about with what, cot. The men looked like they were wearing some sort of make-up or costume, but she knew now what they were. Not human men, no, Shifters, but these weren't like the ones she met with Hudson.

These men had no honor. They'd sold themselves to serve whatever dark plans the crazy old man she'd worked for had concocted. Fergie had no idea what Offner wanted from her, but she was going to find out.

"Hey, frog boy," she taunted one of the men, "so, you like dressing up in women's clothing?"

"What?" hissed the easily goaded male.

"Where the hell are my new Louboutin's? This is the second pair you guys have tried to steal from me," she taunted.

"Lady, I ain't no frog, and I wear men's clothes," the man grunted, and took a step towards her.

"Really? Then what's with the deep V? You trying to bring back disco too?" she snorted.

"My dear," the impatient sigh of their boss entering the room had both goons turning around, "I hired you for your background in research, but that quick wit of yours would've gotten you the job on its own," the two men parted to allow him through.

Mr. Offner, still stooped and old as ever, wore a grotesque smile on his withered face. Fergie had always tried to think kindly of people because looks weren't everything, but there was something seriously wrong with this man.

His entire person was just wrong. She saw it somehow. It shrouded him like a dark cloth, or cloud. Fergie blinked rapidly. Her breathing became shallow, and she felt her stomach cramp.

What was going on? She'd never had such an averse physical reaction before. Her head began to ache.

Everything in her wanted to get away from the vile man, but she couldn't move. Stupid handcuffs.

"Well, if I knew you were going to turn out to be a kidnapper and a lunatic, I would have passed on the job offer. Seriously," she struggled to sit up and exhaled in frustration, "would you mind letting me up at least?"

"Not until you tell me where my property is, girl," he sneered.

"Girl? Really? Okay Mr. Politically-Incorrect-Pants, I realize I might have missed protocol with the company laptop, but that was because these goons of yours attacked me in the parking lot of the library before I could bring it to you. Was it my fault there was absolutely no service in that place and their phone lines were down?" she reasoned.

"Why did you not simply give it to them?"

"Because they never asked for it," she retorted.

"Tell me you lot identified yourselves when you approached Ms. McAndrews," he slowly turned towards the two men who went a little bit pale when his attention was focused on them.

Fergie swallowed, their lizard green skin turned the color of faded scrubs after a moment or two. She realized they weren't breathing quite right and her eyes widened.

"Uh, you see, boss," one began to try to explain, but he was barely able to suck in any air.

Fergie had seen enough. Maybe if she distracted Offner long enough help would arrive. Maybe Hudson would find her. Hope sparked inside of her and she wanted so desperately to fan it, but who was she kidding?

No one knew where she was or what was happening to her. No. She didn't want to think about that. The way Fergie saw it, if she was going to die, she was going down swinging.

"No, they didn't tell me who they were. They never asked for my laptop either. What kind of criminal mastermind are you anyway? I mean, you made *me* take a test before you hired me. How on earth did these morons get their jobs?" she growled and rattled the cuffs against the metal frame of the cot she was lying on.

"You know, I think you are right, Ms. McAndrews. Perhaps a late test?" the old man turned slowly, curving one of his gnarled hands in the air and Fergie bit back her gasp.

"Holy shit," she whispered.

It was like when Darth Vader choked the Imperial Admiral in *Empire*. She trembled with revulsion and fear as spittle dripped from the Shifter's mouth. Offner moved his hand once more, the angle bent and unnatural, and the sound of something crunching reached her ears. Fergie closed her eyes as the goon fell to his knees before collapsing in a pile on the floor.

"He's not dead," Offner explained, and wiped his hand on his pants, "yet. Now you," he addressed his other minion, "untie Ms. McAndrews so we may have a civil conversation."

Fergie was too stunned to speak. She felt the cuffs loosen and fall off, allowed that to register before she scrambled off the bed and to the other side of the room aware that Mr. Offner's yellow gaze was following her the whole time.

"I believe you were inquiring about your shoes?"

She nodded. Born with genes that ensured she would remain on the short side, Fergie had always believed a woman was at a disadvantage without proper footwear. It was one of those sayings the women in her family had passed down to her. Well, not her step-monster, but her father's sisters and cousins. The McAndrews' women's unofficial slogan when it came to shoes was sort of go big or go home.

Of course, she'd updated it to reflect her own personality. She remembered the look on Jessenia's face when she'd said it to her a time or ten. Good times. Would there be any more of those left for Fergie?

Life's short, bitches, make sure your heels aren't. Her own words flashed across her mind and she clenched her jaw. Right then, she really wanted her shoes. The floor was cold under her bare feet, and Fergie hated the feeling.

"You will find your Christian Louboutin's under the bed," Mr. Offner leaned on his cane and gestured with his other hand.

"Thank you," she said, shocked he knew the designer's name.

She bent and looked under the bed for her red heels. Closing her eyes, she took a second and pulled them out from under the bed.

"Aren't you going to put them on?"

"My feet are dirty. I'd like to wash them first," she said.

"I see, well that will have to wait, my dear."

She nodded and clutched the shoes to her chest. Watching him for any sudden movements, Fergie waited for him to continue.

"Ms. McAndrews, where is my laptop?" he asked.

"It's in the boot of the truck I was driving," she answered.

"I can assure you, it is not. You see, Ms. McAndrews we have tracking devices installed on all our equipment. Which is, of course, how we found you at the library after you'd been sent to the courthouse," he closed his hand tightly over his cane and the sound of splintering wood seemed loud in the close quarters.

"What? But that's where I left the computer. In the little lockbox in the back of the pick-up," she said again, aware of a growing unease inside of her.

"And I am telling you, Ms. Mc. Andrews if you insist on playing this game with me you will not recover from what I will do to get the information, do you understand?" he flashed his yellow teeth at her and Fergie's skin crawled.

The old fucker wanted to hurt her. She knew it in her bones. Her eyes darted around the room looking for anything she might use to defend herself, any chance she had to escape, but once more she came up empty.

"Do you want to know why I released you from the cuffs, my dear?" he asked, handing the cane to his remaining minion.

"Why did you?"

"Because you are no threat to me, you insignificant human," he spat the word at her.

Fergie squeaked. She watched in disbelief as the bent and crooked old man began to take off his jacket and shirt. Mr. Offner, her elderly boss flashed his yellow teeth in a parody of a smile that made her want to hurl. His offensive odor grew stronger. The sweet stinking scent of death seemed to cling to him as more of his flesh was revealed to her eyes.

"Oh my God," she whimpered and tried to shut her eyes but she couldn't.

She felt almost compelled to stare as those yellowed teeth cracked under and fell from his bleeding gums under the strength of his own jaw. What the fucking fuck?

"Open your eyes, little human. Did you think I was some weak old man? Come now and see who it is you truly work for," Offner straightened his spine.

He seemed to grow before her eyes, a tall twisted monstrous thing. Fergie's own horror rose inside of her. The sounds of his bones breaking and muscles tearing was loud, too loud. She tried to cover her ears, but something, some unseen force held her still.

Eyes wide, Fergie wanted to scream as the horrible display continued. Tears flowed from too much air hitting her sensitive corneas, but she was unable to blink.

A mash of holes and fangs replaced the teeth in Offner's mouth. When he was finished, he was much bigger and taller than before, though he still had a slightly misshaped hunch even with his newfound veiny musculature. Fergie swallowed down a gasp of fear.

He nodded his head and the invisible force that had held her still dissipated. This monster that stood before her wanted something. Whatever it was, she was not inclined to give it.

"I want the information you researched for me and I want to know who else knows about it," his voice was deeper, more guttural than before. It made shivers race down her spine.

"I told you, as far as I know it's in the laptop in the truck."

"My scouts tell me your truck was compromised last night when those damned Guardians interfered with your retrieval."

"So you did have them attack me?"

"The Gila Shifters are under my employ. They were simply to retrieve my property, but they have failed me. This is what I do to those who have failed me," he reached for the remaining goon, closing his gnarled claw over the Lizard's throat.

Fergie almost felt sorry for him. Almost. Until she remembered he was the one who'd licked her face with his poisoned saliva and rendered her unconscious.

"This is your last chance, now, secure the female,

while I ravage her mind," he hissed and thrust the man at Fergie.

The gasping goon grabbed her wrists and pulled her forward to a rusted folding chair that was near to where she'd been standing. She held her heels firmly in her hands like they were some kind of lifeline, then inspiration struck.

"Let me go," she demanded but he simply hissed and shoved her into the chair.

He pushed her down and kept his hands on her shoulders. This was it. Fergie had to try. She grabbed one shoe in each of her hands and held them tightly with the heels facing up. She closed her eyes and said a little prayer to whoever might be listening then she used all her strength and bent her elbows, plunging the sharp stiletto heels into the tops of the Shifter's hands.

His screeching bellow nearly deafened her, but she scrambled out of the chair and ran to the door. Of course, it was locked. She cursed and banged on it, screaming for all she was worth. The sound of clapping from behind her made her turn around.

"Are you finished now," Offner asked with a calm look on his face, "Get up!" he ordered his minion who was currently bleeding from both hands.

"Let us try this again. You, secure her to the chair and you, sit quietly," he waited as the grunting Shifter walked over to her. Fergie met his angry glare and narrowed his eyes.

"*Yessss, ssssir,*" hissed the Gila Shifter.

"The Guardians took you home," Offner said.

He was talking to her again, but she was too busy worrying about what this goon was going to do to her now that she'd hurt him. His bloody hands grabbed at her and shoved her hard into the seat.

"You must be important for them to do that, but I don't have any time to waste,. I must strike before the penumbral eclipse occurs with this next full moon. The darkness will make the magic ripe for the picking."

"What does that have to do with me?"

"You've confirmed the location of the vein of magic I intend to leech from the earth, you stupid filthy human, and now, I will take that information directly from your mind."

"No," she struggled against the Lizard man, but he was too strong for her.

Of course, now he had an ax to grind, and that made him all the more immovable. His claws dug into her shoulders, tearing her pretty new dress. She yelled and struggled, but it was useless. Exhausted and panting, images of Hudson raced through her mind as

Fergie tried to wrap her head around what was about to happen to her.

"Don't worry, dear, this will only hurt a lot," Offner's vile grin made her stomach turn as he approached her with gnarled claws outstretched in her direction.

His yellow eyes blazed with power and something that looked a hell of a lot like hatred. Fergie had no idea why the man would hate her, and she did not want to find out.

Offner was muttering something in a language she did not recognize, dark gray tendrils of what she could only assume was magic seemed to spread out, filling the room. The tips of them inched towards her, faster with every word he uttered. The smell of rotting flesh made her gag as it grew more and more with every foul word uttered from his cracked lips.

Panicked, she bucked and pushed against the Lizard man holding her, fighting past the rising bile in her throat, but he was a mountain she could not move. Dammit no. She would not succumb to this. She couldn't.

"Aghhh," Fergie screamed.

It felt as if someone were scraping the inside of her scalp with a hot poker, sifting through her brain, carelessly discarding things he considered useless. Fergie howled in pain. She wouldn't let him invade her mind. But what could she do? She tried. She did. Fergie fought desperately to block him, but she knew she couldn't last forever.

A deep, menacing growl started to build up inside of her. Anger and fury accompanied it, along with real fear and panic. Images of a huge Wolf with blue eyes filled her. The Wolf was angry, and he was desperate to find her.

Hudson. It was Hudson. He was trying to reach her, busting through the smoky ropes of what she somehow knew was dark magic. Her mate was using his blinking power, as she'd called it. He was accessing the shadows and the black spaces between them like secret tunnels to get to her.

I am so sorry, my love, she thought.

Her fierce, handsome Wolf was coming, but he would not be in time. She only hoped he knew it wasn't his fault. Her chest squeezed, and a sob built in her throat. It was too late, but he still fought, valiantly tearing the dark magic binds to shreds.

Fergie wanted to tell him how much she appreciated it and him. She wished he could know just how much she wanted to be with him. To give *them* a chance.

The constant scrapping of her mind eased, and she breathed a bit better now. Hudson had freed her from the incessant pain. The probing of the crazed man she'd thought was her boss stopped, but Fergie could not move.

Sounds of fighting, screams, flesh tearing and bones crunching reached her ears like gory whispers on waves from a faraway shore. That sounded kind of nice, she thought. Fergie embraced the image, she felt as if she was floating.

The whispers grew nearer, but they were still muffled and she couldn't make them out. Her head hurt. She was so very tired. The black Wolf howled long and deep beside her. The sound so pitiful it brought tears to her eyes. She wanted to comfort the beast, but her poor broken mind was worn out, her body too. Fergie was completely exhausted.

Sleep now, float away and sleep, a strange voice whispered in her mind and she nodded.

Yes, sleep sounded good. That deep, black ocean of unconsciousness called to her, and Fergie was powerless to stop the tide from taking her out and swallowing her up. She would miss her friends and the life she could have had.

She would miss Hudson too, her sweet, handsome Wolf who'd shielded her from harm, but now it was time for her to sleep.

THIRTEEN

"Did you find her?"

"What do I look like? I'm a Stallion, he's the blood hound," Furio snorted at the dark-haired Jessenia.

Storm closed his eyes and breathed in deep. His supernaturally enhanced canid sense of smell was greater than the other Shifters in the room. He didn't give a rat's ass about the electric current pulsating between the Horse Shifter and the kitchen Witch. They could figure that shit out on their own time. He had a mate to track.

The group of Guardians had left the coffee shop with Jessenia and walked the two streets over to the garage where Fergie had last been known to enter. The pick-up truck was still there, and the engine was warm.

That was good. It meant she hadn't been missing for too long.

"She got to work a little late today, and like I told you, she asked me to meet her for lunch. I was early," Jessenia pulled open the unlocked driver's side door, "someone has been in here. She wouldn't have left it unlocked."

Storm growled as he stalked over and sniffed the interior. Gila Shifters had been all over the fucking thing. His Wolf pressed against his skin. The need to run, to hunt down the fuckers who'd been in his mate's vehicle were strong, but first he had to figure out where they'd taken her.

"Storm," called Furio from the bed of the truck, "they busted open the lock box here. Probably looking for the computer I took out of it last night, huh?"

"What? That's what they wanted? Why did you take it in the first place?" Storm barked at the man.

"Hey, don't yell at me. I thought it was strange when she asked me to grab it, but that was the only reason why I did," he hopped down from the bed of the truck, "she told me to before she passed out from that scratch. She looked at me and said, 'I need my purse and my laptop' and then you picked her up. I went and swiped it before we left for the Keep."

"Where is it now?"

"In my room. Sorry, *cump*, I didn't think to bring it," Furio rubbed a hand over his face, a sign he was agitated.

"Okay, so that was her work laptop," Jessenia offered, "this new company was really uptight about security. Fergie told me all about it. Maybe this company isn't what she thinks it is?"

Kingston stepped forward from where he'd been inspecting a drain in the middle of the garage. He seemed extremely interested in what Jessenia had to say.

"This company, what is it called?"

"L-Corp," she responded.

"L-Corp?"

"Loyalists," snarled Storm.

The enemies of everything they stood for. Now it all made sense. The Gila Shifters were mercenaries, guns, or rather, claws for hire. The Loyalists had paid them to hunt down his mate.

"Gila Shifters' are notorious sell swords," grunted Kingston, "you should've seen this."

"What do you want me to say? Want an apology. Fuck, they have my mate!" Storm's Wolf threatened to swallow him whole in a tide of fury and pain. What were they doing to her?

"Storm! You have to get control of your beast,"

Kingston commanded in his Alpha voice, and for once Storm welcomed his unit leader's authority, "I don't think they've left the building. Come on, focus. I need your nose."

Storm followed Kingston to the drain. He dropped to the ground and breathed. He sifted past the mildew and metallic scents of the actual vent, searching for things he'd find familiar in water drains. Only he was coming up empty.

"It's dry," he muttered and sniffed deeper, "Kingston, this isn't a storm drain. It's an air duct."

"Why would a garage have an air duct on the floor?"

"Makes about as much sense as a drain in this garage," added Furio, "this is an indoor garage and there are gutters outside. Water doesn't get in here."

"You're right. I think there's a room below us and," Kingston pressed his toe against the duct, "this must filter air to it. Can you hear anything? Catch a scent?"

Storm dropped to his knees determined to use his extremely sensitive hearing and olfactory senses to bring his mate home. Worry gnawed at him, but he forced the rising panic to quiet. Even thinking he could fail was unacceptable.

He ripped the grate off the vent and stuck his head

as far inside as he could. He took a deep swallow of air and his Wolf tensed. The soft tones of almonds and sugar were there. They were laced with her emotions. Confusion, fear, pain, and sadness being the strongest. All hers. All fading.

Grrr.

"Fuck, she's in there," he took a deep breath, "she's not alone, Kingston. I smell three others. She is suffering, goddammit! The Gila Shifters are there, and someone else. Wait. No! It can't be," he looked up and met Kingston's glowing Dragon eyes.

"Who?"

"Someone we thought was dead," Storm growled, "the Warlock Offner."

He stood up and started searching the walls and the floors. Calling his Wolf, Storm used his enhanced strength to break a hole in the asphalt. Blue orbs of power circled his claws as he ripped apart the ground searching for a way inside. If Warlock Offner was there, Fergie was in serious danger.

"It can't be," Kingston said as he joined Storm.

His golden eyes flashed with fury as his Dragon pushed him. His leader inhaled to try to pick up the scent of their nemesis, but Storm knew he was right.

"The Warlock is alive?" Furio joined them with Elena and Byram with him.

"Who is this Offner?" Jessenia asked.

"He's a Warlock, sold his soul to practice dark magic. He is a dangerous man, a Loyalist," snarled Storm.

"He is their leader," growled Kingston, "and he killed my mate."

"Oh gods, I'm so sorry, but what does he want with Fergie? She isn't magic," Jessenia's voice rose an octave with hysteria.

"The Loyalists are trying to gain as much magic as they can to force the supernatural world into doing as they bid," spat Furio, "she must've found something out."

"They want to amass enough power to control the whole of magic," Elena chimed in.

"I've heard of them, but she's a normal," Jessenia looked from one Guardian to the other.

"I don't know, but he hired her for whatever reason and she must have something on that computer he wants. If they find out she's his mate there is no telling what they will do," Kingston stated grimly.

"We need to find a way to follow this drain," Jessenia said, her panic rising as the implications of what her friend was facing became real.

Dread filled Storm. What if he was too late? His heart pounded and his stomach clenched. No. He would not think like that. He stopped in his tracks, opened his arms, and closed his eyes.

Concentrate, he commanded himself. His fists clenched at his sides. He couldn't just bust up the floors with no purpose. Fuck. He had to try to locate their matebond and follow it. It was his only hope.

"What is he doing?"

"I think he is trying to track her."

Storm pushed the whispered words out of his head. He had no room for them. His mission was to find Fergie. She was the only thing that mattered. He exhaled slowly and breathed in once more, allowing the hints of her fragrance to dance across his tongue.

Finally, beneath the haze and fog, separated from the anger and fear, he found it. Softly pulsating, the ethereal link between himself and his mate was there. He saw it, felt it, and he would follow it.

"Storm!"

He heard his leader shout his name, but it didn't matter. Storm allowed the swirling black shadows to swallow him as he held on tight to the thin rope that would lead to his mate. Focusing all his energies, every last fiber of his being on finding her, Storm used his newfound powers to blink out of the garage.

When he opened his eyes a new wave of fury threatened to drown him. His mate was pinned down by a Gila Shifter and Offner was looming over her menacingly. That sonovabitch would die for this.

In an almost berserker-like rage, Storm engaged the Warlock. The bastard was currently attempting to hurt his sweet Fergie using some kind of black magic.

"You bastard," he roared and rammed the misshaped fucker into the wall, enjoying the satisfying crunch of bones when he hit the prick into the cinder block wall.

Next, Storm dug his claws into the sides of the Gila Shifter who still had hands on his mate. The man screamed in pain as he gutted him then turned to face the onslaught of more of them.

Gila Shifters filled the room, and Storm was outnumbered, but he still liked his odds. He placed himself in front of Fergie's limp form. He would be her shield, her protection, until the end if need be. The image of her pale face was burned into his mind.

"Do you still think you can beat us? Didn't your leader already make the mistake of underestimating the Loyalists? I got his mate, and your bitch is dead too! I will win, dog," Offner spat and lifted himself from the floor.

"I hope it was worth whatever you promised the Devil, because I'm about to send you straight back to Hell," snarled Storm.

One arm dangled limply from Offner's side, but he was laughing for some reason. Storm growled as the once normal looking man he'd recognized as the Warlock the Guardians had fought and killed months ago began to grow larger. Offner's cackle deepened, and he addressed Storm in a guttural voice that he hardly understood. He'd been a fanatic before, now he was positively demonic.

"Remove my head or don't it does not matter. You can't kill what is already dead."

"No? Well, I can try!"

"Get him!" Offner screamed, and the other Shifters attacked.

Storm half-shifted, bulking up in size, speed, and strength with blue energy surrounding him, he defended his woman like a knight fought for his lady. He tore through flesh and bone with fang and claw, taking hits left and right.

Finally, he heard the arrival of his fellow Guardians. Good. He was in need of reinforcements. His heart pounded and blood coated his limbs. Some of it was his, most theirs. Fucking Gila monster blood contained venom, but their saliva was what got you.

He'd avoided most of the bites, but it was a close thing. He'd never thought he would be so fucking glad to see the unit of ass kicking Guardians come to his rescue.

Kingston led them all through a hole his Dragon fire had burned right through the ceiling. One by one, his friends dropped down to fight the oncoming wave of Shifters.

Storm barely had time to register Kingston going after Offner which gave him time to tend his mate. The Warlock snarled with their arrival and scrambled with his broken arm in hand to the far wall. Reaching into his pocket, he took out a piece of chalk and started drawing runes on the paint while chanting in what Storm knew was an old dark tongue that had not been spoken centuries.

"Kingston!" he howled at his leader who went after the piece of shit.

The Warlock had truly embraced dark magic. Disguising himself as a Loyalist was genius really, but Storm hardly admired the bastard. He snarled and fended off another Gila's attack. The bastard smelled of Fergie.

"You are going to pay," he promised.

"You know your mate's skin is sweet as her scent, I always did like almonds," the soon to be dead man taunted.

Storm had no time or inclination for suavity. With

quick efficient movements he slashed through the Gila's defenses. His Wolf demanded vengeance and Storm was right there with his beast.

With each resounding hit that echoed off the walls of the confined space, Storm's Wolf called for blood. Finally, he used his middle finger and thumb to rip the bastard's throat out. A deep growl filled his chest, but he took no time to glory in his kill. His mate needed him.

"Go to her, we've got this," Furio grunted.

In three moves he ended another of the endless stream of Offner's minions. Storm turned and went to Fergie's slumped form. He grabbed her face in his hands and brought her forehead to his as emotions, he'd never felt before threatened to overwhelm him.

"No, no, no," he muttered, "I won't let you go. Not now. Not when I've just found you. Come back to me, love, come back."

Then he tossed his head back and loosed an ear-piercing howl that had every single being in the vicinity dropping to the ground, even his own team. When he'd finished, the Guardians had rounded up those of their enemies that still breathed.

"Come on, we need to get her back. I know some herbs that will help," Jessenia spoke from his side, and he nodded. He would not give up his hold on her.

"Is she?" Furio clapped him on the shoulder.

"She is alive," he murmured, "barely."

"Then she has a chance," the Horse Shifter said.

"She's got more than that, pony boy, now let's get the hell out of here," Jessenia snapped at him.

"You three go, I will stay with Elena and Byram to clean up the mess," Kingston said, and Storm nodded his thanks.

He was in no state to do more than that. Fergie was in his arms, but she was unwell. He could feel her internal struggle and cursed himself a fool in a million different ways.

FOURTEEN

Back at the Keep, Storm settled Fergie back inside their room. He could no longer think of the space as his now that she was in his life. Though truth be told, he'd leave the keep. He'd change his entire life if it meant he'd get to keep her.

Fergie, his heart called out to his mate and Storm dropped to his knees beside the bed. Jessenia had retreated to the kitchen with Furio on her heels. For whatever reason, the Stallion was behaving oddly and crowding the woman.

Storm growled at him. He wanted nothing to interfere with her thought process while she was preparing a healing potion for his mate.

"Will this work?" he sniffed the cup when she'd finally returned an hour later.

Fergie had made no movement or sound in all that time. Her breathing was shallow and her color had all but left her cheeks.

"Storm, why don't you go clean up while we sit with her?" Furio offered.

"No, I appreciate your offer, but I can't leave," he shook his head.

He refused to move from his place at her side, not even to clean the blood and gore from his skin and change his clothes. He simply couldn't. Not until she opened her eyes. Every moment he watched her suffer, every second that passed without her opening her eyes, was pure torture. Seconds felt like days, and minutes were eons.

Please gods, let her wake, he prayed.

"It won't hurt her," Jessenia hedged, "but I can't make any guarantees that it will rouse her either."

"Hey Storm, it's better than doing nothing," Furio said rising to the kitchen Witch's defense.

"Alright, give it to her."

Storm carefully lifted Fergie's head up. His sweet mate resembled a princess out of a fairy tale. The one where the prince had to kiss her to wake her up. If only that would work, he thought, and placed the cup at her lips.

"She can't drink. I'll spill it," his voice cracked.

"Here," Jessenia came forward with a medicine dropper, "let me try with this."

He nodded and stood by anxiously while she ministered to his mate. The woman was a true friend. He could sense her closeness to Fergie through their *matebond*. He was grateful for her help.

"She's my life," he said to the Witch who nodded at him, sympathy shining in her big eyes.

"My mother was mated to an Eagle Shifter after my natural father had died. I know how it is between mates," she said, "there now. She will need rest."

"Thank you," Storm said and resumed his place.

He took Fergie's soft, limp hand in his and brought it to his lips. The throb in his various bruises and cuts were nothing compared to how painful it was for him to see her so pale and weak.

She was always so full of fire. Beautiful and brave, sensual and earthy, she was everything he'd always wanted in a mate. His perfect match in every way.

This was not fair. He couldn't have found her after all these years to have her ripped away by that fucking fanatical asshole of a Warlock bastard. And the fact he'd gotten away made him all the more angry.

Storm promised he'd hunt down Offner after she was better. He would rip the fucker to shreds. Make him pay for even thinking about touching her.

"I get first dibs," the softly spoken whisper brought his startled head up.

Eyes the color of whiskey met his, and he watched in disbelief as they warmed to molten butterscotch. Fergie furrowed her eyebrows and reached to touch his face.

"You're bruised," she said.

"You're awake," he countered and this time he let the tears flow, "thank the gods."

Storm dropped his head onto her belly and kissed her over the sheet that covered her body, holding her as tightly as he dared. When her arms came around him, he exhaled a great deep breath of relief. She was awake now. She was better, and that was all that mattered.

He dropped more kisses on her stomach over the bedspread, moving upwards to her chest, her neck, her chin, her cheeks, her mouth, every place he could reach, whispering senseless words of love and promises.

Nonsensical phrases and touches that she met and echoed in response. He could hardly believe it, but he was so grateful, he didn't dare question.

"I'm so sorry, love, my love, my mate," he said.

"Don't be. I should have asked more questions instead of running. I was scared," she said, and he saw tears trickle down her cheeks.

The pain they caused him nearly undid him. He

took her face in his hands and dropped his forehead to hers. Breathing in her scent he willed himself to calm.

"I am so sorry you were scared. Where did he hurt you?"

"No, that's not what I meant. I mean, yeah, we can talk about that later, but I need to tell you that I am sorry I ran from you. I was scared of what I was feeling."

"What do you mean?"

"I mean, I thought I would sound crazy or desperate or both if I told you that, well, I think I love you," her watery-eyed smile reached him and he held her tighter.

"You do?" his eyes widened and pride filled him as she nodded.

"I love you so much, mate," he growled and claimed her mouth in as gentle a kiss as he could muster before forcing himself to release her.

"Why didn't you say that before? I would've never walked out this morning," she smacked him, then hugged him tighter.

"I was an idiot," he apologized, "but I will never keep anything from you again."

"Good," she said and sat up, "will you do something for me?"

"Anything," he vowed and helped her to stand.

"I want a bath," she said and her eyes glittered at him in the dim room.

Storm steadied her with a hand on her elbow when she would have wobbled. His breath hitched and cock hardened with her presence. Fuck, he was an animal, but it couldn't be helped. He would always want her. That didn't mean he would do anything about it. She needed to get well first.

"Okay," he nodded.

"With you. I want to take a bath with you," she whispered, and he watched in awe as heat filled her gaze.

"Are you certain you are strong enough?"

"Hudson, that man tried to rape my mind. Evil tendrils of whatever filth he's filled himself with scratched at the inside of my head, and I need to chase the remnants away. I need to remember that I am alive, help me," she covered his mouth with her hand when he snarled in response to her frank statement, "No more anger. I need you to help me feel good. I want to connect with you. Please," she begged.

How could he ever say no? Simple. He couldn't. He would always give her what she needed.

"Mate," he growled the word, "whatever you need, I will provide," he lifted her off her feet.

"Shit," she frowned, and he stopped in his tracks.

"Are you hurting? Do you need a doctor?"

"No, dammit," she growled, and he followed her gaze to her feet, "I lost another pair of shoes! I stabbed that green freak with the heels," she snarled.

Relief flowed through Storm and he laughed aloud. He walked to the adjoining bathroom and cradled his sweet, sexy, shoe-loving mate in his arms.

"My love, I will buy you a truckload of them if it makes you happy."

"A truckload, huh?"

"Yes," he sat her on his knee, and turned on the water watching it cascade like a waterfall into the tub.

"I'll hold you to that," she unbuttoned the dress and slipped it off her shoulders, and he helped her into the tub while removing his clothes.

"Let's rinse off this muck before we plug the drain," she said.

Storm removed his soiled clothes and joined her. Fergie reached for him and he allowed her to wash his frame with her tender, loving hands while he did the same to her.

Together they bathed and rinsed, then he did as she'd suggested. Storm plugged the drain and filled the tub with steaming water. He added a scoop of unscented healing salts and sat with his legs on either side of her supple form, loving the feel of her lush shape cradled in his embrace.

"Feel good?" he asked.

"Yes," she sighed and relaxed, allowing her weight to press against him.

"Good," he kissed her shoulder.

"Hudson?"

"Most people call me Storm," he said.

"That's why I call you Hudson," she bit her lip and they both smiled.

"Anything you want, love."

"Okay, I want answers."

"Shoot."

"How does this work? Us being mates, I mean," she frowned.

"Well, I've never been mated before," he began, and his heart swelled with love for her, "but I think we can figure this out together."

"Yeah?" she teased and splashed him.

"Yes," he said, letting the truth in his eyes speak for itself.

Storm tugged on a lock of her hair bringing her closer until their faces were perfectly aligned, then he mashed his mouth to hers. Softly, slowly, he poured all of his love for her into his kiss. Again and again his lips met hers, tongues tangled and breath mingled until they were both trembling with desire.

"Need you, mate," he whispered, teasing her tongue into following his as he traced the seam of her plump lips.

"I want you to need me, Hudson. I've never felt so safe and loved in all my life," her eyes darted to his, and he felt as if he'd been struck by lightning.

His pulse raced as Fergie turned in the water and straddled his legs. Her skin was slick and hot as it rubbed against his.

"Good cause I do need and want you. I always will and I vow to always keep you safe as well, love you, mate," he growled and skimmed his hands up her arms to her vulnerable throat.

Storm caressed her skin, nibbling on her mouth while she rolled her hips, stroking his sex with her own. The heat of the water was nothing compared to the blood boiling in his veins. She was a siren, a goddess, and all his. His Wolf growled, and the man wanted to beat his chest in triumph.

"Now, Hudson, want you now," she moaned into his mouth.

"Anything for you, mate," he promised.

"Hudson," she moaned his name and Storm's entire body trembled.

His cock twitched and his brain short-circuited. All he wanted was to bury himself deep inside of her welcoming heat, to lose himself in the pleasure only she could give him.

After almost losing her, it was heaven to be able to hold her, kiss her, love her like this again. He'd been scared that he would never relish her in his arms again.

"You'll always have me, Hudson, if you want me," she read his thoughts and he welcomed the exchange. Mated couples could sometimes communicate telepathically and he couldn't help but think that would come in handy as she positioned herself over his hard length. She held his gaze, waiting for his response and Storm tightened his hold on her bountiful hips.

"I will always want you," he grunted and entered her slick heat with one strong flex of his hips, "mate."

Pure pleasure, the kind he only ever tasted with her, touched every cell of Storm's being. He knocked the drain from its hold, needing less water so he could control their movements better. Fergie clutched his shoulders, their slick skin made it hard to find purchase, but they made it work.

Storm intensified his thrusts, following every twitch and moan his mate made like a roadmap to ecstasy. Both hers and his. She was breathtaking like this. Eyes lust-glazed, cheeks pink, hair a wild mane of fire.

Yes, Storm thought, she was normally gorgeous, but in the throes of passion she was a goddess. His goddess. He was hardly able to keep himself from spilling his seed like a green pup, but even he had the presence of mind to make sure his mate was satisfied before he followed suit.

Her walls clenched around his length, stroking him deftly with every swivel and grind of her sexy as fuck body. Storm's balls drew tight against his body, ready to spill his seed deep into her healthy womb. But not yet.

First, he would make her see stars, then he'd follow her into oblivion. Grind, swivel, thrust, and repeat. Water splashed around them, the sounds of their passion echoed off the tiled walls. Fergie's moans grew louder, more erratic as he added power and speed to his thrust.

"Do you like that, mate?" he grunted, and she nodded, unable to speak.

Good, he wanted her speechless. Loved her desperate and panting. Fuck yeah, he gave her more. He drove deeper and deeper into her tight sheath. Every move, every whimper, every scrape of her nails on his shoulders, every shudder and moan was his.

Only his. He wanted them all. He'd always been a greedy fuck.

"Come for me, love," he growled.

Large hands gripped her hips, he lifted his mate and brought her down hard on his cock. Again, this time faster. And again.

Storm worked her into a frenzy of passion and movement. He thanked fuck for his Wolf's speed and strength in this. Pleasuring his mate would always be a priority for man and beast.

"Hudson, gonna-" she slapped her hands against his arms.

Her mouth fell open in a silent scream, Fergie arched her back. Storm felt his fangs extend, and he leaned forward and pierced the flesh just above her perfect breasts, marking her again and claiming her once more as his own.

The tangy sweetness of her life's source rushed down his throat and her sex squeezed him. His eyes widened as a sharp burning pain seized his shoulder. It was soon replaced with pleasure so sweet, he could hardly breath. Fergie rolled her hips dragging a deep moan from them both and lapped at his skin.

Blinding white lights filled his vision and Storm dropped his head back and howled. Sinking into her was as close to heaven as his Wolf's soul had ever been.

Pure bliss, he thought as he filled her with his seed, changing her scent, and mixing their essences for all time.

"Mine," the word reverberated in the bathroom, only it wasn't his voice. It was hers.

Satisfaction warred with pure wonder. Both emotions raced for dominance as he opened his eyes to look upon his glorious mate. Fergie's blood tinted lips were opened and her fangs peeked through. She was breathing heavily, her butterscotch colored eyes glowing as she viewed him.

"Mine," she said again, and he hardened once more inside of her.

This time, he would love her slowly and properly. And in bed.

FIFTEEN

"So, what you're telling me," she said between bites of a very large, very rare ribeye steak.

It was so large she'd needed a second dish for sides, which resembled most of the Shifters' places for those of them gathered around the long table in the dining room of the castle, also known as the Keep. Except for Furio. The Horse Shifter was a vegetarian and was currently munching on an enormous cauliflower seasoned with garlic, olive oil, and sea salt. She recognized it as a specialty of Jessenia's.

Hmm. That was weird. She was certain her BFF hated the man. Besides the magic kitchen did all the cooking.

"What were you saying?" Hudson asked, and she resumed her train of thought.

"Oh, uh, so you guys are telling me I'm a Shifter now?"

"Yes," said Kingston, their leader, "sort of."

"What do you mean sort of?" snorted Jessenia.

Fergie growled at her so-called BFF. Turned out, she had quite the secret too. Jessenia Banks was a Witch. And not just because she ate the last strawberry Poptart or finished the coffee.

Hmm. She was a rather ballsy Witch too. Seeing as how she just turned and blew a raspberry at her newly growly and furry former roommate.

"Shifters aren't made with bites. We are not actually Werewolves or what have you. Not the way the humans tell in their legends and myth. However, it is written that true mates can sometimes awaken their significant other's *anima animalis* or animal soul," the Dragon Shifter said.

Fergie frowned at the hard-looking man. His meat was burnt to a crisp. She couldn't really be expected to trust someone who preferred to char their meat black, could she? The fluffy ginger colored Wolf inside of her shook her head. Seemed she didn't like that either.

"You okay, love?" Hudson, or Storm as he preferred his friends to call him, asked.

Fergie supposed that in company she could think of him by his nickname. She nodded at him. Her lover, her mate, her Wolf who'd shielded her with his very body when she'd been under attack.

Good mate, her Wolf pushed the thought at her, and she hummed in agreement.

"Okay, so I'm a Wolf Shifter now and you are all members of an elite group of supernaturals called Guardians of Chaos?"

"Yes. Our job is to preserve the natural free state of all magic for the betterment of supernatural peoples," Kingston explained.

"Yes, but *nushe*, if you want me to give up my vows," Storm began and everyone at the table stilled.

"Are you kidding? This is totally kickass," she said, and she meant it, "And just think, being mated to me means you get to keep your new *blinky* superpowers-"

"Fergie," Storm looked pained at her description of his new enhancements.

"Well, love, you blink in and out of the shadows and when you throw punches your hands glow blue with your Wolf's added energy," she shrugged.

"I like it," Furio grinned, "we can call you *blinky* now!"

Storm growled at the Horse Shifter and tossed a fork at his head. Furio was quick though, and he caught it.

"Manners," Elena, the only female in the Guardians said in a sing-song voice.

"Only I can call him *blinky*," Fergie announced to end the argument, but Storm still didn't look happy.

Whatever. He would get over it. And if he didn't, then she could help him. Later. In bed.

"I would like to go over the contents of your laptop, after dinner perhaps?" Kingston asked.

"Well, sure, but it's no secret. L-Corp wanted as much research as they could get on old land surveys in Hudson, Bergen, and Essex counties. I'd only just begun, but I'd compiled some pretty extensive files with documents and references surrounding each of the GPS coordinates given to me. They took my computer each evening, and supposedly wiped it clean so I wouldn't have access after I handed it in, but I was able to save everything to my cloud before that so I have copies of everything they asked me to research."

"You saved all the information to your cloud? Like a corporate spy?" Storm said, and she was kind of miffed at his incredulity.

Fergie punched her mate in the arm and frowned at the number of open-mouthed faces in the room. Only Jessenia winked.

"What because I like shoes and haven't been able to hold a job makes me a fucking idiot or something?"

"No!"

"No."

"Of course not."

She snorted and rolled her eyes. Fergie stood up from the table and placed her utensils in her now empty plate.

"Thank you, Keep!" she shouted, and the rest of them looked at her like she was certifiable.

"Just because the castle seems to magically prepare everyone's meals, and it automatically or magically cleans up after you all, doesn't mean it doesn't have feelings."

"Uh, love, the castle is an inanimate object," Storm began.

"Is it? Well, inanimate objects don't cook like this and they don't take suggestions from my friend there because I know that is her cauliflower recipe."

"That's true. I just kind of thought of it and here it was," Jessenia added, "who built this place anyway?"

Fergie waited for someone to answer the question, but they all simply looked at one or the other. Unbelievable.

"I can't believe that whatever magic you all are in the business of protecting, none of you ever thought to research the origins of the Keep's magic?"

The number of blank faces around the room

answered that question. And they thought she was an idiot. Sigh.

"Whoever has my laptop should disable the GPS tracker before turning it on, but in the meantime here, I can give you access to my cloud, I just need your email address," Fergie picked up her cellphone and waited.

"Sure, send it to KBaldric001 at goc dot org," the Dragon said and cleared his throat.

"Done."

"Thank you, and can I say, uh, welcome as the first official *conpar* to an anointed Guardian of Chaos."

"But I thought you, *oof-*" Furio grunted from the fist Jessenia planted into his stomach.

The pained look in their leaders' eyes had every one of them frozen in place. Except for Fergie. She stepped forward, aware of Storm tensing at her movements. It was against Shifter decorum to touch someone else's mate, but she'd been a human first, so she figured she'd get a pass. Fergie opened her arms and hugged Kingston briefly dropping a platonic kiss on the man's cheek.

The lights in the room glowed brighter, warming them with its intensity for a brief moment, as if the Keep itself wanted in on the friendly gesture. Fergie stepped back, into the arms of her mate who'd stood when she did. He gripped her tighter than was necessary in her opinion, but she secretly liked it.

"Thank you, Kingston, I am honored."

"My *conpar*. Hmm. It is a bit formal, but I like it, *nushe*," Storm grinned.

Kingston nodded at her once, then stood to leave the room. Before he exited, he placed his big hand on the wall of the dining room and looked up at the ceiling with one eyebrow raised.

"Thank you, Keep," growled the most powerful Shifter amongst them, to the astonishment of everyone there.

Fergie just smiled.

EPILOGUE

S torm gazed at his mate in the light of the rising sun as it filtered into their bedroom through the new gauzy drapes she'd had him install. It was one of the several pleasant changes his sweet Fergie had made in his life and he couldn't help but be grateful for each of them.

"Love," he whispered and brushed his lips over her smooth cheek, tucking a stray behind her ear. "They're here, my love, wake up."

Fergie moaned and turned towards him. He couldn't really blame her. Poor thing. She was more than likely worn out from the exertion of the night before.

Together they'd run through the pine barrens in

their fur by the light of her first full moon as a Wolf Shifter. Her red fur had gleamed in the silvery light of that magnificent globe, and together they'd chased shadows and rabbits. They'd ventured to all the magical places nearby and partook in the cool, clean waters from the mystical *Blue Hole*. A favorite swimming spot for local supernaturals.

His mate was as beautiful and fierce in her Wolf as she was in her skin. Larger than their wild cousins, Wolf Shifters burned a lot of calories in their animal forms. He was thrilled to discover their telepathic abilities were strong in that shape as well.

Projecting his thoughts to his other Guardians was something Storm had gotten used to out of necessity but being in his mates head especially during lovemaking was positively thrilling. He'd never tried to talk in his fur before, but with her it was as natural as breathing.

He'd been so concerned about her transformation, he hadn't realized he was projecting until she'd responded inside his mind's eye.

I am fine. It did hurt, but it's okay now, love. Will you teach me how to run? Teach me to be a Wolf now, she'd pushed the thoughts into his mind and he'd welcomed both her voice and the challenge she presented.

Storm had never been much of a mentor to anyone, but Fergie was so full of life and curiosity. He'd shown her his favorite places and hidden trails. They'd spent hours wandering the forest. Then they'd returned home and slipped back into their skin. Afterwards, they'd made love and re-sealed their matebond by moonlight. It had been the best night of his life. Bar none.

"Mmm, what is it?" she asked

"Hello there, beautiful," he said and kissed her nose.

"Hello, yourself," she smiled and opened her arms, to which he eagerly went.

His mate was one hell of a *cuddler*. Who knew he'd grow to like that sort of thing? He never had before, but then again he'd never had a mate before. She wiggled closer and his body responded immediately and predictably.

"You asked me to wake you when they came, well, they came," he said and nipped her ear between his teeth.

"They're here?" Fergie yelped.

She practically toppled him over in her haste. He had to remember her new strength, but for now he'd just thank the gods for his own wolfish reflexes.

"Where? Where are they?" she pulled on a short

robe he found ridiculously sexy and pinched his arm impatiently.

"Ow," he frowned, "that hurt."

"I'm sorry," she said, and kissed his chin, her whiskey eyes sparkled mischievously.

"Come on, I can't wait either," Storm tugged her hand and walked her across the floor to the new door that had appeared in their room just after she'd moved in.

It seemed the Keep was happy with his little *nushe*. His *conpar*, he corrected himself though both terms of endearment were perfect for his Fergie.

He'd never heard the term *conpar* before, but now that he knew it meant 'beloved mate', it was the only way he thought of his sweet Fergie.

She squealed excitedly when he opened the door with flourish and he was glad he'd thought to add a few more surprises to her order. She deserved them. Especially after what he'd done to three pairs of her panties this week. Darn claws.

Who was he kidding? Storm loved it when his mate squealed with delight whenever he tore her panties from her sweet body.

"My lady," he bowed and grinned as Fergie entered their brand-new two-thousand square foot walk-in closet.

Technically, it was theirs, but he only took up a small part of the enormous space with his clothes and weapons. The rest was all hers.

"*OH MY GAH!* I love you so much," she jumped at him and kissed him hard on the mouth before leaping off to open her goodies.

Storm sat on the velvet chaise at the bottom of the spiral staircase that led to the second floor of the expansive room. Fergie gasped and awed at the bounty before her and joy filled him as he watched her open gifts like a child on Christmas.

"I am not a child," she mock scolded, "but I so enjoy presents. These are so beautiful and there are so many of them!"

"Fifteen pairs, and a few selections from the lingerie department," he nodded at the pink packages on the side of the mountain of shoes.

He was proud of his haul and anxious to see her wearing them. And nothing else, of course. Fergie dropped the box of the fourth pair she'd opened and leapt onto his lap. His hands closed around her bottom and he hugged her close, worried she'd fall and hurt herself.

"Don't you want to open the rest?"

"Not now, now I want my real present," she said and pressed her mouth to his.

"Fergie," he nibbled her lips unable to resist the sweet temptation she presented.

"I love you, you know, even without the shoes," she whispered and his heart pounded in time with hers.

"It makes me happy to make you happy," he returned squeezing and caressing her spectacular ass beneath the silky robe.

"I only need you for that, mate," she wiggled against him and he immediately rose to the occasion.

"Let's open the rest later," he said.

"Best idea you've had so far," Fergie agreed.

Damn, he loved her. And he would make it his business to show her. Again and again. He swallowed her moan as he began to exhibit the extent of his immeasurable feelings.

Sometime later...

Only fourteen pairs of luxury heels, including all six Louboutin's, had survived. One pair of Jimmy Choo's had unfortunately broken beneath his body. But, hell, was it worth it. He'd replace it later.

"Damn straight you will," his *conpar* moaned aloud.

Then she was speechless, and finally, she was gasping his name, which was coincidentally just how he liked her.

"Mine."

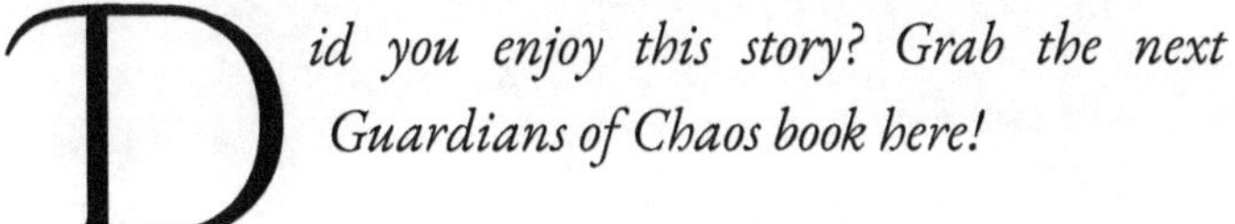

Did you enjoy this story? Grab the next Guardians of Chaos book here!

Dragon Shield

Guardians of Chaos 2

BLURB

He's the leader of an elite force fighting a supernatural war, she's been under a magic spell that's kept her captive for centuries, can they find peace in each other?

Kingston Baldric is a Diamond Dragon Shifter and the leader of the Guardians of Chaos. Holley Mount is a Witch trapped in the walls of the Guardians' Keep for almost three hundred years. A devoted soldier, Kingston has already paid the ultimate price for duty causing him to seal off his Dragon's heart for good. But can Kingston resist the call of his fated mate?

When the Loyalists murdered his beloved Neela to tip the scales in the war to gain control of all magic, he never thought he would recover. Chaos is Baldric's only release until the day when the Guardian's own Keep reveals a secret room to him alone.

In it, he finds the most beautiful woman he has ever seen trapped inside a spell. Holley's body was imprisoned for centuries, but her mind has been very aware of the beings inhabiting the walls of the Keep during that time. She's learned much about modern life and longs to be freed to take her place in the real world. Especially when the pull of her mate is so strong.

Will Kingston accept her after the Fates had already dealt him the harshest of blows? Can Holley keep her freedom without him?

GUARDIANS OF CHAOS PLEDGE

I am the watcher in the storm.

I am the iron shield.

I protect against those who seek to control the wild nature of magic.

I am the guardian of chaos.

To thrive, we must be free.

From chaos comes creation.

PROLOGUE

2*00 years ago...*

The cold, gray walls of the dark rectangular room seemed far too close for comfort as Holley slowly blinked into consciousness. Her head pounded. Pain reverberated throughout her entire body.

How did she come to find herself in this place? Memories tried to break through her bruised mind, but they were foggy. She heard voices whispering around her, but they stopped as her eyes gradually opened.

"What is happening? Where am I?"

"Quiet, heathen spawn," someone hissed followed by a vicious slap to her face.

Holly gasped at the explosion of pain in her cheek.

Frightened did not begin to describe how she felt. It was dark, too dark for her to see. But then a light came, a torch, she thought and squinted against the sudden onslaught to her sensitive eyes.

"Ah, the Witch awakens?"

Holley stilled at the sound of the one voice guaranteed to terrify her. It could not be, but it was. Preacher Milton hovered over her with a lantern held high. The glow from the candle was bright, hot too, as he held it close to her face. But that was not why she trembled.

It was his angry pale eyes that glared at her from beneath the darkened hood of his cloak. The man who'd hit her was sneering beside him. There was something off about his color and his movements.

His other followers stayed back so she could not make out their faces. A shame, she thought, she would love to have names to go with the hexes she was determined to rain down on their foolish heads.

The townspeople hated her and for no real reason. They did not know her. Never took the time. But why would they? She was half savage in their eyes.

Tainted. Unclean. Holley had heard it all. She'd learned not to care, to be unaffected by the stares of those too arrogant to ask questions and too ignorant to listen to the answers.

The fact she was a Witch only made matters worse.

Of course, she did not advertise her powers. That would not be wise at all. Granny Rose taught her better than that.

Oh no. Granny.

"Why am I here? Where is Grandmother?"

"Your grandmother has been hanged for your crimes," he spat, "and since the fires could not take you, Devil-worshipper, this shall be your prison till you die of starvation or the air runs out!"

He opened his arms wide and multiple lanterns along the walls flared to life, manned by his followers. Holley struggled to sit up, horrified when she realized she couldn't.

"You brought me here? To the forest Keep?" she asked, shocked at the preacher's gall.

This place was ancient and sacred to her father's people. Though her dealings with the Lenape tribe were few and far between, she knew the stories. Heard of the strange supernatural beings that had built this place many hundreds of years before Europeans had come to live on this side of the world.

The Keep had been built long ago by a secret order of Witches and other creatures. Or at least that was what she'd been told.

Holley played on the grounds surrounding the enormous stone structure when she was a child. She'd visited the castle with her Granny Rose to meet with her paternal grandfather. Traditionally, Lenape children went to the mother's tribe, but because her mother was a settler, Holley had been all but shunned.

Only her Grandfather Katonah had agreed to meet with the half-European child to see if she possessed the magic of his line. That had been a cold and eye-opening lesson for young Holley.

Grandfather Katonah had met with her seven times after that day. He'd explained in stunted terms about the magic of their people, and Holley had listened. The old man had died some years ago now, but Granny Rose made sure she did not forget his lessons.

Holley had been doubly blessed, *or cursed* depending on how you looked at it, with magic on both sides. Granny Rose did not possess any particular magical talents, but her mother had. She'd spent her own childhood listening and learning how to make salves, healing balms, potions and the like.

Two very different traditions and customs, but both told the story of who she was.

Holley Mount. Native. Witch. Settler. But she was more than that. Holley was a granddaughter and she had loved her Granny Rose with all her heart. Sadness filled her chest and she sobbed quietly for a moment.

Enough child, it's not the time to be lost in memories, a familiar voice whispered to her.

Holley shook her head. Granny was right. She needed to find a way out of this situation. Her eyes scanned the room, but aside from Preacher Milton who was giving orders to his men who seemed to smear paint or was that blood on the walls, there was nothing of any use.

Beaten and chained to a stone slab deep in the belly of the castle in the pine barrens, Holley was truly trapped. Terror eked its way up her spine. That this place would now be her tomb became quite clear. She struggled against her bonds, but to no avail.

"You cannot escape," Milton smiled wickedly in her direction then nodded at his hooded brethren.

"They're writing a spell!"

"Yes," he hissed and lifted a quill as if he were toasting her.

Preached Milton finished a symbol with a flourish of his wrist, "Do you recognize this cast? No? Oh well, still, I thought an eagle feather suited the occasion," he waved the quill still dripping fresh blood and she winced as droplets hit her face.

Holley suddenly felt as if she'd fallen through ice on a lake and was submerged in some freezing, dark depths she could not see. Her teeth chattered, the cold painful to her, and she screamed her agony.

"The searing pain you feel would be the blood connection you now have with this spell, but you should know that Witch," Milton spat the words at her as if they too could harm.

But what they did was reveal a very terrible truth. The blood they used to cast their magic was hers. Blood magic was the darkest of all arts, Holley knew this and struggled harder against her chains.

"I have harmed no one! You are supposed to be a priest!"

"Your very existence is a harm. You are an abomination and since you will not confess-"

"Confess what? I cannot change my circumstance of birth," she pleaded, but the hatred in his eyes chilled her to the marrow.

"Can't you? Pity. Then you will die here."

Holley closed her eyes and pleaded her case to the great Creator. During one of her grandfather's visits, she'd learned how her ancestors spoke to their kin through the veil between life and death. he'd taught her how to access that plane.

Pity she never practiced. Relying instead on her healing skills to put food on their table. Poor Granny

Rose was gone now, and Holley would follow her into the void. But she was not ready. Not yet.

Life was strenuous within the settlement of Puritans who hated the likes of her. Holley was shunned and treated as an outcast for her tanned skin and black hair. They had tried to tell her that her Puritan mother had been raped by a savage and died in childbirth as punishment for not taking her own life before she could bring her daughter into the world.

She understood it was all lies. Granny Rose and her grandfather had taught her that. She even suspected why Preacher Milton hated her so. Though it did not make this any easier.

"You cannot kill me because my mother did not love you," she screamed as the cold began to seep inside her very bones.

"She should have killed herself before you were born! Devil's whore!"

"My mother loved my father."

"He was a dirty savage!"

"No. He was a young warrior. Descended from shamans. They loved each other, and I come from that love."

"He was a rapist and she a whore!"

"You are wrong Preacher Milton," she defied the

man who had frightened her ever since she was a little girl.

"Your soul shall burn for this!"

His blotchy skin turned beet red in his fury. But what had she to lose? He had killed her grandmother, turned the town against her, and was now set on killing her in this place. The very same castle she used to dream about living in as a child.

"Look at me, Demon spawn," Milton hissed as he drew back his hand.

Holley ignored the stinging on her cheek after he delivered one final blow. She glared at him with hardened eyes. Anger was not an unknown emotion for her. She knew it all too well. Had felt it for the likes of the preacher and those small-minded members of the settlement they'd begun miles away in *New Ark*.

Times were changing. Talk of revolution and breaking away from England were all the rage. Holley was a fan of this search for freedom. Although, she doubted those men had the same ideas about it as she.

She was tired of being told she couldn't do things because she was a woman, a half-breed, a Witch even. They feared her, cursed her name, and as such Milton was able to slander her to where her murder would go unquestioned. She would never understand how people who'd left their country to find freedom could be so unforgiving of those who differed from them.

Her heart squeezed with regret as her body trembled violently from the chill. Puffs of white formed from her breath, and she felt tears rolling down the sides of her face. So cold. So dark. Fear threatened to control her mind, but no, she fought against it.

"Struggle if you will, but I have finally found a way to purge your soul of the evil that inhabits it. My men have traced the images in your heathen books here for you to gaze at until you can see no more. True, you survived my attempts at burning you, and drowning the Devil from your blood, but here you will remain within these walls until you are only a memory!"

"No! No!" she screamed as the hooded cowards began to fill the gaping hole in the wall with brick and mortar.

Holley was going to die. Milton was right. Her wrists ached where the manacles cut into her skin. She'd been beaten and bloodied, starved, burned, and drowned, and finally chained like an animal only to be buried alive behind brick.

She did as he said she would and stared at the runes on the walls inscribed with her blood, wondering at the stupidity of men not for the first time. Closing her eyes to the numbness that had settled over her, Holley knew she did not have long. She chanted the words Granny Rose had taught her.

She could trace their ancestry back to the Lancaster Witches of England. She had magic in her veins on both sides. Power pulsed through her blood and she used that and the words she remembered to tap into the spirits of the Keep. The *manetuwak*.

Hear my call. Answer my need, great manetuwak.

The room warmed and pulsed as the power that resided therein seemed to take a liking to her.

Please, spirits of the Keep. I need your help.

She sensed them listening and wondered for a moment at their origin. Magic in and of itself was neither bad nor good. It was how it was used that determined its affinity.

As if it knew her doubts, the *manetuwak* began filling her head with information. Yes, it was built as she'd imagined, by *supernaturals*. The Keep was for an order known as the Guardians of Chaos. It was created with the intention of aiding and protecting all magic. Yes, it was a positive force, but remained empty as the New World had been overrun by *normals* far too soon for it to be used for its rightful purpose.

Abandoned to the piney woods that surrounded it, the Keep had noticed Holley when she and her grandmother had come across its lands.

Yes, she answered, *we took many walks through your woods to collect herbs under the light of the full moon and I fell in love with this castle and built fairytales in my head around it.*

The collecting of herbs was of course, just another mark against her and Granny. The locals called them Witches and had tried and found them guilty.

Holley had been hanged, drowned, and burned at the stake. She survived all three attempts at ending her life. Granny was not so lucky, she shuddered once more at the loss.

Please, I beg you, do not let them murder me. Protect my flesh, and keep my soul tied to thee, oh keeper of my body. Until the time comes when it is safe for me to awaken. Let me see through your walls and hollows, allow me the freedom to take space and shelter inside your heart, great manetuwak. Keep me safe, keep me hidden, as I will, so mote it be.

Holley felt her own magic rise and swell with each statement and every entreaty. She'd never tapped into quite so much, afraid of the consequences. Above all magic required balance, but this was necessary.

Her mind raced forward for a moment, it was lit up like the sun, then plunged into darkness. The pain went away. Her bruises and cuts healed as far as she could tell. Holley saw a miracle of stars and swirling clouds and mists. She heard a steady hum fill the spaces around her.

There was not one being there with her, but she felt the *manetuwak's* presence and knew she was cared for.

Incredible, she thought as peace began to fill her.

The preacher might have imprisoned her here to die, but she would not perish. She would survive and one day she would walk the forests once more under the light of the moon. Holley would taste fresh air again, she swore it.

Even as she felt her human body freeze and grow still beneath the power of her entreaty, the spell of the *manetuwak* or the spirits of the Keep kept her mind focused and awake.

Until the moment when it was safe for her to awaken, Holley's body would remain frozen in time within the very walls Preacher Milton used to try to kill her.

She was part of the great stone construct now.

Of course, Holley had no idea then that it would take nearly three-hundred years for that time to arrive, but each day she used her magic to try and reach the one man with the power to free her. The one man she had never expected to appear.

Her mate.

ONE

"*It's time. You must move on,*" Neela's voice called out to him through the veil.

He stood there for hours, days, sometimes weeks inside his dreams, waiting to catch a glimpse of his fallen mate.

Kingston Baldric could only visit that metaphysical place where the realm of the undead met reality in that precarious state between sleep and wake. It was there that he sometimes caught a glimpse of Neela, his fallen mate.

As time went on, her image began to fade. The vibrant blonde she-Dragon he had known in life was nothing but a pale shadow now. Was he responsible for that too? He could only wonder.

Their connection was less than it had ever been.

The call to move on was too strong for even her fiery spirit. He was helpless to stop it, and yet, he still came to this place seeking forgiveness for sins of the past.

The vows he made were over, but how could he let go? His heart grew tight and his Dragon hissed. The great beast did not like it there. He hated being so close to death. It was something any near-immortal creature would naturally find repulsive.

"I can't. I can't let go."

"You must," she whispered.

"Why must I? Without you, I am alone, Neela. So very alone."

"You must be strong, Kingston. I am so sorry, so very sorry," her whispers grew more and more faint with every word.

He tried to reach for her, but the veil slapped at his still-living soul. It was powerful, as it should be. That barrier would not allow any being with ties to the physical realm entry. Not even a mighty Diamond Dragon. Kingston growled deep in his throat but stopped when he could no longer make out the silhouette of his mate.

"Neela! Don't go!"

"I have to go. It is time. I am sorry for everything. So sorry..."

"I don't care about that now. It was never important."

"I am sorry," her whispered voice continued to diminish, "so sorry. Be happy, Kingston, be loved."

"Neela! No! No! Noooo!"

Kingston Baldric, Diamond Dragon, Alpha and team leader of the Guardians of Chaos stationed at the Keep in the Pine Barrens of New Jersey, woke with a start. Sweat beaded his brow and soaked through his sheets.

His room was unnaturally warm, almost stifling. He tossed off the covers and sat on the edge of the large mattress. He ran his hands over his face roughly, wiping away all traces of that torturous dream.

Fuck. He'd been to see Neela, or *her ghost*, as she was now beyond the physical realm. It was not the first time he'd visited his mate in his dreams, but something told Baldric it was the last time.

His heart squeezed desperately inside of his chest. She'd been taken from him far too soon and there was simply no right way to deal with the loss of one so worthy and deserving of all his best.

Neela had not been a Guardian of Chaos. She'd spoken no vows and had no place in battle. The precious female should have been off limits in this endless war the Loyalists had been waging against the supernatural world.

The Guardians did what Guardians do, they

protected magic in an effort to preserve it for all *super-naturals*. They were not like the army or the police. That bit was left up to the Enforcers. If the Loyalists wanted to simply fight, they should have gone after them.

Only, they didn't. Now, Neela was dead. His enemies had decided she was fair game and the rare she-Dragon was targeted.

She'd died far sooner than she should have and with more pain than she'd deserved. He could still hear her crying out his name as she succumbed to her wounds that fateful day. Bloodied and left for dead on the side of the road, it appeared an accident to locals. But he knew better.

Even worse, he was responsible for her suffering and her death. No matter how many wrongs he righted, Kingston would never forgive himself. He would never forget that he was the reason she died so tragically.

All his promises were for naught. Images of his brother, Edgar, raced through his mind. They'd been inseparable once. Since they were young Dragonlings, the brothers shared everything they had. Secrets, toys, games, books, and as they grew older, even women.

When they met Neela, things changed. The lovely Sapphire Dragon was beautiful with her blonde hair and sparkling blue eyes. She'd captivated both brothers and they'd happily dueled for her affections. Edgar won Neela's splendid heart, but Kingston had delivered the mating mark. Now she was gone and the pain was too much. For a hundred years, they lived together as mates, and now he must learn to be alone.

Shame washed over Kingston as he recalled their last argument. Their relationship was complicated to say the least. He was a private man and could not share this with any of his Guardians, but he knew the secrets he kept would be the death of him someday if he did not learn to let go. Even in death, Neela was still smarter than him.

The sound of her pleading voice echoed in his brain, his refusal, followed by her resolution to find happiness within her life. He never held it against her even as he abstained, but it hurt him to think that she was on her way to meet her lover when she'd been killed.

Of course, he told the others she'd been going shopping. He might not have saved her in the end, but he could preserve her reputation at the very least.

With her soul firmly on the other side of the veil, Kingston had to wonder if she was right.

Was it time for him to forgive himself and move on?

Doubt began to rear its ugly head, but his inner Dragon hissed at the debilitating fucker. Kingston had too much on his plate to start giving in to weakness of any kind.

He needed to be strong for his Guardians. Good leaders could not breakdown in the middle of a war. And that was what this was.

Offner had succeeded in killing Neels, kidnapping Fergie, and overall, pissing him the fuck off. But it wouldn't be long before he met the evil Warlock again. Then Kingston would truly make him pay.

Magic was not the Warlock's personal plaything. He'd destroyed the reputation of the Loyalists, but there were still those who believed heavily in the fundamentals of their credo. Mainly to be dicks.

"Where are you with the search?" he spoke into his cell phone and waited while Elena updated him on what she'd found out.

"There are several warehouses that have reported suspicious spikes in magical use over the past week in Newark, Kearny, and Harrison."

"Get over there and investigate. Take Byram with you," he told the Panther Shifter.

Kingston rarely used his Alpha voice when giving orders to his Guardians. He preferred to trust in their loyalty and respect for him and their mission. After all, they'd all taken the vow. Each one of them chose this life. For better or worse.

He checked the time. Four hours. That was about all the sleep he got just lately. His dragon puffed out a smoky breath in annoyance. The enormous beast would have liked to snuggle up for a week or two, but he had no time for that. The hunt was on, and it was only a matter of time before Offner was captured.

Meanwhile...

"I need the location damn you," spat the aged Warlock.

"Master, we have not been able to locate the files. If you would just let us try to get the female-"

"We tried that already," he slammed his gnarled hands onto the stained table and pointed at the long scar on his cheek, "see what that blasted dragon left me with last time? No, I will not take the risk of kidnapping the redhead again. Just find me the map she located the first time," he commanded.

His blood pumped sluggishly through his veins. Too much time had gone between his last feeding and a Warlock was only as good as the powers he drained from his last victim. The pitiful Witch he'd happened upon was weak and old, which was why he felt as poorly as this.

Time was running out. The Demon who owned

his soul would be coming for him soon and if he could not satisfy the beast with a supply of magic, he was as good as gone.

It must be done now. He had to find that vein of magic deep within the lands. He'd almost forgotten its existence, but he knew it was somewhere. He just had to find it first!

Failure was not an option. After he settled his account with the Demon, he would make the Guardians pay and magic would be his to rule!

Two

"What the fuck are you talking about?" Furio shook his pony-tailed head at his best-friend and fellow Guardian.

"I am telling you, I am not *just* using my Shifter abilities, *cump*. Check it," Storm demonstrated by holding his right hand high and balling it into a fist.

Black, smoky tendrils began to wrap around his hand almost immediately, and when he threw the punch he'd been winding up, his fist sent that power to the far wall where it shattered as if it were sheetrock instead of the huge eighteen-inch-thick cement bricks.

All of the walls inside the Keep were constructed of the thick, stone blocks. The building itself seemed to take offense at the attack. Immediately following the display, the room grew colder and darker.

No sooner had Storm turned around to smile over his supposed victory at Furio, then one of the broken shards seemed to zoom across the room to smack him in the forehead.

"Ow!" Storm rubbed his head and flung the shard onto the floor.

"Awe, *cumpy*, you fucked up."

Seconds later, every bit of the broken remnants of brick and plaster floated upwards and off the floor. The air hummed and buzzed with energy as the pieces wove themselves back together seamlessly, creating the appearance of never having been broken.

"Sorry, Keep," said Fergie McAndrews in a sing-song voice.

She walked into the room at just the right moment as she always did. Catching her Wolf Shifter mate's glowing blue eyes with a mischievous smile on her lips.

The redhead wore her latest pair of spindly-heeled torture devices, these in an alarmingly bright shade of purple, and headed directly into Storm's open arms. She greeted him with a kiss that was far too personal to conduct in mixed company, but they were Shifters. PDA's were kinda the norm.

Their story was legendary, even if it only began

months ago. The love they shared for one another was almost tangible. It hurt to watch, but Kingston remained unmoving and observed the byplay.

He turned his head out of respect once their lips touched, noting with passing interest how the room seemed to warm and glow around the mated couple. It was as if the Keep wanted to bask the lovers in a protective bubble. Odd, he mused. Then again, he'd started to notice something off with the Keep after Fergie had pointed it out over dinner one night.

There was something very different just lately about the place he'd called home for the last few decades. A certain awareness he had not recognized before.

As their group leader and a rare Diamond Dragon Shifter, Kingston was one of the oldest supernatural creatures in the order. The Guardians of Chaos was a well-respected organization, but their numbers were small. He'd been a sworn member for a century. His Dragon hissed as his mind threatened to wander back to the days of his youth.

Don't go there. Not now.

The past was in the past. Best to think of other things. Like hunting for the bastards who'd attacked Neela, then Fergie. The Loyalist problem was getting entirely out of hand. If they refused to accept that mates were off limits then why should the Guardians have to adhere to the rules set forth by the Assembly?

Kingston was in a seriously pissed off mood. That seemed to be his baseline just lately. But what did he expect with little to no rest? A Dragon needed to sleep, but he was anxious. Unsettled. As if he could sense something big was coming.

But what? Fuck if he knew. Kingston was many things, but a clairvoyant he was not. Besides, it was no use. How could he sleep knowing Neela was gone and it was all his fault?

Grrrr. The Dragon inside of him snarled. The beast's claws scratched against his skin, but it was too risky. He could not let the anger inside devour what precious little was left of his humanity.

And just lately, it felt all too little. His fire was burning low, the heat that flamed his soul was going out. Fading. That happened when mates died, but his was no usual mating. He frowned and rubbed his chest.

It could not be that. After all, when he'd woken up that morning he'd been hotter than a furnace.

"Kingston? You alright, *cump*?" Furio knocked on the wall, his inquiry barely making a dent, "you're growling, dude, like loudly," he added, eyebrows raised high on his pronounced forehead.

The Stallion Shifter was unique in Kingston's experience, and he valued him as a member of the team. He silenced his growl and gave the man a curt nod before exiting to his study.

Sometimes he needed to be alone. Now was one of them.

The wall sconces lit themselves as soon as he entered, as did the fireplace. His computer turned on, but the lamp next to it stayed dark. He frowned deeply, pulling his chair out before sitting his colossal frame down.

He waited, but nothing happened. *Hmmph*. He'd gotten used to the Keep taking care of all the little odds and ends he and his team were simply too busy to worry about. Very odd, he mused, the lamp remained off until he bent forward and tugged the little chain.

"You angry with me?" he asked aloud, shaking his head and releasing a long, slow breath.

He was developing Fergie's fancy for talking to inanimate objects. Fucking hell. Kingston ignored his momentary lapse of sanity and logged in to the Guardians network to read the latest reports and necessary assignments.

He never thought New Jersey would be such a hotspot for paranormal activity, and yet, here he was leading one of the busiest groups of Guardians this side of the Atlantic.

Even more amazing were these new confounded machines that were equipped with special, magicked software that protected them against all matters of malware supernatural and not.

Kingston answered his correspondences, updated the proper channels on their hunt for Loyalists in their sector, and took a look at the quarterly reports. He felt like a fucking businessman and that was something both he and his Dragon loathed.

A chiming bell alerted him to an incoming message and Kingston switched tabs to his email. His finger stalled as he rolled the cursor over the new message. It was from the Assembly regarding their meeting over Neela Baldric's death.

"Fuck," he inhaled deeply and clicked on it.

His eyes closed as he read their findings. *Murder. Deliberate. Collateral damage in the war against the Loyalists. Tragic. Apologies.*

"Fucking bastards!"

Kingston stood abruptly, overturning his desk and sending everything on it flying across the room. His Dragon snarled and snapped. Pain lashed at him from the inside out as he balled his fists and took a swing at the wall sending shards of stone flying.

Fuck. He was losing it, he thought as he sank to the floor. The room remained quiet. The stone stayed broken. And Kingston closed his eyes and tried to calm his raging beast.

The door swung opened and Furio and Storm ran inside, halting when they saw he was alone, but enraged.

Smart. Very smart. Kingston was looking for a fight and right then anyone would do. But instead of hurting the very team he was responsible for, he headed for the window.

White diamond-shaped scales began to pop out over his skin and he felt himself losing control over his Shift. And why not? This was a pretty big fucking deal.

With an enormous roar, Kingston tore through the window, breaking glass and brick as his almost seven-foot-tall, two-hundred-fifty pound frame changed into that of a fifty-foot-long four-thousand pound Diamond Dragon. The last of his kind.

Sorrow unlike any he'd ever felt welled up inside him as he shot enormous streaks of flames into the sky and flapped his enormous wings. He opened his jaws and screeched a mournful cry that echoed through the forest.

So much pain, so much anger, he needed to fly. To soar among the clouds to try and forget his sorrows.

His Dragon was hurting. With scales that appeared white to the naked eye, but upon closer inspection they were in fact clear and crystal-like, he used them to hide himself from the *normals*.

When he wanted to be seen he could take on any color in the rainbow. It all depended on where one stood when they saw him. And what mood he was in for that matter. His Dragon preened at the thought. He was a tad conceited that way, but there were not many who could reflect any number of hues.

Cloaked from the humans, he flew for what seemed like hours, employing his own special brand of magic to do so. Diamond Dragons used their powers and their special scales to turn themselves completely translucent, and therefore, invisible to the eye.

It was the only way he could hide himself from modern technology. Right then hiding was the last thing on his mind. He wanted to burn down whole cities and sink the earth in fire and brimstone. To make the world suffer as he suffered.

Neela.

Fuck, he was furiously angry. With himself. With the Loyalists. With Offner. And with the Assembly, those bastards.

Collateral damage? Fuck them. She was a precious

female. Too few female Dragons had ever been birthed and Neela was cherished in her lifetime.

How could they dismiss her death so easily? How could they expect him to stand down and not search for her murderers? But that had been the last line of the missive.

You will forward all your investigative research into this matter to Home Office where our own agents will collect and study your research and launch an investigation. You have been cleared of all charges.

Cleared of all charges. Him.

Well, they might have cleared him, but Kingston would never clear himself. And he would never give up the search.

THREE

Blood poured from the wound on his lip, but Kingston continued to fight his way to the front line. They'd received a tip through a CI of Byram's that the Loyalists had holed up in an abandoned factory in downtown Newark to regroup.

After Elena had scouted the place in her sleek Panther form, they headed in. A dozen and a half of the fuckers were nestled inside. Like the rats, he thought with a snarl.

Petty and cruel, the bastards hurled potion bottles full of bits of wire, nails, and glass with nasty little stinging spells inside that activated the objects when released. Like a supernatural dirty bomb.

After the Guardians had almost killed their leader

for kidnapping and torturing Storm's mate, the group had been wreaking havoc any way they could.

The man, Offner, had been unveiled as a Warlock and as a result, the Loyalists had lost any credible standing they'd had within the supernatural community. No one knowingly backed a soulless oath-breaker.

The Guardians finally denounced them for what they were. Liars and perverters of all that magic stood for.

Byram fought on his left and Furio on his right while Elena engaged their enemies from behind. He'd only taken three of his Guardians with him on this trip to investigate Byram's lead.

The Vampire was inhumanly strong and wicked fast. Elena's prowess and stealth were her finest assets, where Furio's lied in his loyalty. Kingston was honored to have them on his team.

True, he was a fierce Diamond Dragon, but he knew he needed them to win this fight. This war was a long one and required more than speed and strength. It needed endurance, presence of mind, and comrades in arms. The Guardians of Chaos always worked in groups, and this was why.

Still, Kingston felt pretty fucking unstoppable at the moment. Truth was, he'd been feeling off balance lately. Neela's loss compounded with the Assembly's acquittal of his own fault in her death had left him raw and angry.

He'd done his best by the female, but apparently that wasn't good enough. No one knew that more than he.

"Your reign is at an end, Guardian!"

Kingston's head turned just as a green-skinned Gila Shifter leapt into his path. His Dragon snarled furiously in his mind's eye. The fuckers were like cockroaches to his magnificent beast.

"That's where you are mistaken, lizard lips," he reached out with lightning fast hands and had the fucker off his feet and dangling in the air in a split second, "Guardians of Chaos do not rule over anything. We are the keepers of freedom. You are the ones who want to decide who gets to use how much magic, what, when, and where. But that is not up to you."

Kingston growled and punched the Shifter, dropping his unconscious body to the dirty ground before spinning to meet the next attack. The hall was smoky and the scent of waste, human and Shifter, disease, decay, and rot were damn near overwhelming.

"Fuck, they have smoke spells, King," grunted Furio as he delivered a back kick to the head of one Bull Shifter who'd decided to try a half-Shift in the middle of the fight but only managed to make his head swell up like a fucking balloon.

That's what happened to assholes who didn't respect magic. Shifters were a special kind of supernatural who shared their souls with an animal spirit and could access said spirit through a magical bond that was both sacred and unique.

Maintaining a half-Shift was something only a Shifter with a strong connection to his or her animal and who had exceptional control could pull off. Fuckwit here did not fall into the category.

Obviously, snorted his Dragon.

He rolled his eyes and made a mental note to steer clear of Fergie, Storm's mate, for a few days. His beast was starting to sound like her. Next thing he knew, the damn animal would start fawning over footwear.

Not fucking likely, growled the beast.

A rapid succession of pops sounded and next thing he knew, the halls were covered in a thick, black fog that nearly choked him. Kingston smashed his fist through a wall. They had at least six bagged and tied, but the rest of the Loyalists were as good as gone.

Afterwards, he made a call to have the prisoners picked up by the local Enforcers unit where they would be tried and jailed for their crimes in supernatural court.

That part of the job was not his concern, and for that Kingston was grateful. He preferred the hunt and the fighting aspect as opposed to the law and order part of it all.

"You ready?" Furio's eyes were bright red, and he was still rubbing them.

"Yeah, stop that or you'll make it worse," Kingston nodded at the Stallion Shifter.

"Fuck, man, it burns."

He snorted. Yeah, it fucking burned. It always did.. He was more than ready to head back to the Keep. Away from the putrid stink and crowded streets of one of New Jersey's most densely populated cities, he preferred the stone walls of the haunted old manse any day.

"Let's go," he said.

Hours later.

Kingston laid his head back against the enormous claw-foot tub and closed his weary eyes. The water was hot and clear, the way he preferred. None of those pesky bath salts that dried out his Dragon's scales and had him smelling like Furio's fruity fucking head of hair.

The fucking Draft Horse Stallion loved his thick locks to be shiny and well-conditioned on any given day, whereas Kingston couldn't give two fucks about hair. His or anyone else's.

Well. That was not exactly true. There was a woman, *his dream woman*, and he meant that literally as in a woman who appeared in his dreams from time to time. She had the most gorgeous hair he had ever seen.

Thick, straight, and impossibly dark. His dreams about her were vivid, especially where her wealth of hair was concerned. It fascinated him. The way it seemed to hang down her back and across her shoulders, like a velvet curtain running all the way past her waist and hips.

He'd often imagined wrapping it around his hand and lifting it to his face. Wanted to feel the strands slip through his fingers. He wanted more than that of course. To know the lady. To get a whiff of her scent. To kiss her plump, wide lips.

Would she welcome him? Her mossy green eyes appeared curious in his dreams. He felt her desire, her desperation, and it pained him to not be able to help.

For some reason, he associated the raven-haired vixen with wildflowers and herbs. Could picture her in a garden where they grew in glorious disarray. Yes, even thinking of her seemed to conjure images of long hair and swirling skirts, laughing faces while she tended a patch of earth that very much resembled the old kitchen garden he must've walked past a time or a hundred over the years.

Of course, it was grossly overgrown with weeds and the years of neglect shone in its rusted fence and barren patches. He felt a sudden pang of sadness in his chest.

No, that wouldn't do. He made a mental note to tell one of the Guardians to have it cleared and tended. Not that Kingston had the sudden urge to go gardening, but for some reason or other, he needed that small garden cleaned out and made ready.

Maybe Fergie would have some use for it. Or perhaps her friend would. The little kitchen Witch was always hanging out at the Keep now that Fergie had permanently moved in.

Exhaling slowly, Kingston relaxed every aching muscle he had in the steaming hot water. Having already washed the blood and muck from the earlier battle off his skin, this was the Dragon's reward.

He would never admit it aloud, but he was hoping to catch a glimpse of the lovely maiden who haunted his dreams. Of course, those dreams were typically followed by overwhelming feelings of disloyalty to Neela, but he would deal with that later.

Right then, he needed *her*. Needed the dark-haired beauty with the curious eyes and fearless smile.

Yes, he thought, *please. Come to me, little one, comfort me. Make me forget.*

His eyes drifted shut and he felt her all around him. Her presence so real he gasped even as he recognized she was just an illusion, a made-up fantasy.

Still, he welcomed the faraway sound of her voice as she crooned. He felt her touch as she brushed ghostly fingertips across his brow followed by a tender kiss so soft it was like butterfly wings on his lips.

Sleep now, my Dragon. Rest, the time is coming upon us.

Her voice seemed to whisper inside of his brain and his beast rose inside of him. Growling softly, wanting to fully awaken, but she hushed and calmed his Dragon like no one ever had before. The silly beast wanted her as if she were real, but she was not. Sad as that fact was, it was still the truth. Someone knocked on the door to his private bathroom and he opened one golden eye and growled softly.

Fucking hell, what now, he wondered.

"Uh, Kingston?" Fergie's voice rang through the door and he sighed as he made to get out of his bath.

He could not ignore one of his Guardian's mates.

It would not do for a man in his position. Not in the least.

"One moment," he said and quickly dried off and tugged on a pair of jeans and a clean Henley, "yes?"

He pulled the door open and stared in shock at her appearance. The woman was usually dressed impeccably, in designer heels and smart business attire. She was now, with an added addition.

"Um," he was at a loss.

Kingston had never seen Fergie covered in dust from head to toe. She appeared guilty and her new she-Wolf whined loudly so that his Alpha powers picked up on her obvious distress.

"What is going on?"

"Well, you see," she cleared her throat, "Jessenia and I were looking around in the basement, um, exploring really-"

"You wanted faster access to the internet, didn't you?" he narrowed his eyes aware of the current arguments over WIFI speeds within the Keep.

"Okay fine, I admit it. Hudson's room has the worst connection and I thought if I ran an ethernet cable from the router straight to his room I could plug it in to my PC when I'm home and get my work done faster-"

"How is that coming?"

"Work? It's fine," she tucked her dust-covered red-hair behind her ears with her fingers and tried to remain dignified despite her ridiculous appearance, "anyway, the wall we drilled into kind of um, collapsed, and well, I think you need to see this."

"Should I call Furio? He is the best carpenter among us."

"Just come on. Hurry."

Kingston followed barefoot behind the former normal. After she mated Storm, Fergie's animal soul had been awakened and she was now every bit a Wolf Shifter. Still, he wondered how the hell she stood on those things she called shoes.

They looked downright painful to him, and seemed to defy all laws of physics, but she swore by them. Storm also seemed quite taken with the lethal footwear, judging by the way he showered her with new additions to her collection every month or so.

Whatever. Kingston had no interest in the Wolf Shifters' shoe fetish. He simply followed where she led, down to the depths of the basement of the Keep.

"I used a power drill to make the hole, I mean I thought half an inch was no biggie," Fergie continued her explanation, but he was beyond listening for the moment.

Something was happening to him. His Dragon

scratched and snarled inside of him. The walls seemed to close in the deeper he went into the belly of the Keep, and yet, Kingston could not stop himself from investigating further.

Something was there. Something beckoning his Dragon forward. Magic sizzled along his skin, making the hair on his arms and neck stand up. The air hummed and vibrated with power. Perhaps she'd hit some kind of magical vein or ley line?

It was no secret that rivers of supernatural energy and magic dwelled beneath the earth in what were called magical veins or ley lines. Magic was finite. It was recycled and reused, passed down from one person to the next. Inherited, not made.

He could not be sure just what the female had uncovered, but his beast was hissing wildly and his pulse was racing like mad. He inched forward and noted the distinct drop in temperature. It was downright freezing there.

Jessenia was staring through the gaping hole in the old brick wall. He could tell from her stance that the tiny kitchen Witch was in a state of absolute shock.

"Fergie, take your friend aside," he commanded but refrained from using his Alpha voice on the woman.

He had no wish to start a quarrel with Storm, and

the way he saw it she was his Guardian's *conpar*, his fated mate, not a Guardian herself. Therefore, she was not his to command.

Kingston did try to remember his manners when speaking to the woman. Storm was a good man and an even better Wolf. He hated to admit it, but he felt nothing but respect, with perhaps a tinge of envy over the man's good fortune in finding his fated mate.

Yes, he'd been carrying the weight of Neela's death with him for a while now, but it started long before that. He'd tried so hard to honor both the female and his brother, but he had failed them both miserably.

Not your fault, he thought he heard the she-Dragon's voice whisper in his head.

Every single inch of Kingston seemed to stand at attention as he stepped over the rubble, careful not to impale his bare feet on the sharp stone as he entered the small hidden room. His Dragon snarled at the myriad of magic coming at him from every direction. Symbols lined the walls, he sniffed and scowled fiercely. That spell was old, but they had cast it in blood and for obvious, nefarious purposes.

There were too many people there for him to get a good read. Too much noise. Then everything fell away from him as he caught the faint scent of flowers and blueberries on the air.

Grrr. Mine.

He wondered at the thought, but the truth struck him hard. It was the most wonderful fragrance he'd ever smelled.

His eyes landed on the vast slab of winter stone in the center of the small rectangular space. Chest heaving, Kingston put one foot in front of the other and approached the altar.

Yes. Something inside of him seemed to recognize it for what it was. He hated the thing on sight. The stone table was meant to be a coffin, he realized and growled once more.

As his bare feet drew nearer to it, he realized someone was chained to the cold, hard rock. Just like a sacrifice. Kingston sucked in a breath and more of the blueberry flower fragrance invaded his senses. The air was musty and cold, dust motes filled his vision. He waved them away, squinting and calling upon his Dragon's eyesight. The beast had night-vision and as Kingston adjusted to it, he could not believe his eyes.

It was her. The woman from his dreams.

Thick black hair so long it hung off the sides of the altar surrounded her perfect face. She had tawny skin with earthy undertones of golds and coppers, though he could imagine her rounded cheeks with a hint of blush on them. As it was, the cold kept her unnaturally pale. Still, she was, in a word, lovely.

Her wide mouth was slack as if in sleep, but Kingston knew better. He could tell by the furrow of her eyebrows that she was doing anything but rest. Beads of sweat dotted her forehead as she battled with whatever was holding her down and that was when he sprang into action.

Using his Dragon's strength, Kingston gripped the heavy metal chains that were attached to the manacles binding her wrists. He noted with muted fury the bruises that marked the area, a telltale sign of her struggles.

He didn't know who she was or who put her there, but by the gods themselves, he would see them pay! Anger warred with the singular intent to free her inside of him, the latter won out thankfully, and he stretched and pulled the bespelled metal, oblivious to the conversation going on around him.

"Kingston!" someone yelled and he spared them a brief glance as his Dragon hissed at them for their interruption.

He needed the woman freed. Now.

No, not the woman, his Dragon growled, *my woman*.

"Kingston," Storm touched his shoulder.

Kingston turned his head and growled at the Guardian, one word escaped his lips.

"Mine."

"Oh fuck," Storm said and tackled his mate to the ground.

"Hudson," she groaned, but he knew the Wolf would not harm his mate.

He barely spared them a glance. Good thing the Wolf Shifter had such good instincts, he'd known before Kingston what he was about to do. With one well-aimed roar his flames covered the chains, weakening them to the point where he was able to twist the wretched things to pieces.

The metal bits clanged loudly as they hit the hard floor, but he couldn't have cared any less. Whoever had chained this woman was going to die, even if he had to scour the Earth for the bastard!

He rubbed her wrists and hands hoping to bring warmth to her ice-cold body. She was freed from the awful constraints, but still the small woman's eyes were firmly closed. Her face looked pale and in pain. His beast roared inside of him. Carefully, slowly, he leaned down to her face with his hands outstretched but not quite touching.

"Wake up," he whispered.

Her skin began to glow then, and he was helpless

save to watch as she struggled with whatever magic held her captive. Golden eyes darted from person to person in the room. Somehow, all of the Guardians under his care had arrived without him noticing.

"Egros," he summoned the one male Witch in the room even though his Dragon wholeheartedly objected to the male's presence, but Kingston pushed his jealousy aside.

He needed to help her and Egros was the one person there he trusted to have the knowledge necessary to do that. The Witch approached and Kingston's lip furled into a low threatening growl which had the man lowering his gaze and baring his throat to him.

His position as Alpha commanded as much and he was grateful Egros did so without hesitation. The last thing he wanted was to hurt the unmated male for coming near the woman.

Mate, his Dragon supplied.

Holy fuck. He had a mate. A fated mate. The idea was simply too huge for him to wrap his draconian head around. Better to take it one step at a time. First, he needed to free her. Then he could worry about what it all meant.

"She has been here a long while, Alpha," Egros said and examined the chains and the runes on the wall, "these symbols are both Native American and

European. I suspect the woman here is descended from both sides. Judging from her dress, she was probably confined here sometime in the late eighteen-century."

"Why isn't she waking up?"

"I am not sure, sir," he said, "but I have an idea."

The twinkle in the Guardian's eye left Kingston with little doubt where his thoughts were headed. The others all seemed too stunned to speak, and he couldn't blame them. For years they'd thought he was mated to the one the universe had deemed his one and only.

He'd allowed them to believe that. Had lied to them all. Kingston could hardly accept it. He knew deep down he was not worthy of his own mate.

"We are not qualified to decide who is worthy, Alpha," Egros said quietly, "the universe knows better than we do."

"Boss, is she really your mate? What about Neela?" Furio asked and he could hear the confusion in the Stallion Shifter's voice.

It was no more or less than what he was feeling himself. All he could do was nod in answer.

"Shh," Storm hissed at the Stallion.

"You have to claim her then," Fergie said and from the muffled sounds coming after that statement,

Kingston could only assume Storm had covered his mate's mouth with his hand.

"Ouch!" the Wolf growled and hopped on one foot after his mate stomped on his booted appendage with her stilettos.

Kingston wished he had on shoes, but a quick look told him his own mate was barefoot. Perfect. Maybe that would save him from her wrath after he did what he was about to.

Shit. His body trembled and his Dragon snarled. Worthy or not. Time was up. She needed him and there was nothing he would not do for her.

"Kingston," Byram interrupted, but he was not in the mood for the Vampire.

"Everyone leave," he growled, allowing only a fraction of his Alpha's powers to seep into his voice.

When no one moved, he tried again, this time using triple the amount of command as he bellowed, "OUT! NOW"

FOUR

olley could feel her mate pressing in on her in the dank and cold dungeon that had been the prison of her body for nigh on three centuries.

Finally. After decades of visiting him in dreams, he was here, and he was going to free her. She felt the Keep struggling to hold her firmly in place, but this was it. She was certain. He was hers and she was his. Holley was finally going to be free.

Let me go now. He is my mate. She pleaded with the *manetuwak*, but the spirits of the Keep were not as easy to sway as they had been when they agreed to watch over her.

The Dragon Shifter was mighty though, and she felt his power and the sheer brute force of his strength as he struggled to break the chains that bound her to the stone slab. She pushed the thought at him to use his fire and was surprised when he did.

Even as the others yelled in fright, she loved the image of him maintaining his human form while he called his Dragon's fire forth. Very few managed that sort of control and balance. Kingston Baldric was the only Dragon Shifter she had ever seen, but since the first she had recognized what she was to him.

His Dragon brushed across her mind, the splendid beast growling softly to get near her. Kingston aimed his flames at the metal and after they'd been heated, could then tear them apart. The heat to her had been a mere tickle, but she got the distinct impression that others there would have burnt to a crisp had he spat flames in their direction.

But not him. Kingston Baldric was a seasoned warrior. A noble Guardian, loyal and devoted to his cause. She knew they were fated, just as she knew he would fight it. Her ancestors had told her that when she'd last spoken to them through the veil.

Beware the white-scaled beast, for he has the power to destroy what men and centuries could not.

Those had been her Granny Rose's parting words at their last meeting. Holley never thought much about them, but even as her brain registered that she was almost free, her body seemed downright paralyzed with fright.

"I am sorry about this," the voice of her fated mate spoke as though whispers sifting through the sands of time itself.

She could make out the words, but it was unclear what he meant. Well, it was unclear, until she felt raw pain exploding from her shoulder and travelling through her body at an alarming rate.

She felt fire, his fire, in her very veins. It continued to burn and sizzle until her whole being was aflame. Then there was the flame itself. The spicy, smoky flame of her mate's *Dragon fire* pulsing new life into her body.

She felt her own magic, from both her Lenape and her English roots, rise up to meet his. It was beyond anything she could have ever imagined. A lightning storm of fire and sparkles, flames, and starlight like universes blinking in and out of existence in that single moment suspended in time. It was nothing she could have ever imagined.

Then her back arched and she seized. Her entire body was a mass of pins and needles. Cramps and burning pain filled her. Holley tensed, her back was all the way up, off the stone slab as that lightning strike of flame tore through her.

Her eyes opened wide, but she was still lost in that fierce storm. Unaware of the arms that lifted and held her, the chest that cradled her, and the hands that smoothed across her face.

"It will pass. I got you," a deep, rumbly voice spoke into her ear and Holley relaxed, sinking exhausted into his solid embrace.

It was him. Her own mate. She was safe. She could finally rest, but not before she looked upon him. Willing her heavy lids to open, Holley gasped at the golden-hued stare of the most breathtaking man she had ever seen. Of course, she had seen his face before. Had watched the handsome Shifter for years through the hollows of the Keep, and yet nothing could have prepared her for the impact of his unwavering stare in the flesh.

Her body quivered helplessly as she warmed and swelled in places she could barely comprehend. So this was desire, she thought as her mind raced with a million images of the two of them touching and embracing. Consummating their bond as was their right, their need.

The scandalous image of his naked body flitted through her mind and she felt hot all over. It felt so good, so delicious to be warm again. After centuries in the cold and the dark. Her mind immediately went back to the swell of his manhood she felt pressed against her side.

Holley was a Witch, not a saint. Kingston's lips were a hard line across his chiseled face, and how she wanted to soothe them. To make him smile and laugh.

She had tried to honor the privacy of the Keep's inhabitants, especially during intimate times. But ever since she'd known Kingston Baldric was her mate, she'd tried reaching out to him.

So, yes, she'd spied him in the shower and out. Seen every inch of his glorious naked form. He was a work of art. Sculpted and refined by the finest masters and architects of them all, the Fates, and they had done so just for her.

His nostrils flared as his gaze bore into hers and, though she had no strength to speak of, Holley lifted up in his arms and pressed her mouth to the rigid slash that was his. He was still at first, but the second he understood she was kissing him, her Dragon wrapped the steel band of his arms about her waist and returned said kiss tenfold.

"Mate," he growled and pressed his forehead to hers, but Holley could only sigh before she slipped into the first peaceful sleep, she'd had in three centuries.

FIVE

"You need to explain, *cump*," Furio demanded.

"Are you fucking nuts? *Cump*?" Storm mocked his friend and shoved him aside, "He's the leader! Our fucking Alpha, man, and he don't need to explain shit."

"Well, I'd like an explanation," Elena's pink eyes flashed at him, but Kingston was only half listening.

The woman had kissed the common sense out of him then proceeded to pass out. He'd rushed to his suite of rooms and called Egros and Byram to aid his mate. Both had confirmed it was merely sleep.

She was okay. Whoever she was.

Mine, hissed his beast and he closed his eyes against his Dragon's anger.

Possessive fuck that he was, Kingston nodded his head, sating his beast's claim and turned to face his Guardians. What would he tell them? What could he?

Fuck. It was an impossible situation, but they deserved the truth from him.

"I should start at the beginning," he said.

"Good place as any," Fergie smiled, and he snorted at her unique brand of humor.

"Yes, it is," he leaned back in his chair and glanced once at the open door to his sleeping quarters where his mate was curled in the soft six-hundred-thread-count Egyptian cotton sheets.

"When I was younger, my brother and I-"

"You have a brother?" questioned Furio.

"Had," he corrected the young Shifter and his voice filled with sadness, "Edgar was killed many decades ago. A century almost. Anyway, it was before I said my vow to become a Guardian of Chaos. Before I came here to lead you, I was Kingston Baldric of the Skye Clan. I had a brother, Edgar. He and I were more than family, we were best friends, and oftentimes, we were our own fiercest competitors."

"Sounds fun," said Fergie.

"It was," he agreed.

Maybe this wouldn't be so bad, he thought and so

he continued, "We shared everything. Games, toys, secrets, hunts, conquests."

"You mean women," said Elena.

"Sometimes," he shrugged, "Our parents passed into the void together as centuries old Dragons sometimes do. We were the last of our kind, the last two Diamond Dragons in the world. Then there was Neela. She was part of our Clan, a rare and dazzling Sapphire Dragon. We competed for her affections-"

"And you won, right boss?" smiled Storm, but Fergie frowned, shaking her head. Women's intuition was real, he mused as she elbowed her mate.

"No, actually, Edgar won her hand," he huffed out a breath and rubbed the back of his neck, "Back then the Skye Clan had opted to stay apart from the troubles of the world, both supernatural and normal. We had no allegiance to either the Guardians or the Loyalists side in the fight against magic, but as everyone knows Dragons are one of the most pure magical beings around, and we are scarce at that."

"How sad," Jessenia murmured, and Furio put his hand on her shoulder in comfort.

"My kind has been hunted and killed for our magic, our fire, our hoards, for thousands of years. It was not long before the Loyalists brought the fight to us. The very day Edgar and Neela made their vows at sunset on the shores of the Atlantic with me as their sole witness, we were attacked."

"Were you prepared?"

"How could we be? We were young and naïve," Kingston's eyes looked at the wall, but in his mind he was taken back to that fateful day on the beach.

Neela was resplendent in her blue sundress with her blonde hair bouncing around her shoulders. She'd cut it shorter than usual and it suited her, Kingston thought as he walked his brother's bride down the makeshift aisle they'd lined with shells and rocks along the sandy beach to where Edgar stood waiting for them.

Barefoot in linen pants and a button-down shirt, his brother's near white hair gleamed brightly in the orange and yellow rays of the setting sun. Kingston was often taken aback at how different they looked, and yet both were Diamond Dragons as their father before them.

His own hair was a deeper, darker shade of blond, almost brown really. Instead of Edgar's blue eyes, his were gold. Both men were tall and fit, as were most Shifters, and even Neela had the body of an Olympian swimmer. She-Dragons were rare and cherished crea-tures, and envy stabbed at him at his brother's good fortune.

A truth which shamed him, so he buried the feeling deep. He knew in his heart that the Fates were tasked with pairing souls, and as much as he cared for Neela, had even once lusted after her body, she was not his. His fated mate was somewhere out there. He had only to find her. But this day was not his, it was theirs.

It was a simple truth. One he took in stride as his brother's blue eyes glowed with his beast as he took his bride's hand in his. Together, the two young Dragons spoke their sacred vows of love and devotion to one another. Kingston knew the mating marks had been exchanged the previous night, but this ceremony was tradition and he stood and witnessed their promise.

The couple gazed at each other with such perfect love and understanding that his Dragon's heart longed for the day when he would make such promises to his own fated mate. How he would treasure her!

Yes, his beast agreed, but his daydreams shattered into a million pieces when they were suddenly attacked. Ambushed by a dozen or so supernaturals wielding magic and weapons. The three Dragons were caught off guard and unprepared to defend themselves, but still Kingston turned to fight, to give his brother and Neela a chance to escape.

Edgar shifted and clutched his mate in his claws, but he was too slow. While Kingston fought off various attacks, a Warlock hurled a magicked spear at Edgar. He had been aiming for Neela. She was most vulnera-

ble, unable to shift as quickly as her male counterpart, and Edgar had thought to fly her to safety. Instead, he'd put her in greater danger. At the last minute, his brother turned his enormous, scaled body and bared his side where he was most vulnerable, taking the hit himself.

After Kingston had finished off his enemies in a berserker-like rage, he went to his brother. Edgar's head lay in Neela's lap and she cried and held him as his life leaked away. He was dying and there was nothing either of them could do to save him.

"Promise me you will keep her safe, King," Edgar begged, "you will take her as your own and guard her with your life. Promise me," Edgar's grip on Kingston's hand was damned near painful, but not as much as watching him die.

It was the way for most Shifters. And for fated mate's, it was worse. Edgar knew what he was asking. He had to know, but he was counting on Kingston to help him save her.

Neela wept with raw pain as his fire went out, and as she lay gasping, he made up his mind.

"You gave him your word?" Furio asked, jolting him from the past.

Kingston looked up and nodded. Jaw clenched tightly, he looked down at the tight fists he'd unconsciously made on his lap. His claws bit into the soft parts of his palms.

Funny, he didn't even realize he was doing that. Kingston relaxed his fists and watched the droplets of blood well up even as his own healing abilities closed the wounds.

"Oh, Kingston," Fergie said and laid her head on Storm's shoulder, "I am so sorry."

"But you loved Neela?" Elena asked.

"Yes, I loved her, but I was not in love with her. I gave her my bite to heal her, placed her under my protection. I tried. I promised my brother I would save her, and I tried. Afterwards, I joined the Guardians of Chaos to help keep her safe."

"But why? Why did they want her?" Elena asked.

"Because a she-Dragon is rare. They can use her blood and organs in all manner of dark magic," Jessenia whispered the answer and Kingston closed his eyes at the thought.

"That's why she was cut up like that," Furio trembled and Kingston could feel his horror.

"Yes," he cleared his throat.

It had taken hours to tell the tale completely, and the sun was creeping up over the forest. Fuck. He had kept these things buried for so long. It was like having a raw wound. One he wished to never feel again. But even as he metaphorically bled, he felt himself healing. This was meant to be. Kingston understood a little better now.

He'd wanted to shield this truth from his Guardians, but it was time to let the whole truth out. They deserved that much.

"Part of what we have uncovered, ever since Fergie was abducted, is that Offner has had his minions out gathering all manner of information on the history of magic in this area. He wants to expand his dark arts, and he's hunting for ley lines. Magical vortexes to further his own stores for whatever hostile takeover he has planned. Dragon blood would only further his cause."

"But she knew this," said Furio, "she knew the risk, so why would Neela go out alone? I mean, one of us was always with her when she went shopping. It makes no sense!"

"She wasn't shopping," Kingston growled and expelled an angry breath.

It was embarrassing, a betrayal of confidence, and his own fucking fault. The hush of silence was deafening and he hated to break faith with her memory, but they all needed to heal. The truth was the only way to do that.

"I failed in my promise to my brother," he

announced, "Neela was not shopping, she was in the process of getting artificially inseminated. After a hundred years of being platonically mated to me, she desired offspring. I'd dedicated myself to protecting her, and to serving the Guardians, but I was never able to give her that part of myself. I am not sure she wanted it, per se, as she loved my brother. Still, it is my fault she is gone-"

"What the fuck? No. No fucking way. This is bull-shit," Furio pushed off his chair and stormed out of the room.

"I'll go talk to him," Jessenia stood up to follow the Stallion Shifter, her expression somber.

Kingston sighed heavily and looked around the room. Elena's arms were crossed and tears fell from her eyes. She'd known Neela the longest, but not as well as she'd thought.

With his Alpha powers, he sifted through the emotions of his Guardians. He wanted to know how they received this information. Dragons were private creatures. News about his supposed mating to Neela was hard for him to share, and probably just as difficult for them to hear.

"So, Neela wasn't your mate," Fergie said matter-of-factly, "but *she* is?"

Kingston turned to see *her* standing in the doorway. His breath caught in his chest as he took her in. Familiar long, dark hair floated around her like a cape, and he realized she was standing underneath a vent. She licked her lips, gazing at him with haunted, moss - colored eyes.

"Yes," he answered Fergie's question, but his gaze never wavered from his mate.

She wore an old-fashioned, roughhewn dress that had him frowning at its obvious coarseness against her delicate skin. He wanted to tear the offensive material away from her body and shower her with silks and lace.

Images of her tawny skin naked and bare for his eyes only had his beast hissing and his cock hardening inside his sweatpants. Fuck. He needed to practice better control. Stopping his growling was difficult, even as awareness and recognition passed between them in that long, deliberate stare.

Mine, growled his Dragon.

Kingston waited for her to speak. He swore he saw a hint of a smile playing on the corner of her wide mouth, causing a dimple to pop out puckishly. She turned her gaze to the others in the small sitting room and nodded her head in greeting.

"Well then, it is nice to finally see you all in the flesh," her husky voice broke the silence and it was like lightning struck his every nerve.

Her voice was crisper and deeper than he'd expected, but oh so perfect. His Dragon rumbled in pleasure at hearing the dulcet tones. She walked further into the room on wobbly legs, smiling as she steadied her gait. She looked at everyone, with that open expression and held out her hand.

"I am Holley Mount," she introduced herself, "and I have watched over you with the help of the great *manetuwak*, the spirits of the keep for many, many years."

"Uh, I'm Byram," the Vampire moved first and greeted her politely.

He was quick to shake her hand and let go, which was smart since Kingston had gripped the armrests of his chair tight enough to tear the leather and crush the wood. She turned her head and caught his eye with a perfect black eyebrow arched.

He could not tell if it was annoyance or what, but she continued on. As she had every right to do, he reasoned with his dragon. Hell. He didn't know why she was mad, he was a Shifter. They were possessive assholes at the best of times when it came to their mates.

He cleared his throat, and she turned once to look at him. Then she tilted her head at the damaged chair, and he felt his face heat in embarrassment.

Fuck. He'd have to work on that.

"My name is Egros," the male Witch spoke, and his mate, *Holley*, nodded.

"Yes, you and I must chat about your portal. I think I know a way to make travelling through space and time much more efficient and less draining on your stores of magic," she returned.

"Yes," he nodded enthusiastically, "I would love to hear your thoughts on that."

Like any great diplomat, Holley went to each of the Guardians present. She spoke to them of things she couldn't possibly know, but somehow did. She laughed at something Fergie said and remarked on her vast shoe collection. That earned her a fan for life, he mused.

Then it was Elena's turn. The pink-eyed woman tried to remain stern, but once Holley complimented her on the hours of training the feline Shifter put in to her daily routine, she had her on her side as well. No one took training as seriously as Elena.

"I could show sometime," the woman said and Holley nodded.

"You're Storm," she stopped in front of the Wolf and congratulated him on securing his mate.

Then finally, she was right there. Within touching

distance. Kingston held himself very still. One move and he would have her crushed against him.

Fucking hell. He didn't want to scare the woman.

"Hello," she said.

"Hello," he answered.

"So, you said you and the spirits of the Keep watch us?" Fergie asked.

"Yes," Holley said, but remained motionless in front of him.

"Then you do the cooking and cleaning?"

"Not me exactly, but I guide and impress upon the *manetuwak* things that you would prefer."

"Like chicken salad?" growled Storm and Holley laughed.

"Well, it was that, or the manse wanted to suffocate you in your sleep. I thought the food a better punishment, don't you agree?"

"Uh, yeah, sure," he said, and his mate tweaked his nose.

"Okay, you guys have a lot to discuss, so we're gonna go," Fergie announced and began shoving the rest of the lot out of the room.

Thank fuck.

Kingston was barely hanging on to his Dragon. His body vibrated and scales popped out all over his skin. He was hard-pressed not to claim her then and there.

The typically standoffish creature inside of him was snarling like never before. Scratching against his skin with ferocious strength, demanding he fully claim his mate. Now.

Mine.

"I suppose we have things to discuss. Is there anything you want to say to me before we start?"

"Yes," Kingston growled and pulled the woman forward so that she was hovering over him.

He brushed his mouth across hers and it was like the light of a thousand suns burned inside of him. He moaned into her soft mouth as she submitted to his invasion. Tangling his tongue with hers, savoring the flowery blueberry flavor. He kissed her thoroughly before pausing so they could catch their breaths.

His forehead pressed to hers, he said the only word he was capable of, "Mine."

Six

olley woke from her unexpected slumber slowly. Had it all been a dream? Was she still chained within the belly of the Keep?

No, she realized as she slowly came back to herself. She was warm for the first time in eons. Everything looked blurry, and she blinked her eyes again until it all became clearer.

This room, she thought, *I know this room.*

Heavy wood furniture without accent or adornment, large windows facing the piney forest, beige walls, plain coverlet on the enormous bed. Yes, she knew this place well. It was *his* room.

Voices from nearby reached her ears, and Holley remained still so she could listen. It was Kingston's voice that sounded loudest to her. That deep timber soothing and alluring. Her chest tightened in sympathy as his words became clear. Poor man, he spoke of his brother and the unusual and tragic circumstances that led to his mating the she-Dragon, Neela.

This group of Guardians had been living within these walls for only a few decades, which to her was relatively short. Decades were nothing to a group of supernaturals with extended lifespans, and certainly not more than a blink to a Witch who'd been captive within the Keep's hollows for centuries.

Still, she'd had an advantage over the Diamond Dragon. Where his hope of finding his own fated mate had been squashed that day with his brother on the beach, she'd recognized what he was to her from the start.

At first, it had broken her heart. She wondered how it was possible that he already had a mate of his own. In fact, Holley had almost gone mad until she saw what really existed between them. Now, she knew the entire story.

Neela and Kingston were bound by a vow neither could break. He'd given his brother his word, gave her his bite to protect her, and in the end neither had been happy. It was all so terribly sad.

Worse still that in seeking some sort of fulfillment

away from him, the she-Dragon had been killed. Her life's blood harnessed for dark magic. The guilt he must feel was bound to be overwhelming. Her heart ached for the man.

Holley murmured a small enchantment for the she-Dragon's soul, and another that Kingston might forgive himself. There was no hope for them if he could not move on. Her heart stopped at the pessimistic train of thought.

Technically, she was on borrowed time. Holley was only alive because of magic, but her physical body would wither and age rapidly if their *matebond* was not properly sealed. A bite alone was not capable of that. She was grateful for it, but if Kingston Baldric could not love her, then she would be gone before she ever really lived.

It was easier for her to accept what they were to each other. Truth was, she had fallen in love with him years ago. How could she not?

She knew everything about him. His love for French poetry, war films, and good Scotch. She had the Keep prepare his baths and meals the way he liked them. Knew the telltale signs he gave when he was working out some tough assignment or puzzle. It was all in the way his forehead creased and his smokey scent thickened whenever confronted with something particularly troublesome.

Holley had fallen in love with him in a million different ways. He was their leader, but he was so lonely, so very much *alone*.

She could save him from that fate, but he had to want it. She needed him to open his heart to her in order for them to truly be together.

If there was one thing she knew from watching for all these years, it was that mating without love was worse than pointless. It was cruel. She would not wish that on either of them.

After Holley introduced herself to the people she'd been watching over for years now, she turned to face the man himself.

"I suppose we have things to discuss. Is there anything you want to say to me before we start?"

"Yes," Kingston grunted, then proceeded to kiss the breath out of her.

"Mine," he growled, more beast than man when he finally released her.

Holley swayed on her feet. The man was potent, she would give him that. Her eyebrows rose and she laughed, a short bark of a thing, then covered her mouth quickly with her hands.

"I am sorry, I wasn't expecting that," she said and sat down in the chair across from him.

"No, I apologize really," he tugged on his collar and looked around the room before settling his gaze back on her, " that was my Dragon. He is pressing hard, but I understand you need time-"

"Yes, time," she said and wondered if he knew just how precious little she had.

"Tell me about how you became trapped here," he waved his hand at the room, but she understood his meaning well enough.

"Folks didn't much like Witches in the time I was born," she shrugged, "and half-breed Witches even less."

"Half-breed? Who called you that?" he growled angrily.

"I am sorry, I know it is not, what is it called again? Ah, politically correct, but that is what I was called back then. My father was a Lenape shaman. He fell in love with my mother and together they met in secret. He was killed and the white settlers claimed he had raped my mother. She died while giving birth to me. Sorry, this is a lot of information."

"No, I am sorry," he nodded, "you don't need to apologize for anything. Please, continue."

"I was raised by my Granny Rose. I learned of my

English heritage from her. Magic runs on both sides of my family."

"And how were you trapped here?"

"This place was like a fairyland to me. When I was young, Granny took me hunting for herbs in the woods and we came across it. I knew it was special then, but it wasn't until a demented preacher decided I was unfit to breathe the same air as he, that I set foot inside this place."

"Who was he?"

"Doesn't matter. It was almost three hundred years ago and he can't hurt me now," she offered him comfort with her words, understanding that even if he was reluctant to embrace their relationship, his Dragon would demand justice, "I begged the *manetuwak*, the spirits of the Keep to help me and they did."

"I am grateful to them then," he ran a hand through his dark blonde hair.

Holley loved the look of him. His pale skin and light hair, the color of honey, was intoxicating. That and his golden eyes completely through her for a loop.

"I imagine things are going to feel quite confusing for you."

"On the contrary, I have been mindful of the goings-on within these walls for three hundred years, Kingston.

Though I still don't trust tofu, and I am not sure why anyone would 'eat a dick' as Furio is often stating to others, unless he means spotted dick which I know is an English dessert, though I confess it's unappetizing to me, I am very much up to date on current events."

"Uh-"

"I love watching television, and I confess my favorite at the moment are the Jersey Shore reruns everyone binges on in the living room."

"Um-"

"Paulie's hair looks like he got caught in a windstorm with superglue and the women, positively scandalous, but deliciously free. Can I ask what exactly is smushing? I think they mean intercourse, but how exactly is it smushed? And is it related to DTF, or was that GTL?"

"What?"

"Oh, did I go too fast for you?"

"No, not at all, uh, I just didn't know what to expect," he smirked, and she smiled widely back.

The man was simply stunning when he smiled. Holley suddenly felt self-conscious. She tugged on the sleeves of her dress and winced.

"Well, expectations are tricky things. Do you think? Would it be okay if I took a bath? It has been a long while," she looked down at her scruffy looking feet and bit her lip.

"Of course," he stood up, "I should have suggested it first," he wiped his palms on his trousers.

Was he nervous? She wondered in awe as he took out a small rectangular device and ran his fingers over the screen. It was a cellular phone, she knew, though she had no idea how to use it.

He and the others were always looking at those blasted things. She crept closer to him, inhaling that heavenly smoky scent of his and watched as he used his fingers to send a message.

"I'm asking Fergie and the other women to help get you some things you might need for your, uh, your bath," he growled and she noted the flare of his nostrils.

"Ah, thank you. That is thoughtful," she smiled gently and tried not to frown when he backed away from her.

As a Witch, she had a much more defined sense of smell than *normals* but was nowhere near the level of a Shifter. Unlike other *supernaturals*, Witches were a classification that could encompass a huge variety of abilities. Reading minds was not one of hers, but how she wished it was right then.

"What?" he asked.

"Nothing," she turned and pointed, "It is this way, correct?"

"Yes, let me show you."

Kingston crossed the room and opened the door to his overly enormous bathroom. The claw-foot tub she'd seen so many times loomed ahead, and Holley could hardly believe she was there in the flesh.

Her hands skimmed over the cold porcelain and she closed her eyes, thinking of all the times she'd spied on the Diamond Dragon in the clear depths of the large bathing vessel. She'd imagined herself there with him more times than she would like to admit.

"Have you ever had a bath?"

"Yes," she said indignantly.

"No, I just meant do you know how to turn on the water," he corrected himself.

"Well, we had a wooden tub and filled it from pots. Our baths were usually quite cold, and nowhere near as often as modern times."

"I see," he moved closer, crowding her with his body, and Holley's breath came and went in quick succession.

He was so big, so handsome, she thought as he reached around her back. Her entire being seemed to hum in anticipation, waiting to feel the steady warm pressure of his hands on her. Holley waited, and waited, but he did not touch her. Rather, Kingston turned the handle to the faucet and she turned and gasped. She shrieked happily as warm water cascaded from the spout.

"It's so clear!" she leaned down, very much aware of the near kiss they'd just had and touched the water, "I've seen all these amazing innovations for so many years through the hollows of the Keep, but this is different," she said.

"I'd like to hear more about that," Kingston began.

His voice cutoff when she, without hesitation, pulled the strings that held the simple brown dress together and let the hated thing drop to the floor.

"That will be fine. You can ask me anything," she stepped into the tub, sighing and moaning in pleasure as warmth surrounded her on all sides, oblivious to the glowing eyes of her mate as he stood with his mouth open and stared at her nudity.

"This is divine," she said and turned to look at him, but he was gone.

That was strange.

Seven

S he didn't even notice when he left the room. Caught up in her first-ever modern-day bath, Holley was positively delighted with the wide variety jars and squeezable potion bottles that promised silky hair and smooth skin.

When she was finished, roughly an hour and a half later, Holley had managed to use every single one of them down to the last drop. She thanked the Keep and offered knowledge of her favorites so the *manetuwak* would know which ones to refill.

Steam filled the bathroom. She was loathed to leave the water, but it wrinkled her fingers. Besides, she'd avoided the man long enough. Sighing heavily, she exited the tub and pulled the plug, but before she could do more than wrap an enormous, fluffy towel around her body, the door opened.

"Girl, how long you been in here?" Fergie asked and waved her hands around through the fog.

"What?"

"Come on, we got some stuff," Jessenia smiled at her and Holley recognized the kitchen Witch though she'd been absent earlier when she made her introductions, "We got you some clothes and things."

"Really?"

Holley allowed herself to be pulled forward. She motioned for them to use the sitting room and with a wave of her hand locked the door against anyone else.

"Wow, you can do that?"

"What?"

"Just wave your hand and do cool shit like that," Fergie said excitedly.

"Oh," she laughed indulgently, "I can do some things with magic."

"Why can't you do that?" Fergie asked Jessenia.

"I'm a kitchen Witch, Ferg. how many times do I have to explain that? I make healing balms, and salves, potions, and stuff like that. I don't do that kind of magic," Jessenia said calmly.

"Allow me to explain a bit if I may," Holley said

while she sifted through the piles of clothes the two women had started laying out on the furniture.

"I have both Lenape shaman magic and Lancaster Witch blood running through my veins. I was imprisoned in the Keep before I fully developed my talents, but the spirits herein kept me hidden and safe until such a time I could rejoin life on this plane. My magic developed during my captivity, but I was unable to free myself."

"You needed your mate for that," Jessenia nodded.

"Exactly."

"And that's Kingston?" Fergie asked, seeking confirmation.

"Indeed," Holley bit her lip as she perused the offerings before finally settling on a long soft skirt made up of several ruffled layers in the most lovely print she'd ever seen.

"He's a tough one," Jessenia murmured.

"Pardon?"

"Nothing. Shut up, Jess. Now, don't you love Veronica Beard? These oranges and browns are gonna look gorgeous on you," Fergie held the skirt up to her waist and Holley bit her lip.

"I do not know Veronica Beard, but yes, this is beautiful."

"It was difficult to find petite sizes, but I am kind

of an expert being vertically challenged myself," the voluptuous redhead was saying as she handed Holley more things to try on.

She returned to the bathroom, not wanting to disrobe in front of the two females and dressed in the skirt along with a long-sleeved top made out of something called jersey.

Like the state, she thought as she tried and failed to wrestle with the underthings she was supposed to put on beneath the exquisite clothing.

Oh well, she thought, maybe next time. For now, it was enough to be free, washed and clean, and wearing such soft, lovely things against her skin.

"You look so completely hot! Fire breath is gonna bust a vein," Fergie exclaimed.

"Fire breath? Oh, you mean Kingston," Holley felt a deep blush creep across her face.

"Damn straight," the curvaceous redhead pointed to the chair in front of her, "Sit down and we'll help brush your hair."

"Thank you, but I don't want him to bust a vein, do I?"

"Oh, not literally," Jessenia explained.

"It is true I have been watching for centuries, but modern speech is still difficult to pick up."

"I so get that," Fergie said and applied another

potion called *leave-in conditioner* to Holley's long locks.

"Hey, you know this hair is awesome, but maybe you should let us trim it?"

"Oh," Holley bit her lip, "like a hair-cut?"

"Yes."

She hated the idea of cutting her hair. But it had been a very long time. Even in that frozen state, it had grown even longer than when she'd last been awake.

"Just a trim?"

"You won't even notice," Jessenia promised.

An hour, and some tears later, Fergie and Jessenia exited the sitting room with a bag full of tags, receipts, and some hair and nail clippings.

"Well?" Kingston's voice reached Holley's ears and she hesitated before stepping out into the hallway behind them.

"Holy shit," Storm said and got an elbow to the gut from his mate.

"Shush up," Fergie growled.

"You wound me, *conpar*," Storm growled playfully.

"Then I better make up for it," she said then kissed him better.

But none of that mattered to her right then, Kingston's golden eyes had found hers. He broke contact, and seemed to trace every inch of her, from her still bare feet to the top of her head with a thoroughness that left her feeling naked.

"You cut your hair," he frowned.

Holley reached up to smooth her hand over the two, long braids she wore on either side of her face. In fact, Fergie and Jessenia had cut about eight-inches off the length of her long locks.

But that hardly made a dent. Her heavy, thick braids hung down to her hips. Only now, the ends were even and unencumbered by something Jessenia referred to as split-ends. A horrible fate that plagued females who spent far too little attention to their own heads of hair.

"Just a little," she waited for his reply.

For some reason, it was very important to her that Kingston approve of her looks. Holley was unlike any of the people there. Her Native American heritage gave her a sharpness to her cheekbones and was responsible for her unique coloring. These things were simple facts and could not be changed or denied.

Instinct told her she would not find racism here among the Guardians, but old habits die hard. She could not be more different from Neela if she'd tried. Even knowing the she-Dragon was not his real mate did not help. After all, he'd been attracted to her and even vied for her attention before his brother staked his claim.

Where Neela was tall, lean, blonde, and beautiful, Holley was short, with small breasts and round hips, tawny skin, a straight nose, and a mouth that was too big for her face. Her eyes were the only appealing thing about her, in her opinion.

The pale green was unusual. Like the lichen or moss that grew in the Pine Barrens. She and her grandmother had often collected such things for salves and other potions.

Granny was like Jessenia in a lot of ways, more kitchen Witch than not. It was her Lenape heritage that afforded her the more unique aspects of her magical talents.

"She looks great," Fergie said with more than a minor annoyance in her voice, "here, try these on," she said and bent down to drop a pair of heels at Holley's feet.

"Oh, um, thank you," she frowned, inspecting the things which to her looked more like torture devices than anything she'd willingly choose to wear.

"Those are from Manolo Blahnik's new line," she said as if that meant something to Holley who only smiled in response.

With one hand on the wall for support, Holley

stepped into the expensive footwear. She gasped at the difference they made in her height. Then stumbled with her first step.

Her eyes went to Kingston's, searching his for anything. Approval, horror, anything at all, but he remained carefully blank as she attempted her second step.

"This isn't so bad," she smiled right before her heel snagged on the thick carpet that covered the hallway.

Holley screamed before covering her face. Hitting the carpeted stone floor was not something she relished experiencing. Lucky for her, she didn't have to. Kingston caught her first.

The rumbling growl in his chest vibrated against her as he took the shoes off her feet and returned them to Storm with a muttered thanks. She clung to his neck, embarrassment still eating at her nerves while he carried her down the hall and out the door.

"Where are you taking me?" she asked, squinting against the bright sunlight.

"To buy you some sensible shoes," he muttered.

"Wait a moment, please," she asked, surprised by how quickly he stopped in his tracks.

Her heart thundered in her chest and the sound of her blood rushing through her roared in her ears. She was outdoors. For the first time in three centuries.

Nerves danced and her belly flipped, but Kingston was holding her. She trusted him implicitly.

"I got you," he whispered as if feeling her anxiety somehow.

She nodded knowingly and Holley tipped her head back to stare at the November sun shining down on her through the tree line. The Keep loomed behind her, she felt its spirits worry and reach for her, but she shook them off. She had her mate now. Everything would be okay. Or so, she hoped.

The big stone structure groaned louder, reaching out for her, but she pushed the tendrils of magic away easily. The castle's magic had grown dependent on her, perhaps even viewed her as its own plaything, but Holley was neither.

She was not a prisoner anymore. No matter how temporary her situation might be, she decided then and there to enjoy every second of it, starting with this.

Sucking in a deep breath, she felt Kingston's eyes on her and nodded her head. He maneuvered her and she slid out of his arms, loving the crush of leaves beneath her feet.

"It is better than I remember," she whispered, opening her arms wide and spinning in a circle.

"What are you doing?"

"Spinning."

"But why?"

"Because the world is beautiful, Kingston, just look at it!" she laughed and continued to move over the leaves in their rainbow of reds, yellows, oranges and purples.

The colors of fall were everywhere. They were there in the bright blue skies, and the warm yellow sun. In the glint of his golden eyes, and the pearly white skin of his cheek. Holley had not felt so alive in centuries.

On and on, she kept spinning, faster and faster, giggling like mad until she almost went down, but he was there once more to save her from harm.

"You are beautiful," he whispered and bent his head.

Kingston's lips were warm and hard. His smoky scent filled her nostrils as he captured her lips in a kiss that warmed her to her soul.

My love, she thought as she kissed him back, *my only love.*

EIGHT

ine. Mine. MINE!

Kingston's Dragon was half a second away from busting down the door to his own bedroom. What were those two females doing to his mate?

He heard the squeals and the laughs, and though muffled, he was sure there was some crying thrown in as well. If not for Storm's bemused expression as they waited in the hall, he would've knocked the fucking door down.

Finally, the thing opened and he exhaled. Kingston waited with baited-breath to catch the first glimpse of his sweet mate. The first thing he noted was the now familiar blueberry scent that seemed to tease his senses whenever Holley was near.

Delicious. Mate. Mine, his Dragon hissed.

Nerves danced up and down his spine. Where was she? Jessenia and Fergie had exited first. The two women grinned at each other, then him, stopping for a moment in the doorway.

He wanted to pick them up and move them out of his way. But the idea of touching another female did not sit well with him or his Dragon. He waited, albeit impatiently.

Suddenly, she was there. Kingston's mouth went dry. Bloody hell. Nothing could have prepared him for the sight of his sweet mate after a bath. Her skin glowed warmly, so unlike the pale coldness of when he'd first seen her chained to that hated table.

Her eyes danced over him as she stepped hesitantly into the hall. He swallowed. Hard. The soft, clingy fabric of her top outlined her lovely, firm breasts. She was not wearing a bra. Her nipples pebbled against the material, and suddenly he wanted to claw Storm's eyes out for being there, in the hallway, with them.

Fuck. He had it bad. The possessive urge to cover her and hide her from the prying eyes of others was a genetic throwback to the days of yore when Dragons stole away their maids and hid them amongst their treasure hoards.

Of course, that kind of thing was frowned upon these days. Pity, really. For she was a greater treasure than any he had ever possessed. And yet, something held him back from truly claiming her.

A small, niggling measure of doubt whispered inside his brain. After all, he'd failed Neela. He would fail Holley too. The idea of that warm honeyed glow leaving her skin, that bright sparkle in her eyes dimming forever, made his heart stutter in his chest.

Could he risk it? Risk her life for the sake of his pleasure? What if she was targeted next by Offner or any of the remaining Loyalists?

No, huffed his beast.

He would never let that happen. She would be better off if he never touched her. Decision made, Kingston struggled to keep his beast under control. Resolved to never consummate their mating. To never even lay a hand on her enticingly sweet body.

His jaw clenched, he remained rigid. Unsmiling and unmoving. Well, until Holley attempted to walk in those ridiculous heels that Fergie had given her. He was fond of the redhead, but those things were lethal weapons.

The damn spindly contraptions got caught on something, perhaps the carpet that ran throughout the hallway. As she pitched forward, Kingston threw his resolve out the window. He could not allow her fragile, soft body to hit the hard, unrepentant floor. Not while he still drew breath.

With faster reflexes than ever before, Kingston covered ten feet of space in a nanosecond. He heard the surrounding gasps, registered that something unique was happening, but nothing mattered until she was safely in his arms.

"*Cump*, look down," Storm whispered, pushing his mate behind him.

Kingston growled softly but did as asked. Good thing too, he mused. Orange and red glowing flames swirled around him, surrounding his entire body.

"I think he got blinky," Fergie whispered.

"What?" he asked.

"Like Hudson. But instead of blinking, you kinda burned through space and time. I mean Kingston, you were there one second then the next you were over there and carrying Holley," the redhead said unable or unwilling to hide the amazement in her voice.

Yes, his Dragon chuffed.

He had burned across the hall to catch his precious female. Once in his arms, those same glowing tendrils circled the two of them. For a moment, he wondered if the fire would hurt her, but it did not seem to, though the wall was taking a bit of a beating from the heat.

"It's lovely," she said and leaned her face closer to his, laying her head down on his shoulder.

His chest swelled with ride. She was simply beyond his experience with women. Unafraid of fire, perfect for a Dragon. How could he ever let her go?

Mine.

He felt her magic reach out to his. Touching, swirling, moving in and out of one another. It was intimate. It was incredible. And for a single breath of time, it combined, pulsing in time, before it stopped and faded away.

Holley's impossibly pale green eyes met his for a moment before she wrapped her arms around his neck and crushed her small, firm breasts to his chest. He returned the embrace, holding her tight to him. His precious mate.

She felt so fucking good, wound around him like that. Far too good to let go. No, he would not even consider it again.

Fuck those shoes though, he thought and began to stride purposefully down the long corridor with the exit in mind. He knew the Keep had a way of playing with individuals who had no clear destination.

Kingston always had a goal in mind, and this was

simple. Get Holley comfortable, *and safe*, footwear. Done and done.

What he was not prepared for was how beautiful she looked reacting to her first time outdoors in almost three hundred years. The Diamond Dragon inside of him stirred and puffed out a short flame to celebrate her joy.

Fuck yes, she was joyous. Glorious really. Spinning among the leaves, looking for all the world like the brightest, most precious quantity among the jewel-toned world that was New Jersey in Autumn.

Bathed in the warm sunlight and dancing barefoot among the fallen leaves, Holley Mount, the newly freed Witch, captured his tough Dragon's heart without even trying. If he were being honest, she'd had control of the organ since the moment he'd entered the dungeon-like prison where she'd been hidden all this time.

No wonder he'd insisted on coming here, on gaining this assignment. Somehow, deep within, he'd known she was there. His Dragon had recognized the Keep as his home because of her. It all made sense now.

If only he were worthy of her.

Grrr. The beast inside of him hissed at his defeatist remark. The creature wanted to kick his own ass for all his doubt. He knew it was true, the Dragon would gladly pound out any uncertainty that he was man enough for the job of loving her with his own claws.

Fuck. *Am I strong enough?* He wondered for a brief moment, hating his vulnerability.

Only one way to find out, the Dragon growled.

NINE

olley sat stiffly in the strange vehicle, chewing on her lower lip. She had seen cars on television, but she had never been inside of one. The seat was soft and comfortable, and there was some sort of magical inner heating device that warmed her bottom.

She didn't think she would ever get enough of feeling warm, though nothing topped being inside her Dragon's arms. Maybe it was too soon for that, but he had been hers since she saw him all those years ago when he'd entered the doors of the Keep.

So handsome and stern. Then Neela had stepped inside behind him and Holley's heart had damn near been ripped out of her chest. Time had a way of being lost in the belly of the Keep, but she knew it had been many moons before she understood what they were to each other.

Mated, but not. Bound, but apart. Her heart ached for Kingston in those times. He had struggled to maintain balance, to keep the woman, Neela, safe and protected.

Shifters readily accepted *matebonds* as wonderful things, but what they did not perhaps recognize was that the magic that tied two souls was not without a price. Nothing was.

When Kingston had offered Neela his bite to honor his brother's dying wish he had given a piece of his life's force to the woman. That bond that kept her alive and stopped her from following her fated mate unto death had to feed from something. That something was him.

"What you did was an incredible sacrifice, Kingston, for Neela."

"I'm sorry?"

"I know the pain it caused you, the toll it took on you physically and magically, and Neela knows it too. She honors you, Kingston," Holley closed her eyes and allowed that knowledge in.

"How do you know that?" he muttered.

"I know a lot more than you think," she clutched the armrest.

Cars were fast on television, in real life they moved incredibly so. Certainly far too quickly to be safe.

"Are you alright?" Kingston asked from his position behind the wheel of the Mercedes.

"Um, yes?"

It came out as a question, and she supposed it was. Her stomach was in nervous knots. Holley's heart was pounding furiously inside her chest, and truthfully, she did not know if she was alright.

"Want me to slow down?"

"No! Please don't."

The man beside her focused on driving and she allowed him some space. After all, it was probably not easy for him to consider the situation they were in. Though her heart hurt because she wanted him to feel nothing but joy when he looked at her, she understood his melancholy.

Time, he needed time. As for her, there was much to explore and experience. Being back in the world was a gift she had no intention of wasting.

"Almost there," he murmured.

Holley leaned on the leather covered door to stare at the scenery as it sped by as they drove in to the city. She made herself dizzy in the process. So many people, so many buildings. They were crowded and busy, and oh so splendid!

She yelped when the clear glass buzzed and began to slide into the door. Afraid, she broke the thing; she looked at Kingston who smiled and demonstrated on his side.

"This button controls the window. You can lift it up to close it again if it is too cold-"

"Oh no, I love it," she laughed as the cool Autumn breeze flew inside the vehicle, chilling her skin and whipping her braids behind her.

The look on the Diamond Dragon's face as he watched her made Holley's stomach flip. Of course, that was for another reason altogether other than nerves.

She was a maiden still, even after three hundred years, but she understood the heat in his dragon's gaze. That golden glow that spoke of his physical appetites and lust for her. How thrilling!

The Keep allowed her to see many things during her captivity. Though she tried not to spy on private moments, she had not been altogether innocent. Well, a girl had to get her education somewhere.

Mostly, that was from television. Holley arrived at the conclusion that sex was fast, messy, and altogether something she desperately wanted to experience in the present.

The Guardians had eclectic tastes in entertainment. And while she sometimes watched Elena's suspense thrillers, she often found herself watching rom-coms with Fergie. TV was marvelous in her opinion, as were books. But it was hard to open a book when you did not exist in reality.

Now that she did, she had hundreds of volumes on her list. Something she could not wait to indulge in. Kingston enjoyed books, but rarely had time. He never seemed to watch television.

Byram however was an aficionado of something called erotica films that often involved graphicly detailed scenarios that Holley could hardly comprehend. Who knew a human being could contort themselves into such shapes?

Still, something about everything she had witnessed triggered a response deep within her woman's soul. Curiosity mainly, but it was more. Longing, desire, the need to complete the mating bond they'd begun when his bite broke the spell that kept her captive to the Keep.

The spontaneous kiss they'd shared had awakened something inside of her. Something primal and fierce. She knew times were different, but she could not help but tremble at the idea that a woman, that she could want someone in such a carnal way.

And yet she was certain he was the only man she

would ever want. The only man whose body she wanted claiming hers in every way that mattered.

Holley had accepted his kiss with enthusiasm, if not skill. But something had him ending the exchange far too soon for her liking. Maybe her inexperience was unattractive to a worldly Dragon? She would have to ask Fergie or Jessenia about that when they returned to the Keep.

Meanwhile, she would enjoy this outing. Kingston's smoky scent teased her senses in the closed confines of the luxury automobile, and she almost missed his question.

Holley was a daydreamer by nature, but now she was trying to distract herself from carnal thoughts whilst in his company. It was proving a most difficult job. He was so, what was the word, ah, *blazing*.

Yes, that was what Fergie had said. Her delightful vocabulary was the cause of much entertainment for Holley. But she agreed with the she-Wolf, her mate had certainly set her heart ablaze.

"Is there anything else you can think of that you need? Besides shoes," he glanced at her bare feet and rolled the car to a stop in front of a store with an enormous sign that read *Victor's Shoes*.

"No, I don't think so," she answered.

"Right," he nodded and walked around to her side

of the car, opening the door for her and lifting her out of the seat before she could step on the ground.

"People are staring."

"Let them," he replied in a husky whisper that sent shivers down her spine.

Holley leaned forward but the moment was gone. He turned and carried her into the shop, placing her on a bench while he spoke to the proprietor. She saw in the man's aura that he was a Shifter. Badger was her guess from the scent and the general ornery *tsk* that followed every curt phrase.

"So, you need to be measured? Don't know your own shoe size then?"

"I am sorry, I-"

"You don't have to apologize. Victor, you are being rude," Kingston growled.

"Oh hush, I'm just playin' with the girlie. Come on, let's see what you've got. Size nine! For a petite thing you have a big foot, lady. What?" Victor whistled at Kingston's growl and shook his head, "Fine. No more commentary. I'll see what I have in back for you."

"Comfortable shoes, Vic, none of that nonsense Storm's mate prefers," Kingston ordered.

"What if I want that nonsense?" she asked, eyebrows raised.

"Do you?"

"No."

Kingston raised one eyebrow, giving himself an air of arrogance that she would have found obnoxious on anyone else. But he was right. Holley did not want high heels. She did want something though. Not nonsense. Him. Only him.

Kingston's nostrils flared and his golden eyes glittered at her in the dimly lit shoe store. For a moment, a wave of dizziness swept over her. She closed her eyes and steadied herself.

She wasn't prone to headaches, but after all, this was her first adventure outdoors in two-hundred and seventy years. Her stomach rumbled, and she covered her lips at the audible sound.

"Are you okay?"

Kingston appeared at her side.

"Yes. I am sorry, where are my manners?"

"Who cares about manners? You're hungry. I should feed you," concern darkened his gaze, and she gasped.

From what she knew of Shifters, if he accepted her as his mate, his knowledge of her needs and desires would only grow. So far, he'd kissed her once and seemed entirely unaffected, but maybe she was wrong. Maybe he wanted her just as much as she wanted him.

How could she tell? She licked her lips and

watched as his eyes followed the movement. Holley was on borrowed time, but she couldn't tell the Diamond Dragon that. Would not force him into making another sacrificial mating. It would be too much like what he'd already gone through.

She could never do that to him. Not after loving him from afar for all these long years. The way he gripped her hand now was definitely promising. She had some time yet. Perhaps it was possible he cared more for her than he was letting on?

"I am a little hungry, I think," she confessed.

His face remained unsmiling as he brought one long, masculine hand up to caress her cheek.

"We should head back. I am sorry, I didn't think-"

"No, I love being outside."

"Holley, it's too much for you. I should have made sure you ate breakfast first-"

"Please. I want to stay out. We can get something to eat, can't we?"

"Yes. That's a possibility."

"Thank you," she whispered huskily, "You have no idea what it was like."

"I can't imagine," he smiled kindly.

"Here you are," the stout shopkeeper came into view with a wheeled cart full of boxes.

Holley laughed in delight as he opened each one,

displaying a variety of different shoes and boots all made to fit her feet. Imagine that!

"In my day, common folk were lucky to have slippers made of woven cloth or rough leather with thin soles that wore out quickly," she exclaimed as she lifted shoe after shoe out of boxes made of something called cardboard.

"In your day? What are you, twenty-five?" Victor rolled his eyes and walked away to answer the ringing phone.

"Sorry," she grimaced at Kingston who waved away her concern.

"Don't worry about him. Go on, I like hearing about your day."

"Well, only the rich had heels and soles, and those were made of wood covered in silk and calfskin with buttons and lace. Not me, of course."

"Why not you?"

"Oh," she frowned, "Well, I was an outcast for my entire life. Granny Rose kept us fed, but only just."

"I am sorry."

"Don't be."

It was true, there was a time she had hated her circumstance of birth, but only briefly.

"I was angry about it once, but I don't feel that way now."

"How come you're not bitter?"

"Because," she shook her head and stood up, walking over to him, "I have a chance at life now. I spent decades just watching, but I am here now, and I am breathing the same air as you, hearing the same sounds, seeing the same things-"

"You can't possibly see what I see," he said, and his eyes glittered as they seemed to devour her from head to toe in the closed confines of the shop.

Holley's chest heaved with the efforts of breathing, and she understood then what it was to be in the eyeline of a predator. Kingston was part beast, and his Dragon was watching her from behind golden eyes that seemed to see far too much.

"I like these," she grabbed a pair of something called Converse and held them high.

"Those are classics," he grinned.

"But how does a shoe converse with its wearer? Perhaps a Witch created these?"

"She wants those?" Victor came wheezing back into the room and looked sideways at her choice.

"You heard the lady. Get her a dozen pairs, one in every color. How about boots for the snow and rain?" Kingston asked.

Holley nodded demurely and accepted his offer of

the extra pairs of shoes. It was extravagant, in her opinion, but he insisted.

"Well, you're gonna need socks," Victor waved to the wall where dozens of clothing called socks hung on tiny plastic hooks.

Holley was amazed at the variety. Each one was so different! There were tall socks, and short, something called no-sees, and dozens more.

"They're like stockings," Kingston explained when the little man left to gather her things.

"Yes," she nodded.

The colors and patterns were extraordinary! Holley had seen them on television often enough, but in actual life, they were something else.

"Can I, uh, can I touch them?" she asked and held a hand out tentatively.

"Of course," he sounded angry, but she was so intent on a pair of little white socks with tiny dragons in every color of the rainbow to notice.

"Take as many as you want. Victor! Add these to the total and bill my credit card. I'll carry these boxes to the car."

"Okay," Holley bit her lip and made her selections once he was out of sight.

By the time Kingston came back inside, she was tying the laces to a pair of forest-green Converse into two lovely although misshapen bows. A plastic bag filled with her secret hoard of dragon socks sat next to her, but she carefully avoided bringing any attention to them.

"You ready?" Kingston grunted.

Holley nodded and stood up, moaning loudly at the sinfully comfortable shoes. He growled in his throat and headed for the door, shoving it open with a loud crash.

Holley jumped and followed happily oblivious to his state. Kingston strode purposefully towards the car, leaving her to follow behind him, and she suddenly wondered why he was so angry. It had happened out of nowhere!

He didn't look at her. Wouldn't talk to her. And why? What had she done wrong? In her opinion, not a darn thing. But still, she worried and frowned, chewing on her lower lip as she did whenever she was nervous or contemplating something puzzling. The scenery was not that interesting anymore, not when faced with the conundrum of a Dragon's moods.

Sigh. First hot, then cold, not hot for a different reason. Would she ever understand this man? Could she win his heart? Perhaps honesty would be best. Maybe she should just come right out and admit her feelings.

It was new to her, this uncertainty on how to proceed. Nothing had ever mattered so much to her. Yes, Holley had fought for her life, but this was different. Now, she was fighting for her love.

She played with the little button that controlled the window as she contemplated her situation. Kingston was a man and man followed base instincts. Perhaps she could appeal to those first, then make her case. But how?

She was not exactly schooled in the arts of seduction. And the idea of using feminine wiles to woo the man left her mouth dry and goose pimples running up and down her arms. Up and down, she flicked the button only stopping when he slammed on the brakes and caused her to spill forward slightly in her seat.

"Up or down. Pick one," he growled.

"Fine," she answered with no small amount of cheek, opting for down.

The glass was clear, but she'd been gazing at life from behind a veil for far too long. The air had grown chilly while they were shopping, but she didn't care.

It felt good. Time to save her worry for another day, she decided. Holley smiled and waved to people as they drove past. She didn't understand why they frowned and pointed, but that was alright. She was free. She was happy. And she wanted to share her good spirits with the entire world.

The traffic light ahead of them flashed red and Kingston stomped once more on the brakes. Holley held her hands out to keep from slamming into the dashboard this time.

Heavens, he was upset, but her curiosity was soon overpowered by a sudden undeniable hunger. Not for him. For food. Her stomach growled loudly as the most delicious fragrance she had ever encountered filled the car.

"Oh heavens! What is that smell?"

"What? Holley!"

He yelled her name and tugged on her skirt, but she already had her entire head out the window and was sucking in great, greedy gulps of air to satisfy her curiosity. The aroma was cleverly executed. A delicate balance of several fine ingredients. The result made her mouth water.

Contrary to the Guardians' belief that the Keep's kitchen was operated by one source of magic, Holley knew that was not true. Yes, she had coaxed the castle into punishing Storm by denying him his favorite meals on one or more occasions. And yes, she did encourage the Keep to listen to their wishes and cravings as it was her firm belief happy stomachs led to happy Guardians. But she was not the cook.

Not being able to taste anything would grossly inhibit her ability to produce anything edible. To be honest, cooking was never her forte. She did dabble in the kitchen arts, her talents lie mostly in healing salves and ointments, and some other areas. Like precognition and necromancy.

"Are you talking about *Pizza Palace*?"

She turned and looked at him. He was staring with one eyebrow raised perfectly in inquiry. He was so handsome.

"Pizza?" she turned back to the window, "is that what smells so wonderful?"

That was pizza? She had seen it on TV but had never smelled such deliciousness in life. Unfortunately, food in the eighteenth century was more perfunctory than appetizing.

Oh my. Was that fresh garlic? And yeast dough? Oh yes. With tomatoes? And basil? Sigh.

Holley was practically drooling. Her stomach rumbled once more. She felt her cheeks blush and hid her face when Kingston's lips quirked. She peeked though. Couldn't help but watch as his emotions flitted from shock, to amusement, and finally, indulgence.

"I suppose I can take you to lunch, since I did rush you out the door without breakfast," he put the vehicle into park once more.

"That would be lovely," she answered.

"Yes," his gaze watched her hungrily, and for a moment Holley thought perhaps pizza wasn't the only thing that appealed to the big man.

The possibility made her shiver in awareness and anticipation. But first things first.

"Hi! Sit anywhere you like," a woman dressed in jeans and a t-shirt bearing the Pizza Palace logo waved them to the dining area.

"Is this a date, then?" Holley asked when he guided her to the booth and helped her slide in.

"A date?" he cocked his head and his dusky blonde hair brushed his shoulder, "I suppose it is."

Oh my.

TEN

Bloody fucking hell. He should have just kicked his ass earlier like his Dragon wanted to. It would have been less painful than what he was experiencing at the moment.

Reaching beneath the table, he adjusted his jeans, but it was no use. He was cramped and stifled in the tiny booth, and his dick was harder than steel, and the woman across from him was the cause. Of course, it wasn't the booth's fault. Not exactly. It was the woman sitting across from him. She was the cause of his current state.

His Dragon growled. He was conflicted. There were too many people there. Too many witnesses to her sweet moans as she sampled bite after bite from the three large pizzas he'd ordered, along with a huge antipasto salad, and a basket of garlic knots.

The feast was spread out between them across the table and Holley seemed to be having the time of her life.

"All this is just for us?"

"Yes."

"Well then, let's eat."

She seemed particularly fond of the veggie lovers' pie, where he was strictly a pepperoni and hot cherry pepper kind of guy. She'd *oohed* and *aahed* her way through almost every dish. Her reactions dazzled him. He'd never seen someone enjoy food so much. And he was a Shifter, for fuck's sake.

Of course, he wasn't even going to mention the pineapple topped monstrosity in front of them. That was the one item that still remained untouched.

"Don't say 'I told you so', honestly, I meant to try it."

"Yeah, I know, but, *I told you so,*" he winked and took another well-done slice of pepperoni for himself.

Judging from her reaction to the spur of the moment gesture, he was positive he'd shocked the little Witch. About time. The way he figured, she'd been driving him out of his mind with every excited giggle, soft sigh, and delightful moan that escaped her delectable lips throughout the meal.

"What?" she asked, "Is my face dirty?"

"No. Your face is perfect," he confessed.

It was only the truth. Funny how easy it was to compliment her once he started.

"I had a good time today, taking you shopping, eating pizza with you here."

"Ah, yes, and teaching me to drink through a straw," she blushed and shook her head, but it was the truth.

He'd enjoyed showing her the options and watching as she chose the metal kind rather than the disposable. He wasn't in to killing turtles either, thank you very much.

The simplest things proved to be more adventurous than he'd ever thought through her eyes at her side. Fuck, everything she did turned him on. Her reactions to the modern world were so open and honest.

Refreshing, that was the right word. There was none of that second-guessing or mockery he found in so many others. None of the guilt either. That was all he'd felt at the end with Neela. Terrible, overwhelming guilt.

"It wasn't your fault," Holley whispered.

He nodded his head, a reflex really, but the she-

Dragon had been his responsibility for so long. It felt disloyal to think about her like that.

No, his Dragon rose up and pushed the thought into his head. Holley was his one true and fated mate. His whole purpose was now dedicated to her and her alone.

"Have you tried these?" he leaned forward and held a garlic knot dipped in marinara sauce to her lips.

Holley moaned as she took a bite of the soft, savory dough. She sighed as she slowly chewed the delicious morsel and Kingston was a goner. She leaned forward, took another bite, and his chest vibrated with the force of his growl as he watched.

Great. He was jealous of bread. But what could he say? He wanted to be the one to make her moan like that. He wanted to be everything to her.

Silly? Maybe. Conceited? A little. But fuck it. He had never felt this way about anyone. It was primal and all-consuming, but in the best possible way. She was everything wonderful in the world. Watching her enjoy herself with the food he provided pleased his beast. At the same time, it was also the most torturously erotic thing he'd ever witnessed.

What about Neela? What about the past? What about her, he argued with himself. She was gone. He'd done his best to do his duty by his brother and by her. The only way to honor them now would be to live.

Yes, he wished he could change the past for both his brother and Neela. To be torn apart from your mate was unthinkable. Edgar thought he was saving her, but perhaps it would have been better to let her go into the void with him. But at the time, it was an impossible choice.

Kingston knew with unwavering certainty that if anything happened to Holley, he would much rather join her than try to live without his mate. That was not something he'd wish on anyone. He would have traded places with Neela if he could. But the fact was, he could not.

Kingston was alive, here and now, and so was Holley. The sweet Witch's blueberry scent filled his senses. Tempting him like nothing else. He found the fragrance lingered whenever she left a room in the most enticing way.

His gaze roamed her face, that healthy glow in her tawny skin, those pale moss-green eyes, and her inky dark hair were all doing things to him he could hardly describe.

Of course they were, the Dragon chuffed. He was born to love her. Fated mates could choose to ignore the pull, but they rarely did. And why should he?

Claim. Mate. Mine.

"Kingston? Are you okay?"

"What? Oh yeah, I am fine."

"You are growling. *Loudly*," she looked around at the tables and he noticed some people were starting to stare as well, "I think they heard you," she whispered.

"Shit. You finished?" he asked, dropping bills on the table when she nodded.

He stood up and held out a hand to help her. Electric shocks danced from his fingertips down his spine and straight to his cock, which had been hard as stone since he'd laid eyes on the beautiful Witch. But he ignored it for now and gently nudged her in front of him so he could follow her out the door.

Her hips swayed beneath the silky skirts she wore and a smile played at the corner of his mouth as he took in the green sneakers. She was cute as hell, sexy too.

He wanted her. Wanted to lay claim to her sweet flesh, to stamp himself all over her body, and to rip the eyes out of every man who dared stare.

He turned his head and flashed his too sharp grin at a pair of fuckers with a death wish. They yelped and dropped their sodas before rushing down the street. Shit, he had to calm down. It was too soon for this. She needed time. But he did not know how much he could give her.

"Where to next?" she turned and smiled, and because he hated himself, he opened his mouth.

"I know just the place," Kingston took her hand in his and ignored her curious stare when they passed the parked car and walked over to *Dulce's Gelato Bar.*

"Can I have two please? Double chocolate cherry, and one peanut butter swirl," he placed the order and handed her the first cone watching as her eyes lit up at the sweet confection.

Bloody hell. Kingston's eyes crossed as Holley took the cone from his hands. She moaned loudly at her first taste of the frozen treat, giggling when some dripped over the side and ran down her hand.

"Allow me," he said and took the hand, licking off the dribble of chocolate peanut butter gelato.

It was superb, but not as thrilling as having his lips on her. Her eyes caught his, but she broke the contact. Smiling lightly, she licked her cone and walked with him to a small outdoor bench.

All too soon, there was nothing left of her gelato, so he offered her the remainder of his own confection. He told himself it was because he was a gentleman, and not some pervert. But, *dear gods*, her little moans and groans were doing insane things to him. His Dragon was scratching wildly against his skin. The beast was losing his grip. The primordial imperative to claim her rode him hard, especially when he noticed one or two sets of prying eyes fastened on his delectable little Witch.

Mine. Grrr!

His Dragon was irrationally angry, and there was only one way to satisfy the creature. Kingston stood abruptly and took the cone away from Holley, tossing it in the trash before rushing her to the car.

"I was not finished yet," she licked her lips, frowning at him with a dollop of chocolate still staining the lower.

The urge to bend and lick said lip clean was too much to resist. Kingston wrapped one arm around her tiny waist and tugged her closer to him. Her soft body was so much shorter than his, but still, she felt like heaven to hold.

Mating fever. This was it. That terrible, wonderful madness was taking over, and Kingston went willingly. For her, he would go anywhere.

"I am sorry to rush you, but I have to get you out of here before I do something crazy," his lips pressed into a hard thin line as he bent lower.

"Like what?"

Need rushed through him like lightning as he

placed one hard, urgent kiss against her shocked mouth. But his Witch was nothing if not earthy and warm. She seemed to understand what was happening and opened for him like a flower under the hot sun.

"Kingston," she rested her forehead against his while they both tried to catch their breaths.

"We have to go. Now."

She nodded her head, and he opened the door, tucking her gently inside. Protective instincts he didn't even know he had started to well up inside of him. He drove back to the Keep quickly. The urgency evident in every turn of the wheel and the steady pressure of his foot on the gas pedal.

Scales rippled across his skin only to fade away as he struggled with his beast for control. The Dragon wanted to stake his claim and the motherfucker did not want to wait.

"Calm now," she cooed to that part of him and his physical response was immediate, "I am yours, only yours," Holley placed one honeyed hand onto his forearm and he hissed in pleasure.

Even the most platonic touch from her was better than a thousand erotic touches from anyone else. He felt his gums throb as his fangs descended. Smoke puffed from his mouth, but all he could utter was a rumbling growl.

Gravel flew across the back entrance of the Keep as he managed, just barely, to stop the car and turn off the ignition before he was out of the door.

Everything got a little fuzzy after that. Kingston remembered opening the door and picking Holley up, princess-style. Recalled quite vividly, the feel of her curvy, warm, petite body in his arms. The dreamy look in her impossibly pale green eyes, and the way her mouth felt when she crushed it to his, imprinted themselves on his brain.

Grrr.

Yes, he recalled the kiss and the faint taste of gelato still on her tongue, but even that sweet dessert could not diminish her flowery-blueberry scent. His Dragon hissed and scratched at his skin to the point where his scales and claws were permanently out, but he was careful with her. He would never hurt the woman who was fated to be his.

"Mine," he growled as he raced towards his room with his precious bundle in his arms.

How he got inside without breaking the door down was pure magic. Hers to be exact. The woman was a Witch, least he forget. She moaned in sweet submission as he lay her down on the bed, noting with pleasure how the lamps dimmed, the shades closed, and the doors locked.

Thank fuck for that.

It had been an age since Kingston had wanted someone in this way. Dragons had very long lifespans, but a hundred years or more without sex was still a long time. And this was not just sex. This was something else.

"Mine," he said again nuzzling her neck and pressing her down into the mattress beneath him.

They had on too many clothes, he realized quite suddenly and began to rectify that. Feet first, he decided and sunk to his knees, carefully untying the laces of her new Converse.

Kingston froze once they were off her feet. A smile played at the corner of his mouth.

"What's wrong?" she asked, lifting herself up on her elbows.

The blush that quickly followed told him she knew exactly what he was looking at.

"Your socks," his mouth quirked in a grin he couldn't help but allow to spread across his face, "There are dragons on your socks."

"Oh, um, yes," she blushed a darker shade of red and his heart squeezed inside his massive chest.

She was gorgeous. At some point while he was kissing her, he must've tugged the ties from her hair, because it was in beautiful disarray. Thick and glossy, her inky locks were slightly wavy and mussed from his hands. Her lips were swollen and those crazy sexy eyes of hers were sparkling and bright. He'd never wanted someone so much in his entire life.

He tugged off the adorable socks, kissing her pretty feet before running his hands up the length of her calves. Next came her silky thighs and rounded hips as he rose to kneel on the bed. Again, he stopped, shocked at his newest discovery. Kingston's nostrils flared and eyes widened.

"You aren't wearing underwear?"

"Oh," her embarrassment was evident, but she was brave, his Witch, and continued to explain, "well, I couldn't figure out the thong-thing Fergie gave me. I don't know why anyone would want a bit of string in their crack. Seems pointless really," she bit her lip.

"Oh?" he started to laugh, then frowned as realization hit him, "I took you all over town and you were naked beneath this skirt?"

"Well, I suppose, yes."

He hissed audibly, both turned on and exasperated. The Dragon inside of him demanded he mark her immediately. Then. There. Yesterday for fucking fuck.

His mate went outside without underwear and the knowledge made his beast ready to tear the whole fucking town apart in case anyone happened to catch a whiff of her succulent sweet honey.

Mine.

Speaking of her succulent honey. Kingston inhaled and scented her growing arousal. He was hanging on to his beast by a thread, wrestling for control. He didn't want to frighten her. Sweet little innocent that she was, Holley could not know how to handle a Shifter's, especially a Dragon's libido.

It would be pretty damn shocking the first time around for her. He needed patience, tons of it. The need to bring her pleasure, to make sure she was prepared, welled up inside of him.

"Kingston," Holley grinned, and he was the one who was shocked, "I am not a shrinking violet," she said and sat up running her hands over the scales that were once more visible along the skin of his forearms.

"Holley," his voice was little more than gravel at that point.

"I like that your Dragon wants me," she whispered and tugged on his shirt.

He took the hem and tore it off his body. Fuck, her tentative touches were driving him mad. There was nothing he wouldn't do for her. But he was nervous. She was most certainly a virgin, and Kingston had never had to be careful before. What if he hurt her?

Grrr.

"You are so beautiful, aren't you, mate?" she stroked his arms, shoulders, chest and belly.

The Dragon inside of him stirred, perking up with glee. He liked her words. Preened at the attention and praise. Silly fucker.

"So powerful and handsome. Quite the protector too. You would never hurt me, mate. I know that. I trust you, and I have been waiting for you for so long, my own mate," she nuzzled his nose with hers.

He was breathing like a long-distance runner. Kingston could hardly think. She was weaving spells around him. Wonderful, magical, seductive spells and he wanted to go under with her.

More than anything, he wanted to fall into his sweet, warm, intoxicatingly beautiful Witch. Needed to claim her as his own. To mark her with his bite.

"You know? That we are fated mates? That I woke you with my mating bite?"

Relief coursed through him when Holley nodded. That in turn became something else when next she brushed her wide mouth across his once, and twice, until the temptation was too much to resist.

He caught her lower lip between his teeth, gently tugging until she stilled. Prey to his giant predator. Then he struck, claiming her mouth wholly and fully, and most importantly, with all the desire and feeling he had for her.

"Can I have you?" he asked, as was the tradition with his kind.

"Yes, oh yes," she returned.

After that, it was easy. Phenomenal, but simple. Clothes were shredded, lips were cherished, and bodies moved together in a symphony as old as time itself. Her hair covered them in a warm, thick blanket as Kingston laid down on top of the mattress.

Her kisses left him growling and breathless. He needed her so badly. Wanted her more than air.

Holley's beauty was indescribable through the lusty haze he was under. She was so warm, so bright. All golds and browns, skin like honey against his own alabaster flesh. She was divine, but earthy too. Her magic hummed all around them, cocooning them in a bubble where only they two existed.

It was the only place he ever wanted to be. Kingston suckled her dusky breasts, taking the firm nipples between his lips and using his tongue to make her moan.

Fuck, she even tasted like blueberries and her flowery scent deepened with her growing passion. His Dragon snarled impatiently. He wanted to savor, but his beast demanded he claim her first.

"Want you, please," she said and slid her dripping sex along the length of his cock.

Fuck, he went cross-eyed. She was so fucking hot. Sexier than he'd ever imagined was possible. Running on instinct, not practice, and wasn't that better than anything?

"Kingston," she moaned, and he nodded.

"Yes, take me inside you, mate," he whispered huskily, guiding her hand to his cock.

"Don't know how," she gasped, holding firm to the base of his cock as she continued to slide her heated sex along its length, "oh gods, Kingston, this feels so good."

"Lift up, baby," he coaxed and placed the head of his cock at her entrance.

Her eyes opened and hands gripped his shoulders as his mushroomed head pressed inside of her tight sheath. Holley whimpered in her need and uncertainty. Her nostrils flared, but he was there for her. He would always be there for her, he vowed

"You were made for me, Holley. Press down when you are ready, so you can control it," he spoke through gritted teeth.

Brows furrowed in concentration, it took all his strength and control not to simply thrust upwards, but that would make him a greedy dick. And he would never hurt her or risk what they had by being impatient.

Fuck, this was going to kill him, but it was such sweet agony. Holley's face was flushed. Perspiration dotted her forehead as she did as he said and pushed down.

Eyes bright, she groaned and pushed past the pain. Fuck, she was so fucking tight. He went cross-eyed, but he stayed focused. He didn't want to hurt her. He could never live with himself if he did.

Holding himself still, he allowed her the time she needed to adjust to his size and girth. Kingston reined in his beast and concentrated on her. Sitting up on the mattress, he held her hips between his massive hands and whispered words of encouragement in her ear.

She was so small, so perfect. Holley grunted and clutched his shoulders. Her fingernails bit into the skin there. Her moss-colored eyes held his, and he growled at the pain he saw in them as she took the final plunge. Pushing past the barrier between them, Holley impaled herself on his cock.

Fuck, it felt so good to be inside her heated sheath. She was so tight, so fucking perfect.

"Agh," she cried out.

Kingston held her in his arms and kissed her slowly, swallowing the small sound. Still, not yet daring to move, Kingston stroked her hips and back, the globes of her ass, kissing her lips, then her neck. He caressed and stroked her breasts, kneading the mounds until she was moaning and relaxed against him.

"That's it, baby, you can take me. Relax your muscles, easy," he moaned, praising her and calming her.

He felt her magic pulse around them as her body adjusted to his invasion. Soon she was kissing him back. His hands swallowed her pert breasts. He squeezed and plucked her nipples, loving her groans. His tongue scoped every inch of her mouth. Her response was immediate and sublime.

"So good, baby," he growled and felt a flush of warmth as she rocked her hips. Slowly, he began to move and she with him. Coating his cock with her juices as she accepted him fully and completely.

Thank the gods.

ELEVEN

olley could hardly catch her breath. This was real. It was happening. After decades of watching her heart's desire, she was with him now. Her fated mate was in her arms, and it was the most profound moment of her existence.

His smoky scent invaded her nostrils. The taste of his lips as they moved over hers was sublime. Physical love was something she was very curious about, and now she knew.

Even with her imagination and decades of reading books over shoulders and watching television could not have prepared her for the sensual onslaught that was being claimed by her Dragon. Her heart was liable to beat her to death in the process, but it was worth it. So worth it.

She moaned as Kingston's enormous girth stretched and filled her most secret places. She'd learned a lot about sex during her captivity in the hollows of the Keep. But TV and books had nothing on this.

Holy hell! She'd never spied on the Guardians during their naughty times, but even if she had. Nothing could have readied her for the intensity of his enormous cock stretching and filling her, stroking inside her depths with such precision as to send lightning strikes of pleasure coursing through her veins.

Kingston's throaty growls were doing things to her she could hardly comprehend. He was so beautiful, so magnificent. She wanted to shower him with affection, show him what he meant to her.

Love filled her as she stared in awe at his big, warm body, pale against the bronzed flesh that was her birthright. A fact she could not change or hide. And she didn't want to. People of her time period had sneered at her in hatred, but not him.

The golden eyes of her Dragon lover seemed to covet every inch of her honeyed flesh. Holley was more than willing to give it over to his expert handling. His kisses seared her very soul. He was temptation personified. More than that, he was love. Her love. Always.

"Want you to claim me, mate," she said, egging on his beast, wanting more of him as her magic pulsed in time with her jerky movements.

"Mine," he hissed and flipped them over.

Beneath him now, Holley arched into his flexes. he was able to fill her much more deeply now, and he moaned at the sensual invasion that was Kingston taking over her every cell.

Oh my, he was heaven and hell, angel and devil, all rolled into one, she thought as he brought her heated body to heights she'd never imagined.

"Kingston," she cried alarmed at the sensations rolling through her.

Her stomach tightened, heart raced, and a tingling, burning need began to throb from her sex throughout her entire being.

"I got you, mate, I will always have you," he groaned as he reached between them, flicking her sensitive flesh with his thumb. And then, she saw stars.

A sharp, distinct pain exploded in her shoulder, before turning into the most exquisite pleasure. He did it. He bit her. Making it even sweeter as he lapped at her flesh, sealing the mark from his bite, and completing their *matebond*.

"Mine," he snarled and fastened his mouth to hers as he pumped his hips and spurred on another orgasm that left her gasping for air.

Kingston's body went rigid, and he roared aloud, emptying his seed into her womb. Holley held him through it all. Every shiver and tremble, rippled and convulsion of their joining brought more pleasure and fulfillment than she could've ever imagine. She kissed his face, his shoulders, his chest, anywhere she could reach, even as she struggled for breath. His scales were out once more, and she loved knowing the Dragon was there with them.

"I'm yours, mate," she soothed him with her words, her kisses, and long strokes of her hands on his back, shoulders, and finally, his brow.

"Mine," he said and struggled to steady his breathing.

"Yes," she smiled sleepily against him.

She wanted to stay awake, to talk about what this meant, to tell him what she felt, but exhaustion seeped into her bones and she fell asleep cradled in his arms. Cocooned in his arms, safe and warm for the first time in a very long while.

. . .

"*OMG! They did it!*"

"*They sure did.*"

"*Should we wake her?*"

"*I think we have.*"

Holley blinked slowly against the voices that were disturbing the first good sleep she'd had in a while. She stretched her deliciously sore body and ignored the squeaky yelp that came from her uninvited guests. Fergie and Jessenia were in Kingston's room, and he was markedly absent.

Hmm. So not how she wanted to awaken the morning after being claimed by the magnificent Diamond Dragon, but it was what it was.

Holley turned and blinked at the two women who were facing the wall and not her. Well, at least they were giving her some modicum of privacy. Thank goodness.

"Morning ladies, to what do I owe the pleasure?"

"Holley! Well, I see you were certainly busy last night," Fergie *oomphed* as Jessenia pinched her arm, "What? She was busy."

"Shh. Um, Holley? I was wondering if maybe you wanted to have some tea or something and we can chat?" the kitchen Witch added and glared at her friend.

"Ladies," Holley grinned at their backs and stood up, taking the sheet with her, "How about I take a bath and join you in a few minutes?"

"Perfect!"

"Yes!"

Washed and dressed, Holley walked down the carpeted halls of the Keep by herself to the kitchen. She knew full well to keep her destination in mind. The *manetuwak* or spirits of the Keep were devious tricksters at the best of times, and downright dangerous at the worst. How often had she watched from within as they defeated those who'd dared tried to gain entry without the proper means?

Sigh. Even now, Holley felt the Keep beckoning her back inside, to the safe haven of its hollows that had kept her hidden and secret for nigh on three centuries.

It was difficult, but she was able to resist the pull. She had a mate now. Her connection to Kingston was new, but when she closed her eyes, she could see the ethereal bond that linked their souls, and she knew she was home.

"Thank you, *manetuwak*, you kept me safe, but it is here I belong," she whispered to the Keep as she found the two women sitting at the kitchen counter.

"Please, Keep, I just want to make brownies!"

Jessenia groaned and banged her head on the granite counter.

"What is happening here?"

"Ugh, well, ever since you and Fire-breath were gettin' it on, this is what happened," Fergie said and opened the refrigerator doors.

"What?"

"What do you mean, what? It's empty, Holley! They all are, and I'm starving!"

Holley stared as the bouncy redhead moved to open cabinets and the second fridge, all of which were completely bare.

Darn it. The Keep was angry at her. That much was obvious. But still, it did not explain why she'd woken up alone.

"Um, where is Kingston?"

"How the heck should I know?" Jessenia grunted as she fought to open the oven.

Her bun wobbled on top of her head as she finally got the thing open. But when she went to collect her pan, it was empty.

"What the hell? My brownie mix is gone! Those ingredients were organic, and that was the last of the imported vanilla," she growled and kicked the oven only to yelp in pain.

"Okay, sit down, let me have a look. You know,"

Holley said as she helped the woman to the stool, "this place has a mind of its own and it seems I've made it angry. Still, you should know better than to kick a stainless-steel oven, for goodness' sake."

"I'm sorry. I'm just hungry," mumbled Jessenia.

"Her toe looks fine. Food?" Fergie looked on as Holley inspected Jessenia's foot.

Healing was one of her talents, but they were not needed, she decided and released the appendage. She stood up at once, determining the woman was fine except for a sore ego.

"Let me see what I can do about some breakfast first," Holley announced and was met with a round of applause.

"Is it safe?"

"Of course. That is, I think so," she closed her eyes and channeled those spirits that haunted the halls.

The *manetuwak* were not ghosts, not really, they were *other*. Supernatural creatures, kind of like fairies or very minor gods who used magic to exist on their plane. The Keep attracted them because of where it was located.

Unbeknown to most, the manse was a hotspot of magic. She knew she had to confide in Kingston, had planned to that morning, but he'd already gone by the time the females woke her up.

Typically, the spirits of the Keep offered comfort to those hardworking Guardians of Chaos without whom the particular vein of magic located beneath it would have undoubtedly been plundered ages ago.

You owe it to the Guardians and their mates to keep them fed and cared for, she argued.

But the Keep was being a bit thickheaded. The spirits pushed against her powers. It was as if the manse wanted her back under the spell that had kept her hidden away for so long. She frowned harder trying to convey the importance of her place with her mate.

Please manetuwak, I have a mate now. His job is to protect and shield me. It is not your place any longer. You know I am grateful, but you must resume your duties.

Holley tried for patience, but still the Keep refused to yield. It was taking a toll on her, fighting the thing that had cared and protected her for so long. Her magic was unique, true, but she was out of practice in the real world.

Frowning, she rolled up the sleeves to the soft, pale pink cashmere sweater she wore. The material had felt exquisite against her skin. Especially after such furious lovemaking with her Dragon. She'd relished the smooth, lightweight top the second she slid it over her slightly sore body.

Paired with a long, flowing skirt covered in various

hued blossoms, Holley's attention was held captive by the garment for a moment or two. She couldn't help but simply wonder what it would be like to walk amongst such flowers. Finally, she finished the ensemble with a pair of pink dragon socks and white Converse.

Modern day life had its benefits, but clothing aside, she was surprised at what she found in the kitchen. Her new friends were being downright ignored by the very Keep that was to aid and protect them. That would simply not do. She knew that spirits and magic itself could be obstinate, but this was ridiculous.

"You know better, *manetuwak*," she continued aloud, "A promise was made long before I became involved, and that oath holds even now," she closed her eyes in concentration.

"What is she doing?"

"Shhh."

"She is trying to get the Keep to give us back our food."

Holley ignored the whispered voices and continued to channel the Keep. Pushing words and feelings of praise and thanks to the spirits, she tried to gently remind them of their pledge, asking them to honor that which was set in the very stones of the manse itself.

Unaware of the new arrivals, she could not see the expressions on their faces as her magic pulsed around her in a golden bright aura that was as warm to the touch as it was beautiful. Among them was one particularly curious Diamond Dragon who'd just entered the room to stand with the other Guardians.

Holley felt her hair whip around her shoulders as power pulsed all around her sizzling and crackling like sparks on a fire or some kind of brilliant electrical surge. But she was not cowered by the display, and she had no intentions of giving in to the implied threat. The Keep was throwing a tantrum and she would just have to be stern.

Digging deep within herself, Holley found the thread that tied her to this place. That cord was her connection to the *manetuwak*, the spirits therein. It was what enabled her to live even after being holed up inside the bowels of the manse itself by Preacher Milton and his mad followers.

The memories threatened to shake her nerve, but she pushed them away. He was long since dead and gone. There was nothing left to fear of the man. Grabbing her balls, as Fergie said, she focused with all her might on that single thread.

It was so cold and dark there in that strange realm. The place where magic existed in the physical sense was on a separate plane from the reality she was in now. Holley much preferred the latter, but this place was familiar to her. It was where she'd wandered, much like a ghost, for so many long years.

Watching from afar, waiting for the day she would be free to rejoin the world. The Keep had been both her shelter and her prison. Holley was grateful to the *manetuwak*, but she never wanted to return to the frigid, gloomy place ever again.

Shivers ran through her body the longer she stayed there in that shadow plane. But Holley could not leave just yet. She had to persuade the spirits to honor their path. They had a job to do. They must honor their bargain with the Guardians of Chaos.

Those first warriors who'd commissioned the stone walls and had them built, inlaid with magical properties, had done so long before the Puritans arrived to destroy things one way or another. The *supernaturals* had had an agreement with the native people of the land.

One that would ensure magic remain free and true. The Lenape understood the necessity and sanctioned construction without quarrel. Yes, Holley had learned much about the history of the Keep.

What she did not understand until right then was that it had hidden itself from Preacher Milton once her own bargain was struck. That was why it wanted her back. To keep her safe. Without her there inside, the spell was broken, and the Keep could once more be found.

The *manetuwak* had vowed to protect her. Yes, its doors would always be open to the ones who'd built it and would use it to keep magic from harm. But somehow, she had become the focus of the spirits within the Keep. Now that her spell was broken, she was at risk.

Holley's mind clouded, and she swayed as image after image of how the Keep had protected her and allowed her to live and retain her youth and her physical body, by suspending it for centuries.

She would grow old now, die someday without them. The idea was scary to say the least. She did not want to die. Not yet. Staying did have its benefits. Yes, they seemed to like that, but something nagged at her mind as the small glowing lights circled her and began to tug on her wrists and hair, pulling her clothing, leading her down the chilled dark path.

"Holley?"

She heard a voice through the mist. The lights swirled faster and faster, picking at her clothes and skin. Wait, a second. No. She did not want to go back to that plane. Not there. Not inside the cold, dark place where she was all alone.

She turned her head in the dimly lit ether and something caught her attention. A thicker, brighter, glowing cord that was pulsating with warmth and heat. It was so bright, so beguiling, she moved away from the mist and the now frantic lights.

Kneeling on the moss-covered ground, she lifted the cord and cried out as the most beautiful feeling she'd ever felt encompassed her. It was like being given life. She was amazed as the sound of her name grew louder.

Holley gasped as she was lifted. She felt the place where Kingston had given her his mating mark burn her skin. That sizzle began to warm her icy flesh, and she moaned. When had she grown so cold? In there, with the lights. She wanted to throw her head back and howl in fury. They'd almost tricked her!

"Holley!" Kingston's voice echoed in her mind as she blinked slowly and looked up into his worried gold eyes.

His Dragon was peeking out at her too, and the beast was not happy. That wouldn't do, she thought, and reached up to stroke his handsome, chiseled face with her cold fingers.

"Calm, my love," she whispered and found her throat was dry.

"Thank the gods," he growled and pulled her into

his arms holding her tight to his body.

"What happened?"

"I don't know. We got called away to check out a warehouse for signs of the Loyalists and when I came back you were on the floor, ice cold, and Jessenia and Fergie were trying to wake you up," he said and ran his hands across her face and body, checking for injury but rousing other needs as he went.

"Kingston," she moaned his name and his touch slowed down as he reached her legs.

"You feel so good, so warm," she shivered.

"I'm a Dragon," he growled by way of explanation and she lifted her face for his kiss.

"Ow," she winced as the skin on her shoulder stretched.

She covered her newly opened mating mark with her hand, stunned to see fresh blood there.

"I am sorry, love, I bit you to bring you back," he blushed deeply, and she smiled at him.

"It's alright. I was trying to convince the Keep to take care of you all. It seems the spirits thought perhaps I was not being cared for properly," she tried to explain.

"Well, they can't have you. You," he dropped a kiss on her mouth, "are," and another, "mine," and one more.

TWELVE

orror. Fury. Agonizing pain.

Those words were hardly adequate to describe the abject fear and panic that went through Kingston's nearly seven-foot-tall body when he walked into the kitchen of the Keep and saw his mate lying on the floor.

Her tawny skin was pale and cold to the touch. Eyes shut, body limp, he picked her up and rushed her down the hall to their rooms. The suite had been his since he'd moved in a few decades ago, but it was theirs now.

He might have been mated to Neela, but the she-Dragon had never shared his bed nor any of the rooms in his suite. He still felt pangs of regret when he thought of her, but he knew where he belonged now.

There was only room for Holley in his heart and, for the moment, in his mind. He'd expected his beast to calm after mating her the previous night, but he'd been wrong. The Dragon wanted her even more.

It was difficult to leave her in bed that morning while he went with his team to investigate a lead, they had on the now banned group of Loyalists who had followed their evil leader down a path from which no redemption could be had. Murder, kidnapping, mind-rape, and more counts of heinous crimes than he cared to contemplate could be laid at their door.

Those scumbags needed to be found. Offner most of all. The *sonovabitch* had no morals to speak of. What Warlock did?

He'd sold his soul, broken his oath to magic and to the supernatural world, and now, he would reap the benefits of what he sowed. With any luck, that would be at Kingston's hands or claws.

Claws, huffed his Dragon.

Still, none of that mattered at the moment. Holley's breathing was shallow and her skin like ice. Kingston roared and Egros came running. After the Witch took one look at her, he consulted with Byram, and both were clueless how to help her.

"It's like she's in a coma," Egros explained, "a

magical one, but not as bad as before. I think you can reverse it, Kingston."

"You mean, I have to bite her?"

"Yes," Byram nodded.

"Leave us," he commanded.

The Witch and Vampire did as he asked, closing the door behind them. The first time he'd bitten her there had been curiosity and attraction, perhaps even a sense of destiny. The second time, there'd been pleasure and an urgency of need that was indescribable. This time there was something else. Something he'd been too afraid to say aloud.

"Holley! Holley, I am sorry this will hurt you, my love, but I don't know what else to do," he pulled her sweater off her body, not wanting to ruin it.

She loved getting new, modern clothes. It was something about the way material from this time felt against her skin. He inhaled a breath to steady himself and placed the shirt beside her, leaving her torso clothed in a simple camisole. His Witch still hated underthings, he acknowledged with a concerned quirk of his lips.

Kingston lifted her in his embrace. He brushed her hair away from her face and neck, carefully, methodically, until he could place his teeth over the scar of his mating mark. Then he bit.

Holley jerked in his arms before he had time to seal them properly, but she was okay! His Dragon's heart soared with love for her as she shivered against him and opened dazed green eyes to his. After that, it was only a matter of seconds before he was kissing her.

"Is it too much," he growled as he tugged off clothes and shoes, grinning when he checked to see what color dragon she was wearing on her feet today.

Pale pink. Today she was wearing pink dragons. His beast huffed in indignance, but Kingston thought she was positively adorable.

"Never too much. Please, I need you," she moaned into his mouth, dueling her tongue cleverly with his until he was the one gasping for air.

His cock throbbed in his jeans and before he could properly remove them, his claws popped free and Kingston shredded the fuckers off his body. The scent of his mate's arousal was delicious. It filled the room, whetting his appetite and coaxing his beast to the forefront.

Mine. Mate. Claim.

His Dragon hissed and scratched. He didn't fully understand, but who was he to question. The woman was claimed three times over, but still the creature demanded more.

"Want to taste you, sweet," he growled and laid her down on her back.

Holley moaned, eyes glazed with lust as he ran his hands down the length of her body. His palms heated her still-chilled flesh, and she arched up to get closer to him, seeming to want more of his careful attentions. Her breasts swelled with her arousal and her nipples hardened into tiny little berries he could not wait to sample.

Kingston closed his lips over one, tugging it with his teeth until she moaned his name. Holley pulled his hair, pushing her chest more fully into his mouth. Fuck, she was so hot when she was demanding.

He treated her other perfect breast to more of the same, running his hands down to her hips and thighs. He spread them wide, finding her uncovered pussy with determined fingers.

"You're so wet, so tight," he growled as he stroked the pad of his thumb over her small bundle of nerves, tempting her to madness while he stretched her channel with his other thick digits.

He caught each one of Holley's throaty moans with his mouth and savored them as he kissed her. It was almost enough to make him come right there, but the beast inside demanded more.

Kingston abandoned her breasts and mouth in

search of other treats located further down the wonderland that was her body. Anticipation had precum beading on the head of his cock. He reached down and squeezed his shaft, rubbing that pearl up and down his length, before using both hands to smooth the silky skin of her luscious thighs. She trembled beneath his touch, flexing her hips instinctively, seeking his attention.

She had it. Completely. Now that she was warm, her tawny complexion glowed like bronze in the soft light coming from the fireplace. Funny, that wasn't his doing, but whatever. The Keep had a lot of explaining to do, and perhaps this was an act of contrition.

He used his shoulders to widen her legs and licked his lips at the display before him. She was so perfect. Glistening with her arousal, Kingston could not wait to lap at her honey. And he didn't. He bent his head and swiped his tongue along her lips.

"Oh gods," she moaned and clutched at the blankets beneath her, but he was only getting started.

Slow and steady, with strokes of his long, and sometimes forked, tongue, Kingston made love to his mate with his mouth. He tapped his finger against her clit while he drove into her sweet, hot, sheath. Tasting her deeply for the first time and drinking her down.

She was better than wine, better than anything he

ever had. He was high on his love for her. Intoxicated and bespelled by his sweet Witch. Holley lifted up, pressing herself to him, and he allowed it.

Fuck that. He fucking loved it. He traded his tongue for fingers and returned his attention on her tight little clit. That nubbin was his ticket to making his mate come harder than ever before.

He growled deep in his throat, the sound making a vibrator of his now-forked-tongue as he delivered a myriad of circles, swirls, and taps to the sensitive little bundle of nerves.

Suck, swirl, tap, suck, swirl, tap, tap, tap.

"Oh gods!"

Fuck, she was gorgeous. And his. All his. His Dragon insisted he remember that even as he gripped her hip with his free hand and felt his claws dig into the flesh there, leaving a scratch that would mark her again, same as his bite.

She did not seem to mind. In fact, she pressed deeper against him. Pushing her sweet pussy into his mouth she groaned loudly and covered his hand with hers. Like she knew he was marking her again, and even more wondrous, she wanted it. Holley bucked against him and clutched his hair, but he was relentless.

Pleasuring her was the only goal he had at the moment. And it was goddamn important. He felt the first spasms ripple through her as more moisture gushed forward.

His Dragon growled with pride. She was his. He was going to make her come again, this time on his cock, then he would claim her once more.

Determination set him on fire and Kingston doubled his efforts, licking, sucking, and fucking her with his fingers and tongue until she arched up in a soundless scream that echoed through his heart.

Mine!

He moved up her body before the tremors of her first orgasm could stop and plunged into her silky hot depths. Her sex squeezed his cock like a velvet vise and she wrapped her legs around his waist, encouraging him to move.

"Yes, now, now, now," she begged and who was he to deny her.

Never that. He could only give her pleasure. It was in his fucking DNA. She was the light of his life, his fire, his reason.

"I love you," he said stopping suddenly as the realization came crashing down into reality.

Holley's mossy eyes smiled up at him, though her mouth was serious. She held his face between her small hands and pulled him down to kiss her lips gently.

"I know, mate, I love you too," she returned and Kingston moved deep within her.

So slowly. So very slowly, he thought he would die or maybe kill them both, from the sheer amount of pleasure alone.

She was precious to him, and he would cherish her always. He was her shield. Her protector against all things. Her fated mate. Her Diamond Dragon.

Mine.

His hands held her close as he pushed inside of her welcoming body. The two of them moaned in unison, a symphonic sound that reverberated in the room.

Holley's eyes never left his as they kissed and touched. It was more than bodies, he realized, she was touching his soul. Caressing him so deeply and permanently, he would never be the same. Fuck, he never wanted to be.

"I love you," he whispered once more and brushed his nose against hers while he rotated his hips in tight, slow, circles.

"I love you," he said it again and kissed her lower lip, tugging it between his teeth as he slid his long legs against her smooth ones, grinding his pubis into her pussy, and dragging a husky moan from her mouth.

His Dragon was wild for her. The legendary beast

completely infatuated with his mate, his maiden fair, his one and only.

"I love you," he increased pace, fucking her harder and faster and watching her expression for the right moment to strike.

"Kingston, now," she yelled, and he struck like lightning, biting her once more, marking her flesh, this time above her breast.

He clung to her while Holley's orgasm rippled around him, then Kingston roared with pain-tinted pleasure. Rearing up, he saw his mate's eyes go white as she chanted something unintelligible, something magical.

His own orgasm erupted from him like a long-awaited volcano and he cried out her name as he coated her walls with his cum. Fucking hell, the searing pain finally receded giving way to pure pleasure, though where it had occurred, there remained a dull ache.

When he could move again, Kingston opened his eyes and looked down. Holly was still catching her breath. Her arms were limp above her head, and he kissed her cheek and cradled her close. Then he turned and looked at his bicep. There, like a brand, was a marking. Like a tattoo.

Claimed, his Dragon exhaled a puff of smoke and for the first time ever, his beast was truly at peace.

"I am sorry if that hurt you," she said breathlessly, "I suppose I got carried away."

"It's alright, love," he smiled wide, unable to hide the joy that was bursting from his heart.

Diamond Dragons had notoriously tough hides, even in their human form. No doubt, she had to put a little extra into whatever spell she'd conjured to mark him as hers. He looked down at the angry red marking and smiled. It was a shield with a heart inside it, surrounded by flames.

"I love it and you," he said and meant every word.

"I love you too," she replied sleepily before nodding off.

This time he would stay until she awakened.

Thirteen

"So, what are we cooking today?" Holley inquired.

"Well, in exchange for you teaching me how to make that wonderful skin salve you gave me last week, I thought I would teach you how to make pizza," Fergie clapped.

"*You* will be teaching her?' snorted her best friend, Jessenia and even Holley laughed at that.

"Fine, you will be learning from a certain haughty little kitchen bitch I know."

Holley laughed as the two women continued to tease each other while she started to gather ingredients from the cabinets. The last few days had gone by rather smoothly and she was happy to have some time with the females.

Mostly, she used what was on hand and was incredibly surprised at how rapidly she could order what were once very rare ingredients. Some common sage, local honey, a little lavender, virgin olive oil, and some chamomile flowers made for a very nice salve indeed.

Her mind wandered to Kingston. The man was absolutely wonderful, but she knew he was neglecting his duties to care for her. Last night, she'd assured him that she could stay home without incident. After all, being mated to a Guardian was not for the faint of heart. She did not want him to think she was a hinderance to his vows. He swore an oath to protect magic and she would not be the reason he broke it.

The sound of voices in the living room brought all three female heads whipping around. Holley frowned. She knew from the properly chastised Keep that not everyone was happy she was there. it was something she'd brushed aside, until now. Truth was, it hurt to think one of them saw her as an interloper.

"I don't understand what the fuck he is doing in there with her," growled voices from inside the living room.

"Dude, easy. That's his mate."

"Neela was his mate," insisted the former.

"That was different, cump, he already explained it-"

"Nah man, fuck that. If we can just go around picking and choosing what vows to honor then why are we even here?"

"The fuck did you say?"

The sounds of blows being exchanged and furniture crashing into walls brought Holley, Fergie, and Jessenia, who'd been something of a constant fixture since the unfortunate incident in the kitchen, running. Furio and Storm were locked together in what kind of looked like a hug, but Holley had the good sense to know was a fierce battle.

"Stop it!" yelled Fergie.

"Guys, come on!"

"This is because of me isn't it? Enough!" Holley bit her lip and watched the two friends pound each other into the floor.

"No, it's just," Jessenia hedged, but Holley knew it was true.

She was the cause of the rift between the men. Furio was the sole sour face at every meal and gathering since the beginning. Apparently, the Stallion Shifter held Neela in such high esteem that he did not believe she could or should be replaced.

Even after Kingston had come clean about the truth of his relationship between the she-Dragon and himself, the stubborn Draft Horse Shifter refused to accept Holley! He actually believed she was wrong somehow. Holley's heart ached for the man. From what she knew from her years in the manse's hollows, he was orphaned at a tender age.

With no real family of his own, Furio had made one out of his group of Guardians. With Neela as the maternal figurehead, he felt betrayed by Kingston's actions and Holley's very existence. But that was no excuse to break the damn furniture! She growled and called on her magic.

"I said, enough!" she yelled and her voice echoed off the walls, full of her power.

The two men immediately split apart from one another and were held suspended over the broken remnants of the sofa. Annoyance coursed through her at the mess and she gave them a shake with just a nod.

"Hey!"

"Ow," growled Storm whose teeth had knocked together at the last little jiggle.

"Look at you, two grown men behaving like children"

"Sorry, Holley," growled the Wolf, but Furio refused to look at her.

"Are you finished now? Ready to act like men and not boys?"

Displeasure dripped from every word as she

watched the men look at each other than back at the very angry little Witch. Storm nodded.

"Good," she said and with another nod dropped them both on the floor, "start by cleaning this mess. Then I think you will both benefit from time in the garden."

The small fenced in garden just off the kitchen was Holley's pride and joy. Kingston had made a sort of gift of it and presented it to her just the other morning. Apparently, he had some of the guys clean out all the old vegetation. They even tilled the soil despite it being winter to ready it for planting in the spring.

She'd ordered heavy ceramic pots and large wooden boxes that still needed to be put together. All of that from the computer. She could not wait to see it in bloom. Shopping was one of her new favorite pastimes.

Well, second favorite.

And shopping online meant she never even had to leave the house! While that was certainly marvelous, she did enjoy going to town. But she only ever went with Kingston. Her mate was somewhat protective of her, which she secretly loved.

The crates she'd ordered, along with special seeds and fertilizers, would hold herbs and roots off the ground for easy access. She'd already begun to plan for the upcoming season and had even asked Jessenia's input on several occasions.

"Shit, I mean, okay, okay, I can move some stuff for you," growled Storm, but the second he stood he went to embrace his worried looking mate who growled at Furio.

"I'm not working in no garden," he finger-combed his hair back into its ponytail and stomped away from her.

"Fine, then you can clean in here," she called after him, "you broke it, you clean it, or you will both be eating pickled eggs and sardines for every meal for the next two months."

Storm paled and a sound that was suspiciously like a whinny came from the direction Furio had gone in. Holley turned her back on them and went to the kitchen with Jessenia following behind.

"He doesn't mean it," she drawled, "I mean, Furio is the nicest of the bunch. Always lighthearted and laughing. He was the one who was nicest to Fergie when she first mated Storm. I am so sorry."

"It is not your doing," Holley wiped her face.

She felt foolish for crying, but she couldn't help it. An outcast most her life, it was a familiar though unwelcome feeling to be unwanted. One she wished she could forget.

"Do you think I could show you how to make the salve later?"

"Sure, I'll go ahead and prep the dough and everything for the pizzas. You can help put them together, yeah?"

"That sounds divine," she squeezed Jessenia's arm and walked outside.

The garden gate was newly fixed. The shiny, black wrought-iron gleamed in the morning sun despite it being late November. Holley simply loved the look of.

It was chilly outside, but she relished the cold breeze as it whipped her hair around her shoulders and molded her long skirt to her legs. Fergie had tried to get her to wear something called leggings, but they were stockings for sure!

She was not about to walk outdoors like that. Kingston had pointed out that her penchant for going out without underwear was a tad more risqué, but she wouldn't budge. They compromised on the whole underwear thing anyway. The other day, he took her shopping and she found something called boxer briefs which were wonderfully comfortable and covered her completely.

Whenever he was not home, she promised to wear one of the six dozen pairs he'd bought her beneath her skirts. And when he was home, well, then it was up to him to find out, wasn't it?

The gate was open when she got there, but Holley was too lost in thoughts about her Dragon that she didn't stop to think that anything was amiss. The sound of the gate door banging shut brought her head up sharp and fast.

"You!"

Fright filled her, and she stepped back, but something, or rather, someone grabbed her from behind. Holley struggled against the offensive hold. Her foul-smelling captor struck her across the head, then proceeded to lick her cheek.

The urge to vomit welled up inside of her, but Holley found herself unable to move. The creature holding her hissed, and she recalled Fergie's debacle with the heinous Gila Shifters whose saliva was laced with venom.

"I see time has not changed you, heathen-spawn," growled the familiar though time-ravaged man.

A man she'd never expected to see again. He stalked towards her, leaning heavily on a cane for support and his pockmarked skin seemed to drip and melt before her eyes. Beneath was even more hideous disfigurement. As gruesome and gory an image as she had ever seen.

"I have found you now, and with you, this place. For hundreds of years I searched, waiting, but the magic wards that kept you hidden, also hid the castle from prying eyes. I bet you didn't know that did you? Ha!" the man she knew as Preacher Milton cackled briefly before black spittle ran down his chin.

"At last, I will seize control, and you my dear, are the means that I will use to take my rightful place at the center of all magic!"

She could barely believe her eyes. The man she had known was a religious fanatic at best, but this man was something else. In fact, he was not a man at all. She smelled magic rolling off him, but it was tainted.

Putrid and rotting, the stink stung her eyes even more than the wind. She tried to whimper, but the sound would not come. Still immobile due to the Gila's venom, Holley was helpless to respond.

She could only stare in horror, eyes tearing against the cold, as the Gila Shifter lifted her onto his shoulder and carried her out of the garden to the cellar stairs behind the Keep.

Kingston, she thought, *where are you?*

Fourteen

Kingston's enormous white Diamond Dragon soared beneath the darkening clouds as he neared the Keep. The day's hunt had gone fairly well. They'd found the nest where Offner's Loyalist scum had been hiding the foul Warlock, but of course he was nowhere to be seen.

After dropping off the small Lounge of Gila Shifters they'd rounded up at the Enforcers' compound, he decided to let Byram handle the paperwork and took to the skies. He'd had to work to retract his claws and fangs while handling the criminals.

His beast wanted out. He wanted his mate, and so did he for that matter. The little Witch with the pale eyes and tawny skin was all he thought about. He found heaven in her touch, bliss in her arms, sweetness in her kiss. But it was so much more than that too.

Who knew Dragons were such romantics? But it was true. The Witch was his mate. His everything. He wanted to bathe in her scent. To be in her presence all the time. No matter how impractical. A point she'd made last night in between kissing him silly and loving him until he saw stars.

Kingston flapped his enormous wings harder and faster, using his aerodynamic shape to allow the wind speed him along. He caught sight of the Keep in the distance, hiding among the pines and shrubs of the great New Jersey Barrens.

Odd, he thought as his keen Dragon eyes caught something off about the manse. It was as if the building itself was beckoning him home faster, calling to him as it never had before. Something was wrong.

He searched inside of himself for the *matebond* that connected him to Holley, but it was barely glowing. Kingston opened his jaws and shot a stream of flame into the quickly darkening skies. Lightning flashed overhead and thunder rolled loudly, echoing his growing rage.

Whatever the problem, Kingston was willing to settle it with claws and fire. Dragon fire to be precise. Willing himself to calm, it was no easy feat.

Something primal and not quite tame inside him reared up at the thought of his mate in danger. He had no proof, only this feeling in his gut and it wouldn't let up.

His Dragon's cry echoed through the Pine Barrens, bringing all the Guardians in residence, and their mates and friends, to the backyard where the garden gate was swinging madly in the breeze. He took a deep inhale and snarled.

Something foul had passed that way. Something not entirely human. And the soon-to-be-dead-mother-fucker had his mate.

Rooooooaaaaaarrrr!

"Fuck!"

"Kingston, what is it?"

Summoning as much restraint as he could, Kingston shifted to his human form, catching the pair of sweats someone tossed his way and shrugging them on even as he used his Dragon's eyes to search the grounds. She was there roughly twenty minutes ago he judged from the fading scent. And she wasn't alone.

"Where'd he get that ink?" he heard one of them ask and snapped his head to look at the Shifter who spoke.

Furio. His fastest and at one time most dependable Guardian. The Stallion had not been himself lately.

Looking at him now, in this agitated state, Kingston was stunned to see him clearly for the first time.

"Holy shit, *cump*," the man pointed, and he looked down.

His torso was covered in whirling flames of orange and yellow. White smoke billowed upward and little sparkling lights zipping around him. He growled with a start, but it was his added powers. Those he'd gotten as a result of finding and mating with his *conpar*.

"Uh, you're on fire, boss," Storm added unnecessarily.

He ignored the stares and whispers. Holley needed him to focus.

"When was the last time any of you spoke with Holley?" he growled in a voice so thick with his Dragon he was barely discernible.

"Uh, we were going to make pizza and she was going to show us how to make a salve," Jessenia piped in.

"But Storm and I had a disagreement," Furio bowed his head.

His feelings were like a beacon to Kingston, who as his Alpha and the leader of their team wanted to offer comfort to the man. However, seeing as how his actions had put Kingston's own mate in harm's way, he also wanted to rip him a new asshole.

But his primary goal was to find Holley. Still, regret and emotions poured from Furio into him and he did the only thing he could, he nodded at the man, Acknowledging his repentance and he was glad for it. It was the only thing that saved him from being charred to a crisp by his angry as fuck Dragon who wanted his mate back now.

"The women came in and Holley, well" his lips quirked and Kingston acknowledged it as a sign the Draft Horse Shifter respected his mate, his Dragon growled softly in approval, "she kicked our asses, boss. Took us to task like a pro and made us clean up our shit."

"Yeah, then I, uh, took Storm inside to check him over for injury," Fergie cleared her throat which left the rest up to interpretation.

"She was going outside to clear her head I think," Jessenia added.

"You let her go alone?" he turned to the kitchen Witch, but Furio moved in front of her.

"It's my fault. She asked me to work in the garden and I refused. She was outside alone because of me."

"It was a lot of things, not just him," Jessenia's voice rose as she tried to push her way in front of Furio.

Clearly, something was going on between the two

of them, but Kingston did not care. Not then. He closed his eyes searching for her scent and started to move.

"Listen up," he growled to everyone there, "Holley is my mate. This 'ink' is her mating mark, I can feel her inside the Keep. The spirits, the *manetuwak* are watching but they can't interfere," he said as if caught in some kind of live feed he was getting from the manse itself.

"Can you find her?"

"Yes, I think so."

"Well, what are you all waiting for?" Fergie bent down and picked up one of the spades from the ground, "let's get those fuckers!"

He raised his eyebrow as Jessenia reached into her back pocket and pulled out a small vial. She nodded at Fergie and moved to stand beside her and Storm.

"What? It's an attack spell. Don't worry, Holley showed me what to use," she smirked.

Kingston's hearts welled with pride at the men and women before him. They were willing to risk their lives for his mate.

"Thank you, but I don't think you should all follow me. What if it's a trap? I need someone to stay here," he began.

"No way."

"We're coming-"

"Listen up! I will go with Kingston," Furio stated.

Kingston felt his Guardian's inside of him as he never had before. Their thoughts and feelings projected like a newsreel. Storm's brow was furrowed in worry as he considered bringing his mate back within range of Offner and his vile henchmen. Fergie was frightened, especially because she had a secret. A baby, he thought in wonder and sent waves of calm to the couple.

"You three stay here," Furio pointed at them.

"No way, Buster!" Fergie growled, but Jessenia interrupted her.

"It's better this way Ferg. You guys stay and the three of us will go. Egros, Elena, and Byram should be here any minute. You can send them after us."

"Darn it," she stomped her stiletto on the ground.

"He's right, *conpar*, we will watch their rear and make sure no more men follow them," Storm wrapped his arms around her and pulled her back against him.

Kingston nodded at the Wolf and turned to where Furio and Jessenia were pointedly not looking at each other.

"Come on, we wasted too much time already," he growled and took off around the back of the Keep to where a pair of cellar doors flapped in the chilled breeze.

At that moment, rain began to pour down and lightning flashed once more, hitting close to where he stood. The entire fucking earth could flood and he wouldn't care, not unless he had Holley back in his arms.

Rrrrrrrooooaaaaarrrrrrr!

"Where does that lead?' Jessenia called over the rising storm.

"The furnace room," he growled and took off down the stairs and into the darkness, following the stench of the rot and death, and beneath it blueberries.

Mine.

There was no light but, Kingston was able to see using his Dragon's eyes. Think infrared but without the goggles. He inhaled deeply, wishing he had some of Storm's strength of smell, but for what it was worth, it was like he was seeing in 4D.

Furio grabbed onto Jessenia when the Witch stumbled in the dark and Kingston raised a finger to his lips. They were getting closer. He wanted to use his new powers but hesitated. The last thing he needed was to rush in and put Holley in even more danger.

It wasn't the stink of the Gila Shifters or of Offner himself that told him they were closing in on the men who had his mate. No, it was the pulsing little sparks of light that were zipping all around and practically pulling him forward.

He felt as if his entire body was buzzing with energy. Then he felt her. The first thing he saw was the broken wall where Jessenia and Fergie had accidentally tried to drill to install an ethernet cable.

But this time his mate was not laid out like some sacrifice, trapped and suspended alone by a spell only he could break. Like some modern-day Snow White.

No. This time there were three Gila fuckers holding her down while the mad Warlock Offner recited an incantation in *Demonspeak*. The guttural sounds were harsh to his Dragon's ears and the foul stench they pulled forth from the crack in the floor was polluted and tainted.

Kingston's body began to Shift, but it was too small for a full-sized Dragon. Using his extreme Alpha powers, he did a half -Shift, something only the strongest Shifters with supreme control and balance of their dual natures could manage to pull off.

Yes, he was enraged, but this was his best chance to save her unscathed. The beast recognized that and did not fight him as he called his white, diamond-shaped scales to cover his arms, shoulders and chest. Horns erupted from his forehead, while his fangs descended, and claws popped free of his fingers.

Kingston's skin became pale as alabaster and wings protruded from his back, as well as a spiked tail. In this shape he could breathe fire, and block against just about any weapon known to man or supe.

He moved forward stealthily, in time with the spirits of the Keep. As if sensing his presence and intent, the manse's *manetuwak* seemed to come to a decision. They accepted him, hiding him in the shadows until it was the right time to pounce.

Like right when that evil sonovabitch held an athame over his beautiful mate's face.

Motherfucker. With a roar so loud the basement shook, Kingston emerged. His body was shrouded in spiraling flames as he shot a stream of fire out of his mouth, hitting the first fucker he saw. Furio and Jessenia got to work against the others as he circled his nemesis.

"You are too late! My master comes for the Witch," hissed Offner.

His eyes met Holley's and all of his protective instinct and his beast's rage burst forth.

"Then he shall die with you," promised Kingston.

FIFTEEN

"You will die this time, I shall see to it," Preacher Milton, whom she suspected was the Warlock Offner all along, hissed at her.

With a nod of his wrinkled, misshapen head, his Gila minion slapped her cheek hard. Still immobile from the venom, Holley was seriously getting angry. She closed her eyes and sifted through the layers of bindings looking for a way out.

The bastard had learned a lot about magic since they'd last met. No wonder, what with him being a Warlock now and all. The Demon had given him power for which he of course bargained his soul.

A hefty payment, she thought with disdain.

"You shall not win this time! I will kill you and seize control of your magic. I shall pay my debt to the

Demon with your blood," he cackled as his monsters held her down.

From her position half off the stone slab, she could see a crack in the foundation of the Keep. The *mane-tuwak* was trying to defend her, but it could not heal itself and keep her alive at the same time.

"That is not going to work. You should know that Warlock," she said from stiff lips.

"I will steal your magic from your dying soul before it leaves your body and feed it to the Demon. Then I will plunge this vein myself and reap the benefits of eons of magical energy."

"Doesn't matter if you kill me," she gasped weakly as he continued to siphon her life's force with his evil spell, "the Keep will have my powers. It's part of our bargain. You have to give for what you take in magic as in everything," she smiled weakly and was stunned to realize the venom was wearing off.

"You're wrong," the crazed preacher raised a sharp dagger and Holley tried to gather her energy to move away, but those Gila Shifters were just too strong.

This was not her end. She could hardly accept it as such. Captive for centuries to have emerged for what? So this bastard could steal her life and her love from her?

"Ahh, no," she yelled as her mate emerged from the shadows.

"NO!" Kingston attacked, shooting fire at one of her captors before turning on the Warlock.

That was fine. She was able to hit one of them with her magic while Furio and Jessenia took care of the other. She slid off the table and hit the floor, but not before the bastard's eyes caught hers.

"I have you now, Offner, yield," growled Kingston, magnificent in his half-shift.

"You might have cornered me, Dragon, but I have one play left," he threw the blade at her, but before Kingston could lunge for it, the man had his claws out and was chanting dark magic to weave around his body.

Holley cried out as the knife pierced her stomach. She slumped sightlessly against the stone floor. No, this could not be happening, she moaned as Kingston howled in fury. But the Warlock was not done. Even as he chanted, his body morphed and swelled in the small room.

Black, stinking skin bubbled with poisonous ooze as his gnarled claws struck out to attack. The scent of Kingston's blood as the bastard struck his thigh invaded her senses and Holley yelled for him to watch out.

Time seemed to stand still for a moment as pain filled her. She held his gaze and nodded. Kingston would want to go to her, but he needed to end Offner first.

"Get him" she commanded and her mate roared mightily shaking the room with his rage.

Flames engulfed his body as he turned and grabbed for the Warlock's disgusting form. His claws shredded his diseased skin, but he kept on pulling him closer in a fierce farce of a hug. Offner howled, but Kingston was relentless.

He pulled his magic to him and called on his Dragon's fire to burn the oath-breaker until there was nothing but charred bone. Suddenly a guttural roar sounded from the ether and Kingston turned and hurled the dusty corpse into the maw of the Demon who'd claimed Offner's tainted soul.

That evil had no purchase in that mortal world with oath-breaker dead, and after closing his jaws over the dead remains of the evil man she knew as Milton, the Demon went back to hell. Leaving Furio and Jessenia with two Gila Shifters bound and gagged on the floor. And Kingston, her sweet mate, sucking in air as he recovered from the battle.

He was a mighty warrior indeed, she thought even as her spirit began to leave her physical shape. The pain she'd felt was inconsequential as rivulets of blood flowed from her wound.

Damn it, she groaned. It was her heart that was breaking now. Seeing him one last time meant the world, but she didn't want to leave. Kingston ran to her side, losing hold of his Dragon as he did so.

"Holley! Holley!" he roared and shook her, gathering her in his arms.

His body trembled as he sobbed openly, pleading with her to return to him. She wanted to. Oh gods, how she wanted to.

The cold shadows of the veil beckoned her forth and she tried to slow her pace, but it was no good. She was dying.

"No," a voice said, "you must go back to him, make him happy."

The shape of a lovely blonde she-Dragon came into view. With the beauty was the spitting image of Kingston, only this Dragon was platinum blonde and blue-eyed. His grin was the same as he held the woman's ghostly hand in his.

"I am Edgar, sweet sister, and it is my pleasure to meet you. Go back now. Tell Kingston to be happy, for us. And remind the Keep every now and then to honor their deal. The others are watching," he added facetiously.

Holley nodded. She could not speak, but she felt their peace and good will flow through her like a thousand wishes and dreams. She rushed back to herself and inhaled a great gulp of air back into her lungs.

"Holley! Thank the gods, thank the gods," Kingston gripped her tighter, kissing her face and hair. "What do you need? Tell me, please, anything at all. I will get it for you," he sniffed, wiping at his tear-stained cheeks and nose.

He'd never looked more beautiful to her. Holley cupped his face in her hands and marveled at his fierce, unwavering devotion.

"You. I only need you."

EPILOGUE

"Are you shittin' me?" Furio snorted and dropped the piece of broccolini he was munching on back onto his plate.

The entire group was in heaven with the superb meals the *manetuwak* made for them. With a fully stocked kitchen, the Guardians and their mates, *and guests*, were more than happy to resume their duties, respectful of their sacred responsibility to the spirits of the manse.

A happy Keep meant happy Guardians. And that meant "cutlet time" as Holley was fond of saying after binge-watching several seasons of *Jersey Shore*. She was familiar enough with modern terminology, but every now and then there was a phrase that threw her. Like the one Furio just uttered.

"What does that even mean? Does one shit on one or near one?" Holley inquired and Kingston choked on a bite of the savory chicken dish Jessenia had cooked up.

"Nice," Jessenia said and shook her head.

"At any rate, Furio, I am not shitting on anyone. The fact is, the Keep was built on a very powerful ley line that was sacred to my father's people and known to the *supernaturals* who commissioned this place to be built."

"Were they Guardians?" asked Storm.

"Yes, and no," she took a bite of the chicken and moaned in delight.

Jessenia had lost the rental she and Fergie had together and because she was always there anyway, Holley had invited her to move in. She was not a Guardian, but she was quickly becoming family.

The Witch smiled around the room and sighed to herself. They were already a family indeed.

"Well, who were they then?" Elena chimed in.

"From what the *manetuwak* told me, they were Guardians of Chaos, and Enforcers too, and also a few local Witches and Shifter groups. You see each had claim to the land, but they knew it was being targeted. They built this place to protect it."

"Really?"

"Yes, I suppose they weren't counting on the Keep having a personality of its own," she smirked and the lights flashed.

"We thought it was all you," Fergie grinned.

"Well, I communicate with the spirits, but I don't control them."

"Magic isn't meant to be controlled," Kingston added and her gaze met his.

"Indeed, it is not," she agreed.

Later that night, wrapped in the arms of the man she loved more than her own life, Holley sighed contentedly.

"What are you thinking about?" his husky voice broke the serenity, but she remained peaceful, secure in the warmth of his love.

"I was thinking about the first time I saw you."

"When I bit you?"

"Oh no. It was decades before that. You were so serious, so set in your ways."

"You knew," he lifted his head and what she saw in his eyes made her heart swell, "You knew for all that time?"

"Yes," she said because lying to him would never be an option.

"I am so sorry," he held her tight and she smiled.

"I am not. It gave me time to know you. Time to observe you unnoticed. I fell in love with you like that, Kingston. Fated mates or not, I have loved you for many lifetimes," she reached up and kissed him.

Savoring the feel of his lips as they opened and his tongue swirled around hers. Holley moaned and moved until she was astride the big man. Lifting her body, she slid along his shaft and accepted Kingston's hard length deep inside of her.

"Holley," he growled, hands on her hips as he guided her into a frenzy of motion and passion unlike any.

Each time better than the last. And this was only the beginning, or so he kept telling her. So far, it was true. He thrust upwards, in time with her downward swivels. Each repeated motion sent shards of bliss exploding along her spine throughout every fiber of her being. Her magic closed in around them, wrapping them in a blanket where his Dragon met her powers.

Together they reached untold heights. The ecstasy she found in his arms was pure heaven. Heart near to bursting with love, she moaned his name as her pleasure reached its pinnacle with Kingston right there with her.

"I love you, *conpar*," he growled softly into her hair and she loved his fascination with it.

She always found the most intense pleasure in the way he loved her. And she knew he did down to her marrow. It was in the way his golden eyes caressed her like hands, the way his lips seemed to smile whenever she was around. Yes, they were good for one another.

"I love you too," she replied hugging him tight to her breast.

Holley never had to fear the cold again. Not with her Dragon Shield to keep her warm and safe from harm. He would protect her always. She trusted that with all her soul, and whether he knew it or not, she would do the same for him.

That is what it meant to be mated to a Guardian of Chaos. Together they were stronger, better, and more powerful than anything else.

Loving him was easy, getting his love in return was a bonus.

Give for what you take, she thought as sleep came easily to her now.

"Mate."

· · ·

The end.

Did you enjoy this story? Grab the next Guardians of Chaos book here!

READING ON A BUDGET?

Hello Readers!

I am so excited to be able to offer you exclusive bundles available only on CDGORRI.COM for readers using my BUY DIRECT option.

Right now, I have several bundles available at a whopping 30% off the listed prices and there are several series bundles to choose from.

Orders will be delivered via BookFunnel email. Just download to your favorite app and READ!

Thank you for buying direct. Have an awesome day!

xoxo,

C.D. Gorri

Join the Pack!

Looking for a Paranormal Romance series that is loads of growly fun?

Welcome to the Macconwood Pack!

These stories are split into two series, the Macconwood Pack Novels Series, and the Macconwood Pack Tales. Each story features one or more Pack members their journey to their one true and fated mate. They can be read alone, though they are better read in order, as characters may show up in each other's stories.

Pack is family for the Macconwood wolves, and when you read their tales, you become family too. What are you waiting for?

Join the Pack today!

https://www.cdgorri.com/series/the-macconwood-
pack-novel-series/

No cliffhangers. Steamy PNR fun.
Go and read your next happily ever after today!

Have you met my Bears?

Looking for a Paranormal Romance series that is loads of growly fun?

Meet the Barvale Clan first in the Bear Claw Tales! A complete shifter romance series about 4 brothers who discover and need to win their fated mates!

Followed by two more spin off series, the Barvale Clan Tales and the Barvale Holiday Tales!

No cliffhangers. Steamy PNR fun.
Go and read your next happily ever after today!

BEWARE... HERE BE DRAGONS!

The Falk Clan Tales began as my stories surrounding four dragon Brothers and how they find their one true mates, but when a long lost brother arrives on the scene, followed by a few more Shifters...what can I say? The more the merrier!

Each Dragon's chest is marked with his rose, the magical link to his heart and his magic. They each have a matching gemstone to go with it.

She's given up on love. But he's just begun.

In The Dragon's Valentine we meet the eldest Falk brother, Callius. He is on a mission to find a Castle and his one true mate, one he can trust with his diamond rose....

His heart is frozen. Can she change his mind about love?

In The Dragon's Christmas Gift our attention shifts to Alexsander, the youngest brother of the four. He has resigned himself to a life alone, until he meets *her*.

Some wounds run deep. Can a Dragon's heart be unbroken?

The Dragon's Heart is the story of Edric Falk who has vowed never to love again, but that changes when he meets his feisty mate, Joselyn Curacao.

She just wants a little fun. He's looking for a lifetime.

We finally meet Nikolai Falk and his sexy Shifter mate in The Dragon's Secret.

She doesn't believe in fairytales, until a Dragon comes knocking on her door.

Meet Castor Falk, the long lost brother of our original four Dragons, and his sassy mate Josette. The Dragon's Treasure is full of adventure and laughs.

Nothing can surprise this six hundred-year-old Dragon, except maybe her.

Devine Graystone meets his match in Sunny Daye, an irrepressible Wolf Shifter with a heart of gold. Read their story in The Dragon's Surprise.

He's a hardcore realist until she dares him to dream.

Nicholas Gravestone doesn't know what to think when he spies Minerva Lykos on the property his Dragon covets. Can this unlikely pair come to a truce? Find out in The Dragon's Dream.

Thanks for reading.

xoxo,

C.D. Gorri

*Dragon Mates & Dragon Mates 2 boxed sets are now available in hardcover, paperback, and ebook.

EXCERPT FROM
MARKED BY THE DEVIL

Snap! Flash! Snap! Bang!

"Over here! The Dark Prince is by the window!"

Click! Bang! Snap!

"Oh, for fuck's sake," Avail growled. He could feel that secret part of him pushing to be released. Power pulsed through his veins, his beast demanding to be set free, but he fought the temptation.

Snap! Flash! The horde of paparazzi swarmed outside the entrance to the Leeds Foundation, snapping pictures and banging on the polished reinforced glass doors in hopes of catching a glimpse of him—*like he was their prey.*

If they only knew.

He growled aloud, eyes flashing at the throng below. The man they hunted was not the useless, spoiled playboy they took him for.

Avail Leeds was something more. A predator. Not like those uncouth vultures circling with their cameras and cheap shots.

He was the real thing. A creature humankind built into legend with stories of midnight encounters. He snorted a harsh laugh.

If only I could show them. Grrrr.

They'd been there since daybreak hoping to get a statement or a picture of him, but Avail had managed to dodge them. He was no stranger to this kind of game.

Unfortunately for me. Sigh.

They'd dubbed him the "Naughty Dark Prince" years ago, recording his exploits and reporting them with more than a touch of exaggeration, as a constant source of entertainment for *normals* the world over.

As heir to the Leeds fortune, Avail had been in the spotlight since birth. Especially after his parent's tragic death when he was an infant.

His grandparents had brought him up with the finest education and surroundings a boy could have.

So, yes, he was known to indulge in a bit of luxury

and sport in between his family's foundation and other philanthropic works.

The Leeds family was enormously wealthy. The money had come to the family at first from the land itself. Natural resources like coal and oil had started the family's legacy.

Later on, they'd dabbled in manufacturing, then real estate and development. Now the family was known for their charity.

Avail himself had increased their holdings by playing the stock market and investing in several internet start-ups. He certainly had a marvelous head for figures. The mathematical and the female kind.

He gritted his teeth at the reminder. The latter had, once again, caused him this current headache. Women would surely be the death of him, or so his grandmother promised. Often.

Oh dear. Grandmother is certain to be angry this time.

"Denise!" Avail groaned his secretary's name as he looked out his office window.

So many of them are here this time. Ugh. He slumped back in his Perigold executive chair. The exotic French walnut was highly polished and smelled of lemons. The seat was made from the leather of a sixteen-point stag that his great-grandfather had taken down himself. He remembered that day.

Hunting with Grandfather was often the best time of his life. After all, he'd taught Avail everything he knew about controlling his inner demons, so to speak. He sure missed the old man.

His darling grandmother ordered the leather made from the buck's skin to be turned into this bit of posh office furniture for Avail when he took over as president of the Leeds Foundation. Conditioned with only the best mixtures of Mink and Neatsfoot oils, the chair was fucking amazing, if he did say so himself. Soft and strong, perfect for his six-foot four-inch, two-hundred and forty-pound frame.

He was certainly grateful for it as he slunk down into the buttery depths and cradled his head in his hands. It was only seven o'clock in the morning. How did those vultures find him so quickly?

"What have you done now?" *Why does her voice have to reach that pitch?* He cringed.

"Just the usual, Denise," he answered with a grin.

His silk shirt of the night before hung open revealing a large expanse of his muscled chest, evenly covered in a dusting of black hair.

It matched the midnight dark strands atop his

head that earned him the hated moniker *"Naughty Dark Prince"*.

Of course, if he'd bothered to stay out of the public eye the name would probably be forgotten. *Fat chance.* Avail couldn't help himself. He simply loved life, women, and parties. Usually, in that order.

He didn't bother to button his shirt or his pants as Denise stomped across the floor in those ridiculous heels she wore.

The older woman had seen him in far worse shape. He could use a shower and shave, ooh, and some breakfast.

A bloody steak and half a dozen eggs should do it, but even as he thought it his stomach revolted. *Ugh. See what happens when we mix whiskey and magic!* His Devil growled inside of him and Avail groaned aloud. The magic had been a bit much, but the little Witch deserved it. Taunting him for not being interested in her obvious wiles.

The glare coming from Denise had him refocusing his attention on the motherly woman. *Ouch.* She could singe toast with that look! *So loving*, he thought. His secretary of seven years cared about him. That was nice.

"Well, Denise, I suppose you want to know what happened."

"Oh, a night of wining and dining the little trust fund baby? What's to know? Did *little pookie* not like getting kicked out of bed at 3AM?"

Denise Reynolds stood over Avail with a large, steaming mug of his favorite French roast, served black, in one hand. In the other was a large cup of tomato juice and six aspirin. Otherwise, he might have growled at her insolence. *As if.* He loved the crotchety older woman.

Her white hair was sprayed straight up like spindles guarding a castle. The sight was a bit harsh on his poor bloodshot eyes.

Yes, he'd had far too good a time last night, but it wasn't with *little pookie* as much as it was with the whiskey he'd imbibed.

And the magic he'd wielded.

It was nearing the last quarter moon and Avail's beastie had been up for some good old-fashioned debauchery. As was the little Witch he'd brought along for the ride.

Bambi was a trust fund baby and a Witch. He'd met her at *The Thirsty Dog* where he'd gone to partake in some booze and dancing, perhaps a little nookie with a stranger.

He thought he'd found the perfect partner for the evening in the wicked Bambi. The woman had been down for just about anything. Including skinny dipping in the frigid Blue Hole which was just a few miles from his home.

He'd used a few tricks with some ancient runes and conjured a little light show while they swam. He'd even allowed his Devil to play a little bit as well. Hoping for a little suck and blow afterwards.

Not the card game.

And then it had all gone wrong. Bambi had wanted promises with her sex. That was a serious no in his book. Then the taunting came and out she went.

Like a light.

"Well?"

"Oh Denise, what can I say? She wanted more than an evening's entertainment. I simply didn't see us headed that way."

"Well, normally I'd say the girl had standards, but uh, I don't think so."

He stretched as he swallowed his aspirin and downed the tomato juice. Avail held his hot coffee carefully. Denise had a sadistic side and he'd caught her trying to burn his Devil once or twice over the years.

"Humph. How is *that* too hot for you?" She rolled her eyes and gathered the empty glass as he continued to wait for his coffee to cool down.

"I told you before, I'm not that kind of Devil,

Denise," he murmured and sipped the brew as it reached the perfect temperature.

Heaven.

He continued to sip with his eyes closed ignoring everything but the smooth warm liquid as it slid down his throat.

"Really, Avail? You took *that* silicone doll to the Blue Hole! Your grandmother is going to be furious with you."

"Yes, yes, I know. Wait, how did you know?" He frowned.

The swimming spot had been shunned by locals for decades, but the Leeds family still enjoyed the crystal-clear waters.

They were fed by an underground glacier though some still claim to be baffled by its existence. *Whatever.*

Still, he knew better than to take a normal to one of his family's private haunts. He also knew better than to use magic in front of anyone. But he'd figured it was alright since Bambi was in fact a Witch.

Even better, she had her own money. So, he didn't need to worry about her motives. Ideally, she'd been looking for a little light fun on a Friday night. That was all!

How wrong he'd been.

"Avail, you need to see this."

"Hmm? What?" He turned and looked at the older woman who was staring at the television with her mouth hanging open.

"Pookie took pictures! *Ha!* Looks like you've finally did it this time. And look, an interview too!"

"Oh fuck! Turn it up!"

"Leedsy is a very naughty boy! Mmm hmm. He fed me whiskey and oysters on a silk sheet by the pool...

I tell you the truth I didn't mind spanking him, but the ball and gag was where I drew the line. I like it when my men talk dirty, you know?...

Of course, that's true!...

Well, he insisted on wearing my thong as a choker...

Yes, I'd be willing to go out with him again. He is a big boy after all, and his endurance is divine...

I found his size to be more than adequate though his oral skills were slightly exaggerated...

but that is nothing compared to what happened afterwards...

yeah we both saw him...

the actual Jersey Devil..."

For fucks sake...

Continue to read here https://www.cdgorri.com/series/purely-paranormal-romance-books

ALSO BY C.D. GORRI

Contemporary Romance Books:

Cherry On Top Tales

Her Yule His Log

His Carrot Her Muffin

Her Chocolate His Bar

Wild Billionaire Romance

His Wild Obsession

Jersey Bad Boys

Merciful Lies

***

Paranormal Romance Books:

Macconwood Pack Novel Series:

Macconwood Pack Tales Series:

The Falk Clan Tales:

The Bear Claw Tales:

The Barvale Clan Tales:

Barvale Holiday Tales:

Purely Paranormal Romance Books:

The Wardens of Terra:

The Maverick Pride Tales:

Dire Wolf Mates:

Wyvern Protection Unit:

Jersey Sure Shifters/EveL Worlds:

The Guardians of Chaos:

Twice Mated Tales

Hearts of Stone Series

Moongate Island Tales

Mated in Hope Falls

Speed Dating with the Denizens of the Underworld

Hungry Fur Love

Island Stripe Pride

NYC Shifter Tales

A Howlin' Good Fairytale Retelling

Standalones:

Witch Shifter Clan

Young Adult/Urban Fantasy Books

The Grazi Kelly Novel Series

The Angela Tanner Files

G'Witches Magical Mysteries Series

Co-written with P. Mattern

Witches of Westwood Academy

with Gina Kincade

<u>Blackthorn Academy For Supernaturals</u>

*<u>*Be sure to check out my BUY DIRECT BUNDLES</u> and get
30% off when you buy available only my website.*

ABOUT THE AUTHOR

USA Today Bestselling author C.D. Gorri writes paranormal and contemporary romance and urban fantasy books with plenty of steam and humor.

Join her mailing list here: https://www.cdgorri.com/newsletter

An avid reader with a profound love for books and literature, she is usually found with a book in hand. C.D. lives in her home state, New Jersey, where many of her characters and stories are based. Her tales are fast-paced yet detailed with satisfying conclusions. If you enjoy powerful heroines and loyal heroes who face relatable problems in supernatural settings, journey into the Grazi Kelly Universe today.

You will find sassy, curvy heroines and sexy, love-driven heroes who find their HEAs between the pages.

Wolves, Bears, Dragons, Tigers, Witches, Vampires, and tons more Shifters and supernatural creatures dwell within her paranormal works. The most important thing is every mate in this universe is fated, loyal, and true lovers always get their happily-ever-afters.

In her contemporary works, you will find fiercely possessive men and the smart, confident, curvy women they are crazy about. As always, the HEA is between the pages.

Thank you and happy reading!
del mare alla stella,
C.D. Gorri

http://www.cdgorri.com
https://www.facebook.com/Cdgorribooks
https://www.bookbub.com/authors/c-d-gorri
https://twitter.com/cgor22
https://instagram.com/cdgorri/
https://www.goodreads.com/cdgorri
https://www.tiktok.com/@cdgorriauthor

www.ingramcontent.com/pod-product-compliance
Lightning Source LLC
Chambersburg PA
CBHW061900310726
48972CB00004B/1104